GREED

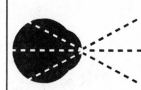

This Large Print Book carries the
Seal of Approval of N.A.V.H.

GREED

A SEVEN DEADLY SINS NOVEL

VICTORIA
CHRISTOPHER MURRAY

THORNDIKE PRESS
A part of Gale, a Cengage Company

Farmington Hills, Mich • San Francisco • New York • Waterville, Maine
Meriden, Conn • Mason, Ohio • Chicago

LIBRARY OF CONGRESS CIP DATA ON FILE.
CATALOGUING IN PUBLICATION FOR THIS BOOK
IS AVAILABLE FROM THE LIBRARY OF CONGRESS

ISBN-13: 978-1-4328-6926-7 (hardcover alk. paper)

Published in 2019 by arrangement with Gallery Books, an imprint of Simon & Schuster, Inc.

Printed in the United States of America
1 2 3 4 5 6 7 23 22 21 20 19

GREED

1

"Just got paid . . . it's Friday night."

I tapped the button on my steering wheel, silencing the booming bass. Even though for years this had been my jam every Friday night when I was at Spelman, I was not feelin' the musicality of Johnny Kemp right now. Maybe part of the problem was that my life was out of sync — today was Thursday, not Friday. I was so discombobulated that I couldn't even line my music (or my life) up right. As I rolled into my assigned parking space, I didn't miss that irony.

I turned off the ignition, leaned back in the seat, and sighed through my exhaustion, remembering those college days a decade ago. These days were supposed to be so much better. In college I didn't have any money, but on Friday nights, I sang this song and hunted for parties as if I did. Ten years out, a full-time job, yet I hadn't made any kind of real strides in my life. My J.O.B.

was truly keeping me just over broke.

Leaning across my seat, I reached for my tote and the envelope that lay on top. Another sigh eased out of me as I slipped out the check and paused before I looked at it, as if that hesitation would change the numbers that followed the dollar sign. But when I glanced down, the numbers were the same as they'd been when my boss had given me my commission check earlier. This was money I earned every quarter over my base salary: $1,557.19 — my best commission check yet. And in the office, this was considered more than decent. Still, it was way short of what I'd hoped, so much less than what I'd worked for, and about a thousand dollars less than what I needed.

Groaning, I slipped the check back into the envelope, then grabbed my tote and slid out of the car, trying to figure out how I was going to make this check stretch so that it could do what I needed this money to do.

If I hadn't had plans for this check, I would've been ready to celebrate. The first time my commission check broke a thousand? Yeah, there would've been a party over here. I may have even gone on a little shopping spree, which for me meant buying more than one item at Marshalls in one visit.

But fifteen hundred dollars was just not

enough.

The weight of that felt like shackles on my ankles as I dragged myself to my first-floor garden apartment. The only thing I was grateful for as I struggled up the path that was flanked by more dirt than grass was that I didn't have to climb any stairs.

Pushing my key into the lock, I didn't even have a chance to turn it before the door swung open, startling me. Before I could take a breath, I was swept from my feet.

"Oh" was all I could get out before my mouth was covered — with Stephon's lips.

And when his tongue pressed against mine and we danced that waltz we'd come to know over the past three years, every single care that had tried to take me down and knock me out this week faded away. Dropping my tote and the check and everything else onto the floor, I wrapped my arms around my boyfriend's neck as he cradled me like a baby, then carried me, stumbling over a couple of paint cans and almost knocking down his easel before we stepped into our bedroom.

By the time he laid me on our queen-size bed, I was ready. That was how it always was with Stephon. He could take me from zero to full throttle with a glance and a kiss.

That was who he was. Forget about whether a woman was black, white, brown — if red pumped through her veins, she was hot for Stephon. Because he had the best of everything: he had the smoldering eyes of Idris, the sexy smirk of Kofi, the swagger of Morris, and just enough gangsta in him like M'Baku (which is the name I would forever call Winston Duke). And then, can I talk about his body? Michael B would come in second to my man. So all I wanted to do was undress him, straddle him, and love him until I forgot that we were on Earth. But when I reached for his T-shirt, he pushed my hand away, then pinned my arms above my head.

He straddled me and kissed me again, just so gently. When he eased up for a moment, my breath had already been taken away.

He said, "Tonight, it's all about you. This" — he paused and glanced around the bedroom — "is for you."

I followed his glance and, for the first time, noticed the candles, even though the softening light of dusk filtered through our bedroom window.

By the time my eyes were back on him, he had already slipped my sweater from my shoulders and unbuttoned my blouse. I blinked twice and he was down to my bra.

Just a dozen more blinks and I was naked, on my stomach, and the soft sounds of Arabesque 1 by Debussy (I only knew that because of Stephon) played from the dock on the nightstand by his side of the bed. My man did his best work listening to the instrumental tales told through classical music. I closed my eyes and inhaled the fragrance of the lavender almond oil (from the nightstand on my side of the bed) that scented the air.

The moment Stephon's fingertips touched my shoulders, I moaned. And if there was any residual stress inside of me, it melted beneath the hands of my man. When he kneaded his knuckles into my back, I groaned through the pleasure of the pain, breathing in rhythm with him. I had no thoughts; my senses all centered on his touch, his scent, as he pressed and plied my skin and my mind to his will. I floated outside of my body, gliding like I was high — my drug: Stephon Smith.

There was no way I would have been able to say how long Stephon massaged me into submission. I slipped into that euphoric state where my body tugged me toward unconsciousness, but I was still aware.

The passage of time . . . and then Stephon lay next to me. Even then, so many

11

moments passed before I was able to flex enough muscles to roll over. When I faced him, his brown eyes, his full lips were right in front of me.

I said, "How did you know . . ."

"That was what you needed?" he asked, completing my thought. And before I could nod, he finished with, "Because on days that end in *y*, I'm in tune to your every need."

If I weren't already lighthearted, his words would have made me so. And since it *was* one of those days that ended in *y*, there was something that *I* wanted to do. "Hand me the oil," I said. "Your turn."

When he shook his head, I frowned, or at least I tried to. I was still so relaxed, the muscles in my face hadn't reawakened.

Stephon leaned so close to me that when he spoke, his lips grazed mine. "I don't want a massage," he whispered. "I just want you."

He had just kneaded me into a noodle, and still, I weakened from his words. "I love you," I told him.

"Beyond infinity," he said, before he sealed our love with a kiss that went on and on and on.

2

I wasn't sure if it was the sun that pressed between my eyelids or the heat that warmed my cheek — maybe it was the sensation of both that awakened me.

Morning. Already.

I stretched, then I remembered. Last night. I sighed. I smiled. Stephon and I hadn't spent a moment making love. Even though I'd craved him, Stephon had loved me in the way I needed most yesterday — he'd just held me.

He'd held me as we first listened to his favorite classical playlist. Then he'd held me when we'd turned on a Netflix movie. The only time he'd released me from his embrace was when he'd left our bed and apartment to get our dinner: hamburgers, fries, and one chocolate shake that we shared from Big Daddy's Burgers (Stephon's favorite eatery). It had been complete love, complete rest.

My eyes were still closed as I reached for my boyfriend, wondering if now, I could do to him what I'd wanted to do last night.

But all I felt was the coolness of the sheets on his side of the bed. I was disappointed, but not surprised. He was already at work.

Pushing myself up, I stood, then lifted the T-shirt Stephon had worn yesterday from the chaise. Slipping it over my head, I opened our bedroom door and the sound of music met me — I paused, taking in the melody of the piano and violin. Mozart's Sonata No. 17.

The fact that I could name these tunes always made me smile. That was just one way Stephon had lifted me up. While I had a profound love for the ole-school jams my dad had raised me on, Stephon had expanded my ear, if not my tastes. I may have been the one with the college degree, but in so many ways, he was far more educated than me.

At the end of the hallway, I paused, and like every morning, I leaned against the wall that opened to the living room, soaking in the sight before me. The living room's light was bright; the blinds were raised and the windows were open, welcoming the warmth and sounds of the birth of the morning. No matter the sun's angle, it always seemed to

14

shine like a spotlight on the highlight of my life. Stephon looked like he was the subject of a portrait himself.

This was one of my favorite things to do — look at my man in his office. Stephon was perched in front of his easel, the centerpiece of our living room. The tan sofa (covered with heavy plastic) and the coffee table faded as if they were created for the background, minor accessories to the main attraction. It was hard to notice anything when Stephon was anywhere.

I loved watching him in the morning, with his bare back to me, his muscles flexing as he glided his paintbrush across the canvas. For the last weeks, he'd been working on this masterpiece — a rendition of the National Museum of African American History and Culture that he'd been commissioned to create for a private school here in Atlanta.

Only half-done, his painting looked like the actual museum already. He'd been so excited when he'd been asked to paint this — if Stephon hadn't been a painter, he would have found a way to be an architect. So this was the merging of his two loves, and in the image that was unfolding, he'd captured the African and American elements of the design — the three-tiered crowns used in Yoruba art and the intricate ironwork that were distinct American aspects of the architecture.

He was working with a ribbon tip, moving the brush with the precision of a surgeon, the grace of a maestro. Like always, I watched with wonder. His focus that could not be broken, his discipline that was unparalleled — this was where Stephon and I differed so much.

Often I asked myself, Who was the soul inside of Stephon's skin? Where did he find his passion? Was it his education versus mine? I'd sat inside rooms off the hallowed halls of the preeminent college for African American women. Stephon had spent almost six months in a juvenile detention center for continual truancy when he was in middle school, and his high school diploma came not at a graduation ceremony, but as a GED certificate delivered in the mail.

Or did his commitment to his craft come from being raised by a single mother, which was the opposite of my upbringing — raised by my father alone?

Really, I couldn't blame my education or my parentage for the way I was wandering through my life. I'd chosen a career in sales over what I really wanted to do because I wanted to make money to live a certain kind of life, one that was worthy of a Spelman graduate.

When Stephon tapped the edge of his paintbrush on the corner of his easel, his biceps popped like he was a construction worker who lifted bricks rather than an artist's brush. And those bulging muscles served as my invitation.

Moving behind him, I wrapped my arms around his chest and pressed my lips against that soft spot right beneath his ear. "Good morning."

He twisted, turning his torso toward me long enough to give me a peck on my cheek. Then his attention, his focus returned to the canvas.

With a sigh, I stepped back. I wasn't annoyed or anything like that. Stephon was already at his office, and the truth was, I needed to get to mine.

So, after another long stare at my man, I returned to our bedroom. It was a quick ritual for me, and in less than forty-five minutes, I had showered and was dressed in a cream suit (my nod to the beginning of spring) and was once again standing in the middle of our living room.

I kissed the top of Stephon's head. "Have a great day, babe."

He twisted once again to give me another

quick kiss, then lowered the music playing through his iPhone. When he lifted the envelope from the sofa, I couldn't believe that I'd forgotten about that check.

"Oh, yeah. That's my commission."

He nodded. "I hope you don't mind, I took a peek." He grinned. "Congratulations."

"Thanks." I took a breath. "It's less than I expected, though. I'm sorry."

"Babe." He frowned a little. "What do you have to be sorry about?" Standing, he crossed the living room to where I was, pressed me back against the door, leaned into me, then covered my lips with his. "This check is great; it's your best one yet, and I know it'll only get better."

"But our vacation with Audra and Joseph."

He shrugged a little as he backed away. "Well, we won't be able to go this time around."

My shoulders slumped. We hadn't been able to go the last time around, nor the time before that, nor the vacation before that one.

He said, "But those two take so many trips, we'll catch them on one of these islands."

As Stephon slipped back onto the stool in front of the easel, I sucked my bottom lip between my teeth. "I was thinking," I began.

He looked up at me.

"I know we don't have much in savings, but I was so looking forward to this vacation."

Now it was his shoulders that slacked a bit. "I know, I was looking forward to it, too, but the only way we would've been able to go was if . . ."

He stopped short of telling me that I'd failed, even though I knew he didn't see it that way. Those were my feelings I was projecting.

"I know," I said, and now my words rushed out. "And I'll figure out a way to make it up next quarter, but we can take a thousand from savings and go to the Cayman Islands just this once."

I took in a breath, and Stephon blew out one as if he thought that was better than speaking the words he wanted to say. Words that he'd told me before. Instead, he said, "Zuri, we barely have three thousand dollars in the bank, and you want to take out a third of our savings? Not to mention the spending money we'd need once we got there."

"But it's not like we won't be able to put that money back. We'll have the rest of the money you'll receive from this painting." I pointed to his easel. "That'll be five thousand, right? And my commission next quarter . . ."

"But we don't know what your commission check will be," he said in a tone that sounded like he was explaining this to a two-year-old. "We have to have a backup. We've had to take money out of savings for the last six or seven months to pay our bills. It would be crazy to go on vacation and then come home and not be able to pay our rent."

I crossed my arms and wondered (not for the first time) how I'd ended up with a man who was an artist, but acted like an accountant.

Bouncing from the stool, he pulled me into his arms again. "Come on," he started, "you know I wanted to take that vacation, too, but the fact is we can't. But that doesn't mean we will never go on vacation; we're just not going right now. Our time will come. For lots of things."

When I closed my eyes, he kissed my eyelids.

"Don't be mad," he said.

"I'm not mad; I'm just . . . I feel stuck. We never go anywhere; we never do anything. We're always concerned about money."

"Correction: *I'm* always concerned about money."

Even before he smiled, I knew he was trying to make a joke, but I found no humor in being told we couldn't take this trip that I'd been looking forward to since my best friend had told me about it last month. I'd worked hard, brought in two new accounts to the advertising agency, and now I was standing in the middle of my living room, blinking back tears because I was way too old to cry over this.

"This is just the season we're in right now." Stephon's voice was softer, as if he knew my emotions needed to be soothed. "We're doing what we're supposed to do now so that . . ."

"We can do what we want to do later," I finished the quote he always said to me.

"Exactly. So you go out there and make that money. I'll be right here painting up some money. And then soon, we'll have lots of it to do whatever."

I nodded. "Okay." I tried not to sigh as I turned away from Stephon. Right before I got to the door, I said, "Oh, I'll be a little late tonight. Remember I have that appointment with the woman from the Girls First Foundation."

"Oh, yeah. Great. I'm so glad you'll be

doing that. Have a great day, babe," he said as he came to the door to give me another quick kiss on my forehead. Then he slid back onto his stool, turned up the music, and now *The Marriage of Figaro* filled the apartment with notes so crisp, it felt like the orchestra was in our living room.

Stephon didn't even look at me when he picked up his brush, and I'd been dismissed. I left Stephon to his passion and hoped one day I'd actually pursue mine.

3

The quick knock startled me, made me sit up straight in my chair and swivel toward the door.

"Hey," my supervisor said as he peeked his blond-spiked head into my office. "You're gonna have those forecasts to me this afternoon?"

I nodded, then tapped a couple of keys to awaken my computer. "Working on that now, boss."

He gave me a thumbs-up and a grin, and I returned the gesture, holding the pose, until he stepped away. Then my smile faded and I stood and closed my door. That was something I should have done hours ago, when I walked into Silver Sky, the advertising agency where I'd worked for the last year.

Returning to my chair I plopped down, feeling as if my energy had been drained even though I hadn't flexed a single mental muscle since I'd walked into this building. It was hard to get my professional juices flowing when all I was doing was calculating forecasts and scouting new clients. What was creative about that? My sales account job here wasn't much different from my last job in medical equipment sales, and the one before that in textbook sales, and the one before that in skin-care sales.

It was all the same, including my boss, always a blond-haired white boy (that was why I called all of them *boss,* never bothering to commit their names to my memory), ten years or so out of college like me, but already running things while I was still skipping along, trying to find my place.

Pushing myself from the chair, I wandered to the window, taking in the downtown Atlanta skyline. I had such dreams ten years ago, always imagining myself on the thirtieth floor in one of these high-rise buildings, conquering the world (or at least Atlanta, since I'd never even been on a plane).

I sighed. There seemed little right with my life — except for my man. That thought turned my sigh into a smile. My shirtless artist of a boyfriend . . . who never budged from our budget. But even with not being able to convince him to take this vacation, there was little I could find wrong with that man. He was the blessing that God had chosen for me. It was so clear that he was God's gift, beginning with the way God had brought him into my life — or should I say the way God had brought him back three years ago . . .

My eyes were blurry and the Riesling was sweet.

And this sweet wine was the reason why I wasn't slumped over this table wallowing in my misery.

Audra said, "See? You're having a good time. And you didn't even want to come out."

I had to squint a bit to bring her into focus even though she was sitting right in front of me on the other side of this small round table. The blue light made her look like a ghost, and that made me giggle.

We were at a club called Blues — and it was either a corny name or the best marketing ever. Audra had chosen this place because she and Joseph loved the local blues performers who were here on weekends, mostly students from nearby colleges.

I'd agreed to come because the place matched my mood. The only light inside was blue, and that was how I felt tonight

25

— just blue, just pathetic.

"See, this isn't a bad birthday." Audra leaned across the table and squeezed my hand before she settled back into her husband's arms.

Didn't she realize how crazy this was? Her words and then the way she was able to snuggle back into her man's arms? She was having a better time than I was, and this was my thirtieth birthday. But my celebration options had been few — either dinner with my father or hanging at this club with my best friend. Since I was older than twelve, dinner with my dad on my birthday was out.

For a while, this wine had made the night great. Then Audra made me remember what I was trying hard to forget. My eyes were blurry again, but now the haze was from the heat of my tears that pressed behind my eyelids.

Just pathetic.

But I, at least, needed to be happy that my best friend had dragged me here so I wasn't with my dad or in my bedroom, wallowing in my latest breakup, this time with Chris. I was only thirty, and I'd had more boyfriends than I had shoes — and my closet was filled with those.

Someone from the outside might think I

was doing a poor job of searching for my father. But my theory was that this was all about my mother. I didn't remember her, not really since she'd passed away the day before I turned five. I was doing all the things she'd never been able to teach me not to do.

The thought of that made a tear drip right into my wineglass.

"You want another drink?" Joseph asked.

At least there was a man here to ask me that.

Before I could wipe away my tears and tell him, Yes, get me two more glasses, Audra said, "Babe, let's get something to eat." She gave me one of her hard, full-of-knowing side glances, a look that was meant to say she thought I was on the way to drinking too much. Not that I did this very often, but she'd been my college roommate, so she knew secrets, the kinds of things that all college roommates knew about each other.

Joseph glanced over his shoulder and looked at the line for the food. This was one of those old-school clubs where the waitstaff served drinks, but there was a buffet line for the soul food that went along with the soul blues. "Okay, I'll get us plates."

"I'll go with you." Audra pushed back from the table, and I sipped the last of my now-tear-flavored wine. When Joseph reached for Audra's hand, I sighed. That was what I wanted in my life.

"Zuri?"

I glanced up at the sound of a man's voice and again squinted through the fog of the blue light and my wine haze.

"It is you," the voice said with what sounded like a bit of glee.

Now like I'd said, it was dark in Blues, but it wasn't dark enough to hide the black Adonis who stood before me.

"Hell . . . oh!" I leaned back in my chair to get a more unhindered view, my tears totally gone for the moment.

"I can't believe it," he said. "I was standing over there" — he paused and pointed to the opposite corner — "trying to figure out if it was really you. Wow, it's good to see you."

If I hadn't already had two glasses of wine, I may have tried to play this off until I could figure out how I knew this hunk. But because wine always loosened my tongue (and other things, which was why I'd had so many boyfriends), I said, "Do I know you?" and right away, I wanted to take those words back because of the way his shoulders slumped.

"I mean" — I added a lie — "you look so familiar, but it's dark, and this . . ." I held up my empty glass.

The explanation must've been good enough, because he said, "Yeah, I guess it's hard to see in here, and it's been quite a few years since you last saw me — twelve, to be exact," he said as if he'd been counting the days. But there was no way that I knew this man; someone like him, I wouldn't forget.

I squinted, trying to think. He'd said twelve years. That would put me all the way back in high school. Was he a dude from school? Nah, there were some serious guys who strutted through the halls of Stone Mountain High, but no one this fine.

He lowered himself onto the seat next to me. "I'm Stephon Smith."

"No!" My loosened tongue spoke ahead of my mind. And since it had started, I let it keep going. "No way. Stephon?"

He bobbed his head.

"I don't believe it," I said, the words coming out of me a little louder, and a lot faster than I wanted. "Stand up again so I can see if it's really you."

Now I didn't actually expect him to do that, but when he did, I took full advantage of the sight. This man couldn't be Stephon. Not with those shoulders that were the top of the frame for the rest of the perfection that was his body. He was fully clothed, but I felt like I had some serious magical power going on, because I could easily imagine each one of those muscles that gloriously folded together into his six-pack and his thick but toned thighs.

Whew! I shook my head to shake that image.

Looking at my empty glass, I wondered what brand of wine I had been drinking. This was some good stuff, because there was no way that lanky kid who always sat in the back of every classroom with head-phones covering his larger-than-average ears could have developed into the man who stood before me.

He said, "Yeah," as he sat back down. "I guess I grew into my skin, grew into my ears, grew into my body."

I laughed, not remembering him having a sense of humor. "That's one way to put it."

He did that bobbing-of-his-head thing again, like there was music playing in his mind, then said, "You haven't changed a bit."

"Really?"

He shook his head. "You still say whatever you think."

"I guess."

"And you're still really beautiful." He
shook his head. "I always had such a
crush on you."

"Get out of here." I waved my hand,
though I scooted my chair a little closer so
that he could tell me more. "I never knew
that."

"Hello?"

I looked up at Audra and Joseph as she
placed a paper plate in front of me and
Joseph lowered the two he held onto the
table as well.

Stephon stood like a gentleman, and I
said, "This is a friend of mine from high
school."

As Stephon introduced himself and
shook hands, I studied him. No, it hadn't
been the wine. The white crew-neck
sweater he wore told the truth about his
shoulders and even revealed just a bit of
the muscles that bulged beneath. And his
jeans. Yeah, well . . . he'd found the jeans
that did his body (and my eyes) good.

Still standing, he glanced down at me.
"Well, I don't want to interrupt you guys."

"Oh, no, please join us," Audra said, and
I wanted to bump fists with my girl. "We're

celebrating Zuri's birthday."

If I'd bumped fists with her, I would've taken it back. Really? She put me on Front Street like that? What would Stephon think? My birthday, Audra and Joseph together . . . That meant that I was alone — just pathetic.

"Really?" He sat down again. "Well, then if it's just the three of you . . ."

Oh, God! Embarrassing!

"I'd love to join you."

Now I smiled. It wasn't that I was interested in Stephon. I mean, yeah, he looked good, but from what I remembered, we had little in common. He was one of the rougher guys in school. Not in a gang-rough sort of way, because he was more of an introvert than anything else. But he was always in trouble — coming to class late, drawing in class instead of listening to the lesson . . . and every teacher had to tell him multiple times to remove his headphones, which he always had plugged into a CD player. He'd been suspended more than a few times for that, I recalled. I wasn't even sure if he had graduated with our class.

But having a common link or not, I was glad he'd decided to stay. With him sitting next to me, I wouldn't look — so pathetic.

Stephon said, "I just happened to drop in. I don't live far from here, and I love coming and checking out the new talent."

"I remember you were into music," I said. "You and your headphones were always getting kicked out of class."

He shrugged and looked a little embarrassed. "Yeah, that was me."

"You were into music and art, right?" I asked.

But before he could answer, Joseph said, "Oh, really? What kind of art?"

"All kinds. Everything intrigues and inspires me, but what I paint are portraits."

I leaned back. "You're a painter?"

He chuckled. "An artist. If I said I were a painter, you might ask me to come over tomorrow and paint your house, and if I did that, oh, what a mess that would be."

We all laughed, and Stephon went on to tell us what he'd been doing since high school. Painting African American portraits, some posed, some not. "I try to tell a story through my art. Of black people's struggles and our progress. I'm hoping to leave a footprint, a picture of this time in history through my paintings."

He spoke with a passion and a knowledge that was impressive. And in between, we listened to performers stand before the mic and sing their stories. Through each performance, Stephon moved his head closer to mine and, in whispers, explained the blues to me: its origins in the Deep South, the twelve-bar sequence, and its influence on other genres of music and in our lives overall.

I listened with fascination, not because I was interested, but because of the way he sang to me. He was just speaking, but there was a musicality to his voice that made me want to . . . dance with him.

When we all stood at the end of the last set and Stephon grinned at me, I felt pathetic no more.

"So, how did you get here?" he asked me. "Did you drive?"

"No, I rode with Audra and Joseph."

His expression brightened like I'd just told him the gospel of good news. "Well, I can give you a ride home."

"Okay," I said.

But before those two syllables had passed all the way through my lips, Joseph held up his hand. "Look, man, it's been really nice meeting you and chatting it up, but we don't know you like that, so if you don't mind, we brought her here, so we're gonna take her home."

If I weren't so wobbly, I would have

raised my hand and objected. First, I was grown — thirty today. And second, couldn't Joseph see how fine this man was? But Joseph's words came from a pact Audra and I'd made all the way back when we went to a party the first weekend of our freshman year.

If we go together, we leave together. No matter what. That is our protection.

That had been Audra's demand, and I'd always complied.

But really . . . how many years ago was that? There was no way those college rules applied tonight, though from the look on Joseph's face he thought those old rules were good rules.

Then there was Stephon. He wasn't any help. He bobbed his head like he had mad respect for Joseph, and when he gave him dap, it seemed like everyone was cool with Joseph and Audra taking me home — except for me.

Still, I said nothing, and Stephon strolled out with us. When Joseph and Audra walked together to get the car from a lot two blocks away, Stephon stayed behind with me.

"It was really good seeing you again," he said.

"You too. It was cool." And I meant that.

Not only had Stephon changed physically, but it seemed like he'd grown in other ways, too. I'd enjoyed talking to him, something I wouldn't have been able to imagine twelve years ago.

He nodded. "So if you mean that, pull out your phone."

"What?"

"Let me give you my number."

I did what he asked just as Joseph and Audra pulled up in their BMW. He led me to the car, opened the back door, and right before I slid inside, he said, "I hope you'll call me, because it may be your birthday, but tonight, I was the one who got the gift."

That was just the first time Stephon Smith had made me swoon. When I'd called him the next evening to thank him for joining us, he'd said, "Your turn. I spent time with you last night. Now you can spend a little time with me tonight."

After that, there weren't too many nights in the last three years when we weren't together, and when it came to the personal side, this time in my life was the happiest I'd ever been.

From the outside, we probably seemed like an unlikely pairing — he with his passion and love of culture, which he celebrated through music and art . . . and me with my search for my passion and my idea of culture that didn't go much further than the reality shows on VH1.

But even with our differences, we could sit and talk, though I always called it singing. Stephon still sang to me when we talked about the weather or politics, when he discussed a new commission he'd received, or when he wanted to encourage me in my career. He sang when he inquired about my father or when we sat together and did our budget.

He sang, and together we were hitting almost every note.

Returning to my desk, I sat, then hit the mouse and reawakened my computer. I had to get some work done since I was leaving early to meet this woman, Ms. Viv, with the Girls First Foundation.

But once I got through work and this meeting today, I was going to give my life some serious thought. If I wanted things to change, then dangbangit, I was going to have to do a few things to make those changes. I didn't know if it was going to be my job or my goals or what — but I was going to change something. Because skipping along in life was no longer good enough for me.

4

I double-checked the address and then turned off the ignition to my Chrysler. The modest ranch-style brick home with a shingled roof that extended over one side of the house surprised me a bit, though it shouldn't have. This house looked like all the others in this Greenbriar neighborhood, very much like the homes in the Stone Mountain community, where I grew up.

But even after Ms. Viv had given me this address, which was just a couple of blocks from my church, First Greater Hope, I'd expected something that resembled a mini-mansion for the fifty-, sixty-, or seventy-year-old woman (I could never tell with a black woman) who I'd met at the African American Women in Sales conference's meet-and-greet cocktail hour at the Ritz-Carlton last month. Ms. Viv was the first person I'd spotted. She was surrounded by a trio of women, all in the standard take-me-seriously business suits. But Ms. Viv stood tall among them, even though she was the most petite, not more than five two, maybe five three, and that Carolina Herrera polka-dot silk shirtdress she had on that day was no larger than a size four.

I chuckled now as I remembered how after I'd peeped her designer dress, I'd checked out her shoes, and she hadn't disappointed. I didn't even have to see the soles to know what was up.

I'd been so intrigued with her, especially once I found out that she wasn't even in sales. She'd been at the conference to recruit mentors for her Girls First Foundation.

"You would be so perfect, Zuri. You're so polished, so well put together," she'd said to me that first night. "And it's not just the way you look, it's everything. You know what the book of Colossians says: 'We must clothe ourselves with compassion, kindness, humility, gentleness, and patience.' You have all of that, and seeing someone like you is what my girls need."

Her words had surprised me. Very seldom had I heard anyone quoting Scripture at any kind of professional event. It was like whoever you prayed to had to be left at the corporate door if you wanted to climb the corporate ladder.

But Ms. Viv had quoted Scripture that night (several times), and again when I'd met her for lunch a couple of weeks after so that she could tell me more about her mentoring program.

"The Word of God tells us in Galatians that Paul told the leaders of the church to carry one another's burdens and in this way they would fulfill the law of Christ. That's why I started Girls First Foundation. I want to carry the burdens of those whose shoulders are not broad enough yet. This is a commandment — to fulfill the law of Christ."

I had been impressed with the whole package that was Ms. Viv — her love of Christ, her chic appearance, her vision — and her consistent follow-up. She called every two days to see if I was still interested.

"I'm not going to let you get away, Zuri," she'd kept telling me. "You're one of the good ones. GFF needs you."

Sliding out of my car, I checked the address once again before I walked up the path to the house. I had to roll back the story I'd created in my mind about Ms. Viv being the rich widow of some famous pastor.

Seconds after ringing her bell, Ms. Viv stood at her opened door, dressed like the last two times I'd seen her — this time in a mauve St. John sheath, with pumps that looked like they'd been dyed to match.

"Zuri." She held out her arms and greeted me with a hug. "Welcome to my home."

I stepped over the threshold . . . and then paused. As my eyes glanced around the living room, my first thought was, *Never judge a house by its front door.*

"Wow!" I did nothing to hide my shock. This home was fit for any celebrity — or rich widow. It had certainly been decorated by someone who worked for the stars. I knew because this — interior design — was my passion. "Your home is beautiful."

"Thank you. I give all honor to God, all of my blessings flow from Him," she said as she led me to the pearl-colored sofa, which wasn't just a couch but a Kate Spade Drake tufted piece that cost over five thousand dollars. I'd fallen in love with it when Audra let me decorate her home. But this sofa had been too much for the budget Audra and her doctor husband had given to me.

Kate Spade seemed to be the designer of choice for whomever had done this living room: two Pierce armchairs (another five thousand dollars) and then the Elsie table lamps, which popped with their bright red bases and sat atop Sheffield end tables, the only pieces that didn't carry Kate's name, though that was still another thousand dollars — for each one.

From the area rug that sat atop the carpet at the front door to the accessories — the two armed sconces and the chandelier that twinkled with hundreds of crystals and hung above the Rossetto Dune dining table (a ten-thousand-dollar piece) — Ms. Viv had spent somewhere approaching fifty thousand dollars in just the part of the house that I could see.

Who was this woman?

"I'm so glad you could join me," she said, drawing my attention away from taking an inventory of this room. "I love getting to know potential mentors in my home, away from all the distractions of a restaurant or even an affair like where we met. Here is more private, and we can be open."

"Yes," I said, wondering why I sounded a bit breathless. Maybe it was because sitting in the middle of all of this fabulousness did take my breath away.

She said, "Well, you're right on time, dear. Four o'clock. The perfect time for afternoon tea; let me go get that."

When she rose, I said, "Do you want me to help?"

"Oh, no. Please, you just sit and relax, and

I'll be right back."

I nodded as I watched her saunter (yeah, saunter, even for a woman her age) from the living room.

I set my purse onto the coffee table next to what looked like a photo album. I wasn't sure, though — it was a thick leatherbound book with an embossed gold monogram — GFF. Just as I reached for the book, Ms. Viv called out my name.

When I looked up, she held up a silver tea set on a tray. "Would you mind?"

Springing up, I lifted it from Ms. Viv's hands and then, as gently as I could, I lowered the heavy tray onto the coffee table. Like everything else in Ms. Viv's home, the silver service set was expensive; I could tell from the weight and the way the silver sparkled.

As I adjusted the teapot on the middle of the tray, Ms. Viv grabbed the photo album and moved it onto the dining room table. For a moment, I wondered if I'd offended her by almost looking at the album, but when she turned back to me, her smile was as bright as always.

When we sat together, I asked, "Would you like me to pour your tea?"

"Yes, dear, would you? And I hope you like blueberry scones."

"Actually, I love them. I get way too many from the Starbucks in my building every morning before I go to my office. I've gotta stop that — after today, of course."

She chuckled as I handed her the cup. "What are you talking about? You are such a beautiful young woman; you don't need to worry about your weight."

"Thank you," I said as I took my first sip.

I had so many questions for Ms. Viv, but I couldn't just blurt out, *How did you get so rich?* So I was trying to figure out a polite way to get all up in her business when she said:

"So, tell me about yourself."

I blinked. That was what I wanted to say to her. "Well . . ." I began, but then got stuck. What could I say about myself and my life that would interest Ms. Viv?

Ms. Viv prompted me. "I already know you're in sales, with the Silver Sky Agency, right?"

I nodded as I sipped my tea.

She asked, "Do you like working there?"

I shrugged. "I've been in sales for about ten years. Ever since I graduated from college . . . Spelman." I paused when she raised her eyebrows then gave me an approving nod. "I chose sales because a speaker at one of our career days said commission jobs

44

were the way people really made money; commission was the road to wealth."

She nodded, as if she understood. "That's something I learned a long time ago. When you're paid on your performance, you will always earn more money than on a nine-to-five job."

So . . . maybe she'd held a sales position before — was that how she got all this money? I said, "The only thing is, it hasn't delivered the kind of financial security I expected. And I've tried several industries, though I've been most successful in advertising. Still" — I sighed — "relying on a low base and high commission doesn't always pay the bills."

As I set my cup on the tray, not wanting to leave any rings on the coffee table, Ms. Viv rested her cup down as well and then patted my hand before she broke off a piece of scone. "You're just getting started. You're young, you're beautiful, you're intelligent. You have to be patient with life. Romans 12:12 tells us 'let your hope keep you joyful, be patient in your troubles.' " She paused. "Just pray, Zuri. Like the Word of God says, pray at all times, and I know what you're hoping for will come your way."

Okay, I'd been right. Surely, Ms. Viv *was* the rich widow of a pastor. That would explain everything — her home and those Scriptures.

Finally answering her, I said, "I do pray. My spiritual life is very important to me." I paused. That was the truth, even though I didn't go to church as much as I wanted. "And I know what God has for me is for me, it's just that . . ." I paused again, wanting to say this in the right way to this woman of God. "I sometimes feel like I shouldn't be sitting around waiting for God to do His thing. Doesn't He say that He wants us to do our part, too?"

She nodded. "He does. Faith without works . . ."

"Is dead," I said, finishing one of the few Scriptures I knew.

Her smile showed that she was pleased.

I said, "So that's why I sometimes get antsy. I feel like I'm not doing enough to change my life, and that's why I was thinking about getting involved with Girls First. I need to get out and do for others, and maybe some good things will come to me."

"That is a great philosophy to have. But don't belittle the questions you do have about your life; they're good ones. Tell me, what are some of the things you'd like to change?"

I tilted my head. With the exception of

46

Audra, no one had ever asked me that question. And Ms. Viv's words, her tone — she sounded the way I imagined a mother would talk to her daughter. The way a mom would help her little girl dream.

Ms. Viv urged me on. "What kind of life would you like to live? What are the things you'd love to do?"

It was the way she looked at me, her eyes, her expression so welcoming. I opened up. "I imagined that when I graduated, I'd be living in a penthouse in Midtown or in one of those downtown lofts. I had pictured myself being way too busy to cook . . ."

We chuckled together.

"So I'd have to eat at every five-star restaurant in Atlanta. I'm talking about each and every one."

Ms. Viv smiled and nodded some more as if she was right there with me.

"And then, of course, the shopping . . ."

"Oh," Ms. Viv said, "every young lady should be able to shop. I don't have a Scripture for that, but I'm sure the Lord would be pleased."

Again, we laughed.

"I'm not talking about going overboard, like shopping all the time and not being financially responsible. But who wouldn't like a designer dress . . . and a diamond or two?"

With a chuckle, Ms. Viv raised her hand as if she were agreeing, or maybe she was about to testify.

Now I laughed, but only for a moment. "It's all been a dream." My voice was softer now.

Again, Ms. Viv patted my hand. "When I was a young girl, I had the same kind of dreams. I went to college" — she paused — "not Spelman. But when I graduated, I got a job just like you."

Now it was my turn to lean back and listen. Maybe she had some kind of blueprint I could follow.

She said, "But what I discovered was that I needed to do something where I was in charge of my future and that would put me in charge of my finances. So while I was in sales for a little while, after a few years, I became an entrepreneur."

"You own a business?"

"I do." She nodded. "Actually, in my life, I've owned a few. Most of them, I was able to sell after many years for quite a bit of money."

I wondered what her definition of "quite a bit of money" was, but as I sank into the softness of this sofa, I knew however she defined it, it was more than had ever been in my bank account. "What kind of businesses did you own?"

"Oh, some that did this, some that did that." She waved her hand as if that gesture was part of the explanation, too. "It doesn't matter. My point is I made so much more money when I was out on my own."

Because I was just so nosy (or maybe it was because I was still trying to prove my theory), I said, "So you owned a business, but what about your husband?" She was gonna tell me he was a pastor in five . . . four . . . three . . . two . . .

She pressed her hand against her chest and gave me a little laugh. "Oh, no, dear, I've never been married."

Well, there went my rich-widow-First-Lady thesis. That surprised me. No matter her age, Ms. Viv was still an attractive woman. I was sure she'd had more than her share of suitors not only in her day, but even now . . . with the way the Internet was set up.

She said, "But I've lived a very happy and fulfilling life." Then she added with a chuckle, "And it's far from being over." She lifted my left hand. "What about you?" Her eyes scanned my fingers for a ring, I guessed. "You're not married, not engaged."

49

It wasn't quite a question, much more like she was stating a sure fact, and her tone sounded almost as if she was a bit pleased.

I said, "No, not yet. I do have a boyfriend," and smiled because I did that every single time I thought about my man.

"Oh."

Her raised eyebrows made me back up a bit. Ms. Viv was clearly a woman of God, so did I really want her to know that he was more than my boyfriend, that he was my live-in lover? With all the Scriptures she quoted, there would be no way she'd approve.

I said, "Yeah, we've been seeing each other for about three years."

"That's quite a while. And no commitment yet?"

I shrugged, giving myself a little time and space to figure out the best way to say this. In any other time, any other place, I would have been shouting about my love for Stephon from the rooftop. But I didn't want her to ask about our living arrangements.

So, I kept my answer simple, vague, the way she'd done when she told me nothing about her businesses. "We're working it out." That seemed to be good enough.

"Oh" — she waved her hand a little — "it's one of *those* relationships."

50

I nodded, though I didn't know what she meant by that.

"Well. Good. Take your time. Like I said, you're young, so enjoy yourself and this huge world before settling down. Open yourself up to new experiences. You never know what or who may just walk into your life." After a pause, she stood then grabbed a notebook from the side table. "Well, if you don't mind, I want to collect some more information about you — just so I can match you with the right girl as a mentor."

"That's fine," I said as I set my cup down once again.

But even as she jotted down notes, Ms. Viv was a pro because I didn't feel like I was being interviewed; we were just girls, just chatting.

She asked me about everything — more about what I really wanted to do with my life, and I opened up about how my heart's desire was to be an interior designer.

"You really need to find a way to pursue that." She shook her pen, scolding me. "If that's the desire that God put into your heart, then you need to ask Him for the right opportunity to come along. And if you start praying, I can see that happening for you soon."

We talked more about what I had to do in

51

the meantime — my job, and the long hours I worked in pursuit of the money I desired.

"I just want to live a different kind of life," I told her, "where money isn't *the* issue. Where I can take care of some of my wants and not only be focused on all of my needs."

When the conversation shifted to my parents, she shed a tear for my mom when I explained how hard it was knowing her only through photos.

"Cancer is so cruel," she said as she hugged me. "Now I know why God led me to you and you to me." She squeezed my hands. "You know what? I want this to be about more than you being here for one of my girls; I want to mentor you myself."

Her words warmed me like a blessing, and I wondered what good I had done in my life to have met this woman.

She was delighted when we talked about my dad and she realized my father was Oscar Maxwell, one-half of the Oscar and Troy Barbershop, one of the most popular businesses (and social gathering places) in Stone Mountain.

"I can't believe your father is *that* Oscar," she said. "I'll have to meet him one day."

By the time I poured another cup of tea, it was so cool, a few more minutes I might be able to call it iced. I figured that was a sign I'd been with Ms. Viv long enough. Just as I asked if she wanted me to clear the tea set, her doorbell rang.

"Oh." She glanced down at her watch. "I'd totally forgotten the time. I have someone else coming to see me this evening."

"I'm sorry. I didn't mean to take up so much of your time."

"There's nothing for you to be sorry about," she said as we both stood. "This has been so lovely."

I followed her to the front door, and when she opened it, a young lady stepped in, greeting Ms. Viv with a hug. And like what every other woman on Earth did to another woman, I did a quick scan: she was about my age, maybe a little younger, though she was three or four inches taller (which was something since I was five seven), attractive, and had a killer body that was on full display in her leggings . . . and her gold-colored T-shirt tied in a knot at her waist.

The letters GFF were in rhinestones.

I wondered if she was one of the mentees, and I waited for Ms. Viv to introduce us. But after the hug, the woman just moved away as if she'd hardly noticed me.

I guessed that was my cue.

Hugging Ms. Viv, I thanked her again, and

when I stepped back from her, she said:

"I have enjoyed you so much."

"Me too."

She nodded. "What you said about your mom really touched me, but this is what I know. The Lord puts people into your life for a reason, to make a difference. Now, I know I'd never be able to replace your mother, and I wouldn't even try. But understand this: I will always be here for you. You have my number, and I have yours."

"Thank you so much."

"Now, give me some time before I assign you. I have to go through all of my girls to see your best match."

"Okay, that's fine. I'll just wait to hear from you."

"Oh, you will, dear." After another hug, she held my hands and said, " 'May the Lord watch between me and thee, while we are absent one from another.' "

I stood there for a moment, not knowing what I was supposed to do with that. So after a couple of seconds, I said, "Amen?" and she squeezed my hands before she stepped inside and closed her door.

"I like that lady," I whispered as I stepped to my car. Slipping inside, I turned on the ignition, then glanced up at her home once again. That had been some meeting. When I grew up, I wanted to be just like Ms. Viv.

5

Another Saturday morning. Today, the Blue Danube played when I opened the door to our bedroom, and I planted myself in the hallway, my eyes on Stephon as the sun beamed what seemed like a halo over his head.

Like every morning, I hugged him, kissed him, then after feeling like an intruder once a few minutes had gone by, I left my man to his business and left our apartment in search of a way to fill my day.

This was one reason why I was looking forward to joining Ms. Viv; her foundation would give my weekends some kind of purpose. At least, that was my goal.

In the meantime, I started every Saturday morning the same way. After hanging with Stephon for as long as he'd allow, I headed to Buckhead, the neighborhood where I wished I lived, but the way our bank account was set up, I'd need a dozen more commission checks with a lot more zeroes before Stephon and I could even look for a place there. So I ventured out on what I called my standing commitment. Like my biweekly mani/pedis and, of course, my hair appointments, I made my way to Buckhead twice a week — every Saturday and some Thursday afternoons.

My destination: Starbucks. Well, kind of. There was no reason to make this drive for my daily infusion of caffeine; I passed up at least two dozen coffee shops between College Park and Buckhead.

But this was my thing, and I told myself the same thing I said every Saturday morning — this was a great way to get some exercise, walking through either Lenox Square or Phipps Plaza.

This morning, I chose Phipps, and though inside the line was long, after about a dozen minutes, I was sipping my grande vanilla mocha (no whip, no foam) and strolling (my exercise) along my normal path so I would pass all of my favorites: Tiffany, Gucci, and Chanel.

I had never purchased a thing from any one of those stores, but that didn't stop me from imagining the day when I'd be able to stroll down the street wearing a Tiffany bracelet while rocking a Gucci purse over the shoulder of my Chanel jacket. And I pretended I was taking that little walk in all of that designer wear in the Cayman Islands.

After a little more than an hour of getting my mall speed-stroll on, I paused in front of Tiffany and admired the diamonds that sparkled through the window. I knew the prices of these items, and it amazed me that people could walk in and drop what I earned in a year on a whim. That was the life.

"Excuse me."

I lowered my cup from my lips before I glanced up, then leaned back to get a better view of the man who stood in front of me. Now, I didn't have designer money, but what I had was designer knowledge. And just like I knew all about Ms. Viv's furniture yesterday, I knew all about this man's clothes today.

He was dressed casually, but it was casual Armani: from his bright navy houndstooth jacket to his jeans, he wore the Italian designer as if he were a billboard.

"You look so familiar," he said, then snapped his fingers. "Has anyone ever told you that you look like . . ."

I held up my hand and said it before he could, "Like Thelma from *Good Times*."

"No."

I frowned, shocked by that simple word. Because at least once a day someone (mostly men who acted like they still had pinups of Thelma Evans somewhere in their home) told me that, even though I was half Bern-Nadette Stanis's age. But it was like guys thought Thelma had been frozen in 1974.

This guy, though — he was different. "That's not what you were going to say?"

He shook his head. "I was gonna tell you that you look like . . . yourself. You really look like yourself."

We laughed, and he held out his hand. "I'm Michael Porter."

As he reached toward me, a gold-and-diamond watch sparkled from beneath the cuff of his jacket. Taking his hand, I said, "Nice to meet you, Michael Porter."

He laughed. "I see how you did that. So you're not gonna tell me your name?"

"I'm sorry. I have a man."

"I didn't ask you to marry me."

I couldn't help but chuckle. "True, but what's the use in exchanging names when we're not exchanging numbers?"

"We're not?" He raised his eyebrows. "Too bad. 'Cause I like you already. You're quick."

"Thank you." Holding up my cup as if I were giving him a toast, I said, "Have a good day," then walked away.

I didn't even finish my normal jaunt through the mall. There was no need. I'd gotten what I'd come for — I was leaving with coffee, more steps on my watch, and a great big ole smile.

Jumping into my car, I secured my coffee, turned on my Bluetooth, then pressed the number in the first call slot. The phone rang just a couple of times before "Hey, baby girl" sailed through the speakers like the first three notes of a song.

When I heard his smile, I couldn't help but do the same. "Hey, Daddy. What's good?"

"Nothing much. Not much could change between Thursday and today. You know you don't have to worry about me like this, right?"

"What? I can't call you?"

We both knew, though, that behind my feigned innocence, there was a whole lot of worry. My father had painfully weaned me off my daily visits. I was trying to give him his space, but it was so hard — because I worried.

"You can call, but you don't have to drop by." That was his preemptive move because just like I knew him, he knew me . . . and he knew I was on my way.

And my counter: "Daddy, I was gonna

stop by for just a little while."

"Baby girl." The singsong voice that had greeted me was gone, replaced by that you-done-something-wrong tone that years ago had me quivering in my Mary Janes. "You've got to give me some space. I'm a grown man."

I had to bite my lip not to say that he was a grown man who'd just had a stroke nine months before. "I know that. But what about food? Do you have enough?"

"Yes," he said, sounding like he was forcing his patience, "because you went grocery shopping on Thursday morning, just two days ago."

I plowed through his annoyance. "So, have you been cooking?"

"Do you think I've been eating?"

But my dad should have known that I wasn't afraid of the edge in his tone anymore. "I don't know. That's why I want to come by and check."

He sighed, and that made me sorry. I didn't want my dad to think that I thought he couldn't take care of himself, but what was I supposed to do? My dad didn't know that I still had nightmares about the phone call from his business partner, Troy, that had stopped my heart.

"They took him away in an ambulance, Zuri."

61

Troy sobbed. "What we gonna do?"

"Look, baby girl," my dad began, dragging me back from that sunken place that I was sure every child traveled to as a parent aged or got sick, "I'm good. Some of the fellas are coming by in a little while. They're bringing barbecue, beer, and dominoes, so you know what's about to go down. We're gonna hang out, solve the world's problems, and talk about all our women."

He'd thrown in the women just to make me smile, I was sure.

His voice was softer when he added, "I'm trying to make my way back, Zuri." He sounded a bit weary. "But I won't be able to do it if you smother me."

I nodded at the same time that I blinked back tears. "Okay, Daddy. But it's okay if I call, right?"

"What you talkin' 'bout? If you don't call, I'm gonna hunt you down and make you dial my number while I'm standing there."

I laughed. "Okay. So I'll call you later?"

"You better."

"Have a good time today, okay?" And just because I couldn't resist, I added, "And call me if —"

"I know, I know. When I need anything, you're the first person I call."

When I hung up, I sighed and rested for a

few moments in the silence of my car. I wondered if this was what it was like for my dad when he first sent me off to kindergarten, watched me go to the prom, or even drove me to my dorm at Spelman, even though I wasn't that many miles away from home. I didn't understand his concern or the tears in his eyes then, but I sure got it now.

"Okay, Daddy," I whispered. "I'll give you a couple of hours." I hit my Bluetooth again and scrolled through the names on the screen, then tapped the one right after my dad and Stephon. When the phone was answered, I said, "Don't ask me any questions, I'm on my way."

Then I clicked off the phone. My man was working, my father was hanging, so I was going to do my thing, too.

6

The sun was doing its job, arching toward
the top of the midday sky, by the time I
eased my car to the edge of the curb in front
of the first house on the Buckhead cul-de-
sac.

Like any great best friend, Audra had the
front door of her brick home already open,
and she motioned for me to park in the
driveway.

I maneuvered my car, then jumped out,
and before I even stepped onto the walkway,
I said, "I know it's early, but do you want to
run out for lunch?"

Audra held up a bottle of wine. "Is this
what you're really looking for?"

I grinned. My bestie. She knew the truth.

She said, "We're gonna have to do this
here, 'cause I can't leave the house."

I crossed my arms and pouted when I
stood in front of her.

"Sorry; Abagail's off today," she said,

referring to her South African au pair. "And the twins aren't feeling well. They're asleep now."

I frowned as I stepped into the grand foyer of the Spencers' five-bedroom home. "What's wrong with my godchildren?"

"I told you yesterday they had little spring colds." She sighed. "But we're good, 'cause last night, I gave them some Benadryl and each their own bottle of wine. Those five-year-olds can't hang." She waved her hand. "They woke up this morning, took a couple of sips of juice, ate a couple of spoons of cereal, and rolled back over."

I laughed and then followed my best friend across the forever gleaming hardwood floors through the pathway that led to the vaulted-ceilinged family room.

Stepping into this massive space always made me want to dance. And it was only partly because my best friend had hired me (yeah, actually paid money) to decorate this room. Actually, I'd done the entire house for Audra and Joseph. But out of the five thousand square feet, this was my favorite space. It was because of the built-in treasure — one entire wall was all glass, the perfect frame to the backyard. All I'd done was bring the outdoors inside — with the seven-piece modular sectional, which was wicker

(for decor) and had cushy leather cushions (for comfort).

With that bright orange piece and all the plants surrounding the perimeter, this grand room was just an extension of their backyard, which was filled with the thick brush of the trees on one side and a duck pond that spanned over several properties on the other. Paradise in the middle of the city.

I flopped onto the sofa while Audra placed the wine bottle on the table. "Chill for a moment while I get the glasses." Audra paused. "I guess since you came over here looking for a lunch date, you haven't eaten, huh?"

"Nah, I was gonna go over to Dad's and eat with him."

"Wait. So I'm your second choice?"

"Nope, you're third. Stephon's working."

"How am I supposed to take this?" Audra laughed. Shaking her head, she added, "I'll whip something together."

"Don't go to any trouble."

"Oh, I wasn't even thinking about trouble," she said as she stepped into the open kitchen just beyond the family room. "This is gonna be a wine, cheese, and chips kinda lunch. That's all I was having since Joseph is out of town."

"Where?"

"At some kind of Meharry gathering," she said over her shoulder as she turned to the cherrywood-paneled refrigerator, which was hidden, blending in with the rest of the kitchen's cabinetry — all my idea. "He left this morning, will be back on Monday. Mentoring some young doctors. I'm just glad I didn't have to tag along. All that medical talk."

She placed her hand over her mouth as she yawned, and I chuckled. This was Audra's shtick, though I wasn't sure why she performed it for me. I knew who she was — a stay-at-home mom because that was who she wanted to be. And she was excelling at that in the same way she'd shined at Spelman when she graduated summa cum laude with two degrees: a BS in biochemistry and an MRS bestowed onto her by Joseph Spencer, her Morehouse boyfriend, who became a Meharry Medical College graduate and was now on staff at Emory University Hospital as one of the nation's rising oncologists.

As Audra prepared her promised platter of cheese and chips, I did what I always did when I came to her home — I wandered to the window and soaked in the serenity of the view. If yoga were a place, this would be it. All I wanted to do was breathe deeply and feel peace.

After those moments of tranquility, I moseyed to the mantel above the fireplace. The photos were a pictorial celebration of the Spencers' life: our college graduations, their wedding, and then dozens of pictures crammed together of the twins, Lyle and Lily.

A warmth filled me when I held the photo of me, Evelyn (Audra's childhood friend and the other godmother), and the twins at their christening. My friend, the ultimate overachiever in her first pregnancy — a boy and a girl. No need for a repeat — at least that was what she always said. "I nailed that test" were her favorite words when she spoke about her children and the prospect of having more. "No do-overs."

"What are you doing? Remembering the good ole days?"

I glanced up as Audra laid down the silver platter filled with five or six different cheeses, crackers, carrots and celery, and two bowls filled with chips. In the center were a chunky salsa *and* a spinach dip — again, her overachiever-ness always on display.

If anyone had come to my place practically unannounced and I had less than ten minutes to prepare, all they'd get would be a container of yogurt or maybe a bowl of Raisin Bran.

"No, I'm not reminiscing," I said, replacing the photo. "Actually, I'm trying to look ahead."

"Oh?" She raised her eyebrows and did a little lean back. "You tryin' to tell me something?"

I sighed as I sat down and poured the wine, filling the glass way past the line of respectability, especially for an afternoon drink — I had this red wine almost to the brim. "If you're asking me if I'm pregnant" — I raised my glass — "no. Stephon and I are always careful."

"So what're you looking forward to — marriage?"

I smiled through the sip I'd just taken. "Yeah. We talk about it all the time, though we're not ready."

"I'm always surprised when you say that because you've been together for three years and living together for — has it been a year?"

I nodded.

Audra said, "Well, I don't know how much more readiness you need. He's the one, right?"

"I'm sure he is," I said. "And that's before I compare him to all the busters I went out with before him." I shook my head. "Stephon is the reason why it never worked out for me with anyone else. God saved this space just for him and me."

Audra filled her wineglass (though she was far more respectable than me — as always), then settled onto the sofa. "So . . ."

"We still have things we want to work out, mostly financial. And speaking of that . . ." I sighed. "We're not gonna be able to go with you guys next month."

"Oh, no."

"It's money, of course." I took a long sip of wine. "It's always money." Another sip. "Stephon wants to be in a better place financially."

"Well, that makes sense, I guess. Nothing is as bad as starting out a marriage with financial problems."

I tilted my head. "How would you know?" I asked with a chuckle.

She tucked her feet beneath her. "I've read about it." She smirked. "But seriously, what I like best about Stephon is how responsible he is."

I popped a cube of cheese into my mouth, and then, just so I wouldn't have to say anything, I tossed in another.

"What?" she said, knowing me too well.

"Nothing, you're right. He's responsible,

and that's good. It's just that sometimes, I'd like to . . . I don't know. Take a risk, do something without having to think about the money in the bank."

She nodded. "So . . . is this really about Stephon?"

I leaned back and gave a couple of silent seconds to her question. "I don't know. Maybe it's all me. I finally found a sales job where I'm doing okay, but I still don't like sales."

This time, Audra was the one who filled her mouth with wine so she wouldn't have to say anything.

So I said, "What?"

She placed her glass on the table. "I don't know how many times we're going to have this conversation. For the last ten years you've insisted on taking jobs you don't like."

"No, I've taken jobs because I needed money. Isn't that why we all work?"

"True, but if you could just live your passion, we'd never have this conversation again."

I held up my hand, creating a wall against her words. "Going out on my own as an interior decorator won't solve a single problem. It won't pay the bills . . . unless you and Joseph are going to have me redecorating this place every quarter or so . . ."

"That's an excuse you can use." Her words made me do a side lean. "But you're challenged by money now. You don't like your job, *and* you don't have money. So what do you have?"

"Direct deposit."

She chuckled as if she thought I'd meant that as a joke. I didn't. I needed to get that check every two weeks, no matter how insufficient it was.

"Look," Audra began, "how many times have you heard someone say if you find something to do that you love, you won't work a day in your life?"

"The only people who say that are ones who are already making a lot of money." I put the glass down on the table, with a sigh. "I'm tired of living like this, Audra." Standing, I paced in front of her. "For my entire life, this is all I've ever done, and do you know what that's like?" I didn't bother to wait for her to answer because as the daughter of two doctors and now married to one, she didn't know my struggle. "Let me tell you. It's hard facing the first of the month. Sometimes I can't sleep — I can't focus on anything except how are we going to pay our rent.

"And then beyond the bills, there's never

any money to do anything else. I can't go out and buy a new outfit." I paused at the chair by the window. "Or ever own something like this." Grabbing the designer bag I'd talked her into purchasing a couple of months ago, I swung it onto my shoulder. "I couldn't afford the straps on this purse. And talk about going out to eat . . . For once, I'd love to visit a restaurant where the menus weren't plastic." I shook my head. "Do you know how many birthdays, anniversaries, new jobs, and new commissions we've celebrated at Big Daddy's because that's all we can afford?"

And her response to my frustration: "Don't talk about Big Daddy's." She wagged her finger in front of her face. "They have the best burgers in Atlanta."

I threw my hands up in exasperation.

"I'm sorry," she said with a chuckle. "I couldn't resist, but, Z, I understand. That's why I think it's time for you to really consider going after your dream. If you're able to do something in interior design, you'll be happy, and that's where abundance begins. By doing something that you love and then working so hard at it prosperity comes."

I nodded even though I still had only one thought — direct deposit.

She said, "Why don't you start with a couple of interior design classes, maybe from the business side? That may get you going."

This time, I wasn't going to waste the energy to even give her a nod. Me? In class? Again? I'd done a won't-He-do-it dance right there on the stage of that cathedral in Decatur when I was handed my bachelor of arts degree. It was truly a hallelujah moment, because while Audra was acing her biochemistry courses, I struggled through my major — English. If I couldn't ace the language that I spoke, I surely didn't need to be returning to any kind of college for any kind of thing.

"Zuri."

When Audra said my name so softly, I knew something philosophical was about to follow.

"It's time for you to stop being on the sidelines and get into the game. You keep saying you want to play, but you won't suit up. You sit and cheer for everyone else — your dad, Stephon, me and Joseph. But *you* never play. You gotta put on the uniform and get on the court."

Her words made me pause, made me think, made me say, "You're right. Stephon is doing what he loves, you and Joseph are happy where you are, even my dad has a single focus — to get well again . . .Yeah." I nodded. "I'm going to be joining that girls' mentoring group I told you about . . ."

"That's good. Some young girl is gonna be blessed to have you as a big sister."

"And who knows where that may lead. But you're right: in the meantime, I'm gonna figure out how to play in the game for me."

Just as I said that, my cell phone rang, and the pulsing heart on the screen made me grin.

"Must be your man," Audra said, even before I had a chance to press ACCEPT.

"Hey, babe," I said, rolling my eyes at Audra. "What's up?"

"I was just checking on you and wanted to know if you had a little time to have lunch with me."

If *I* had time? "Oh, you're taking a break?"

"I will if you can."

"Okay." This was a bit surprising. Once Stephon got started painting on a Saturday, there were times when he hardly stopped to sleep, forget about eat. "Sure, I'd love to have lunch with you."

Audra raised an eyebrow and pointed at the spread she had laid out for us.

I turned my back on her. "I'll stop and

pick up something. What do you want?"

"You. Just you. Only you."

Without saying good-bye to Stephon (there was no need; he knew I was on my way), I pressed end on the call, then jumped up and grabbed my purse.

Audra grinned. "Single people problems."

"No, this is single people's life." I shrugged as I made my way to the door. "And anyway, I'm not the one with two kids. Just save that wine. I *may* be back. After all" — I turned to face her right before I got to the door — "it's just lunch."

She busted out laughing as I skipped to my car, ready to have a nice, long meal with my boyfriend.

7

Did I really want to stand in this line on a Monday morning? I counted by twos the number of people in front of me in this Starbucks line — twelve. Yeah, this was gonna be a fifteen-minute or so wait. I sighed. Mondays were the only days when I had to be in the office by nine o'clock for a staff meeting. With twenty-five minutes before I'd be late, I decided to stay. That long morning meeting would go so much better if I walked in with this grande morning mocha.

So that I wouldn't be in the line tapping my foot, rolling my eyes, and sucking my teeth, I pulled out my cell and texted Stephon:

I ♡ you.

His cell must have been sitting right by his easel, because not even ten seconds had passed when my phone vibrated:

Beyond infinity.

I smiled and squeezed the phone as if I were holding my boyfriend. What a weekend we'd had, beginning with our "lunch date" on Saturday. The only thing — I'd missed church on Sunday, and I didn't really like to do that. But it had been difficult to peel myself away from Stephon, since I could never get him to go to church with me.

Thoughts of my boyfriend kept me cool — for about three minutes. And then that toe-tapping, eye-rolling, teeth-sucking attitude washed over me once again.

On my phone, I clicked over to Twitter to take myself back to calm, and that was the balm I needed. Twitter had no chill and kept me entertained until I heard the singsong voice of the barista.

"Hey, Ms. Zuri." Her waist-long braids swayed as she belted out my name, sounding like she was about to break into a song. "Are you having your usual this glorious morning?"

Ugh. There were two things wrong with this picture — first, I'd told the young woman not to call me "Ms." anything. I was only five — okay, maybe ten . . . well, it was probably more like fifteen — years older than her. But still, if I let her call me *Ms.* today, it would be *ma'am* tomorrow.

And the second thing — who sang this

early in the morning if they weren't in the shower? She was way too chipper to be serving coffee before nine a.m. "Yeah, the usual," I said. And then I added, "A grande vanilla mocha, no whip, no foam," because there was no way I wanted her to mess this up this morning.

The braided barista tapped the register's screen, before singing, "That'll be five thirty-five."

Before I could raise my phone and point the app toward the scanner, a voice over my shoulder said, "I got you."

I blinked as I turned to face him.

To the barista, the man said, "Give me a tall, no water chai."

For too long, I just stood there because I couldn't figure out what just happened as the man handed the barista his credit card.

"Wait." I finally found my voice and said, "You don't have to do that." My words came out just as the register beeped to let me know his transaction was complete.

He turned toward me with a smile that a decade ago would have had me shedding clothing. "I do one act of kindness a week. Today's Monday. Consider this my act, and I'll be done."

He bowed just a tiny bit, and I chuckled. As I turned to move away, the braided barista caught my eye, and the teenager had the nerve to raise one eyebrow and do a little side lean like she was trying to tell me: *Girl, you'd better jump on that.*

But when he faced her, the barista's innocence was back. "I'll have your orders out in a minute," she said in a tone as sweet as the sugar I was about to put in my coffee.

"Thank you," the man said.

All that was left for me to say was the same. "Thank you."

"You're welcome," he said as we eased our way to the pickup side, which was filled with people yawning, rubbing their eyes, all looking at their phones. "It gave me a chance to say something to you. You've been pretty engrossed in that phone since we've been in that line."

Really? This fine specimen had been standing behind me all of that time? As someone stepped between us to get to the service table, I took the seconds to do what I did best — my assessment.

I had no choice; I had to start with the suit — from the Versace collection, if I had to make one of my usually spot-on guesses. It was dark navy, his shirt was the crispest of whites, his tie, power red — he looked good. I wanted to get a glance of his shoes, spit-shined, as my father would say, I was sure. But I didn't want to be so obvious in my appraisal of him.

This was a man whose clothes did not make him. He was more than fine — he was handsome, in a refined sort of way. *Refined* was not a word that I used for someone who was in the vicinity of my age, but that was the best way to describe him. He was the color of a shiny penny, which seemed appropriate — money. And he emanated power. I could see him growing up to be Barack Hussein Obama II.

"I'm Julian." His voice snapped me back, making me realize I'd been staring. "Julian Stone."

Dang. Even his name sounded like money, full of sophistication.

He said, "And you're Ms. Zuri, I know that much."

Holding out my hand to him, I said, "You can drop the 'Ms.' part. Zuri is fine. Zuri Maxwell." It was surprising to me that I gave him my name. I was stopped by men so often — remember, most of the time they thought I was Thelma, and so I let them just call me that. But I guess since, courtesy of the barista, Julian already knew my first name . . .

"It's nice to meet you," he said, shaking

my hand with a grip that showed he thought of me as an equal.

I liked that. I hated the fish handshake from a man.

"So, are you from around here?" he asked.

"No, I work in this building."

"Ah! I'm working in the building across the street; I'm here on a special assignment. I'm from Miami."

"Miami," I said with a bit of longing in my voice.

"Have you ever been there?"

"No." I shook my head, not telling him that I'd never been on a plane. I was probably the only Spelman graduate in the history of Spelman graduates who'd never taken a flight. I'd never been more than one hundred miles away from Atlanta. I said, "But I've always wanted to go to South Beach."

"Oh, yeah? Well, maybe one day you can get down there and I can show you around."

"Zuri!" a barista called out.

Before I could move, though, Julian grabbed my drink, then turned and handed it to me.

"Thanks," I said. After a moment, I added, "Well," because the silence between us was beginning to feel a bit awkward.

"So," he began, then paused as if he was

trying to think of something else to say. "What kind of work do you do?"

I hesitated for a moment, again wondering if I wanted to share. "I'm in advertising sales," I told him, feeling that was innocent enough.

"Really?" His tone sounded like he'd been searching for an ad sales rep all of his life. Then he explained, "I didn't mean to get all excited, but I'm here on a short-term consulting project, for a tech company, and one of the things I want to look into for them is advertising — getting the word out about their new personal assistant app."

"Wow, that sounds interesting."

"Yeah, you know what? Let's have dinner tonight," he said, just as the barista called out his chai. When he turned back to me, he said, "So, dinner?"

"I'm sorry, but I can't. I'm involved."

He raised an eyebrow. "Aren't we all?" Before I could figure out a way to respond to that, he added, "Look, it's really just to pick your brain. I need some advice, and you might be able to help me." I wasn't sure if it was my expression or my hesitation. "Seriously, strictly for business," he said, holding up his empty hand. "And think of it this way . . . It'll be your act of kindness."

He flashed a smile that made me smile,

but still I hadn't budged.

"And you'll save me from eating alone. Everyone has been recommending this restaurant called Georgia's, and I want to . . ."

"Georgia's?" I hadn't meant to share my longing aloud, but if there was anything I knew better than designer clothes and high-end furniture, it was five-star restaurants, all the places that I'd wanted to visit. Georgia's had for a long time been on that list.

Then, Julian sealed the deal with "Really. Just business."

Just business. Those were the words that did it for me. Suppose I could turn this into an account for my company? That would mean a greater commission check next quarter and a greater chance of a vacation in my future.

"Okay." I tried to sound nonchalant about it all. "If it's for business, then fine. Maybe this'll work out for both of us."

He passed me that smile again, this time showing a bit of teeth that looked as expensive as everything else about him. As he led me away from the pickup counter, he said, "Let me give you my cell number so you can call it."

"Don't you have a business card?"

"I do." He nodded, though he didn't make

any moves to get a card for me. "But this is important," he said. "I really need some advice for this business, and I don't want my card to get lost . . . or find its way to the slush pile . . . by complete accident, of course."

I laughed. "Okay," I said, then dialed his number as he whispered the numerals. Actually, I was glad we were doing it this way because Julian was right — his card probably would have made its way into the trash, and that would have been tragic. Because right now, there were two things on my mind: going to Georgia's and how this might turn into an account for me.

Once I pressed in all of his digits, his phone rang, and he answered as if he weren't right in front of me.

"I'll call you back after I make a reservation," he said into his phone. "Is tonight good?"

I laughed as he kept the phone pressed to his ear. I shook my head. "No, I already have something I have to do. Tomorrow would be better."

"If it's better for you, it's best for me." He clicked off his phone. "I'll call you tomorrow after I get our reservation."

I nodded my agreement.

He reached for my hand to shake it again.

"It was nice meeting you, Zuri."

"Same." And then I turned and walked through the door that led to the lobby of my office building. Julian said he worked across the street, so I knew he wouldn't be following me, though he would be watching me. He was a black man, wasn't he? Black men loved to see us coming, but the pleasure was all theirs when we sashayed away.

Knowing exactly where his eyes were at this moment made me chuckle, though I wasn't looking for his approval. All of the appreciation I needed was waiting for me at home. But it was going to be nice to eat at Georgia's and get a chance to pitch an account and earn a large commission.

Oh, this was going to be good. I couldn't wait to get home to tell Stephon about this.

8

This time, I didn't call. I hadn't seen my father since Thursday, and I wasn't going to let him stop me again. He wouldn't have to worry; I had no plans of staying too long. Mondays always felt longer than any other day in the work-week, and I couldn't wait to get home. But first, there was Daddy.

I slipped out of my car and then traipsed up the long driveway to the front door of my dad's Stone Mountain home. I wasn't really sure why I always referred to this as Daddy's house since this was the place I'd called home from birth until I'd graduated from college, then returned seven years later after discovering that adulting was a huge financial challenge for me. So really, this was my home, too.

I pushed the doorbell and sighed the way I always did because really, I just wanted to use my key, but the rule in Oscar Maxwell's house was that my key was to be used in case of emergency only.

Don't be just walking up in this joint if you don't want to see something that you shouldn't see.

I always became impatient as I waited for my dad to make his way from wherever he was in the house to the front. But this was his joint, his rules, so as I waited, I turned and scanned the block filled with homes that had been the center of my existence for so long. Stone Mountain wasn't the wealthiest suburb of Atlanta, but it was rich in the ways you can't deposit in a bank. Like any Southern city, it had a past — first with the carvings in Stone Mountain park that paid homage to the Civil War generals, but this city was really immortalized in Reverend Dr. Martin Luther King Jr.'s "I Have a Dream" speech.

For me, though, this street on Kenilworth's history was about the families that extended from one house to the other. Mrs. Conyers, across the street, had made sure our kitchen cabinets were full and there was dinner on the stove every night for so many years after my mother died. Then, there was Mr. and Mrs. Powell next door to Mrs. Conyers, who kept me after school and then took me with their daughter (my best friend at the time), Iesha, on all kinds of excursions on the weekends — to Braves and Falcons games, to the CNN studio, to the Atlanta History Center — all while Daddy worked long hours in his barbershop. And I would never forget Mrs. Dole, whose house was on the right side of ours and who took me school shopping every year until I was old enough to handle that task on my own.

"Hey, Zuri."

And then there was Mrs. Lewis.

Turning toward the voice, my memories of Mrs. Lewis were so different from the heartfelt ones I had for everyone else on the street. I think I was about eight or nine years old the first time Iesha and I tried to devise a plan to have Mrs. Lewis kidnapped. And we weren't the only kids who wanted her taken out. Mrs. Lewis was the original head of Homeland Security. She saw everything, told everything, was hated by everyone under the age of eighteen.

"How you doing, baby?" Mrs. Lewis called from across her porch.

I gave her a smile that I hoped let her know I still didn't like her. "I'm good."

"You getting here a little late today, aren't you?" My eyes narrowed. "Don't you usually come by before you go to work?"

Wait a minute? Was she still checking me like that?

As if she didn't expect me to answer her questions, she kept on talking. "Your dad's doing real good. You know I knock on that door every morning and every night."

That made my smile warm up a bit. I really needed to let go of the animosity I held because of all of those tales she'd told on me twenty-five years ago. "Thank you for doing that," I said as I dug into my purse. Now that Mrs. Lewis was standing out here, I needed to get in there; I'd just have to deal with Daddy fussing about me using my key. But just as I pulled it out, I heard the scuffle of my father's feet. After too many more moments, there was the sound of the locks turning, then the door creaked open.

"Hey, Daddy," I said. "Surprise!"

He chuckled. "I knew you'd be here today." He rolled his walker back so it would be easier for me to come in. Every time I saw my father, I chuckled — yeah, he was on a walker and *still* didn't want me walking up into his house.

But when I stepped inside, my thoughts turned to the time capsule that I entered. I'd always felt that way whenever I walked through this door. I was back in 1991, September twenty-fourth to be exact: the day my mom passed away. Because from that day, nothing in this house had changed. The blue chintz sofa (so 1980s) was still the centerpiece of the living room, along with the white rocking chair on one side and then the only piece that had made its way into Daddy's home in this millennium — the dark brown recliner.

Everything else remained as a tribute, I guessed, to memorialize my mother. No matter how many times I offered to update the house for Daddy, even with him knowing decorating was my love, he refused.

I kissed his cheek; then, as I bolted the three locks, my father turned around and shuffled toward the sofa. I studied him as he struggled with his steps and dragged his left foot. When he plopped onto the sofa with a sigh, I smiled.

"So, you're good?" I said, before I crossed the room and sat next to him.

"Yeah, I'm real good," he said; then he leaned back a little. "Can't you look at me and see that?"

I chuckled. "You look wonderful."

At least that was what I said. But now that I was closer to him, I saw the weariness in his eyes, which had once been so bright but were now hooded as if at any moment he might fall asleep. Nor could I ignore the slack of his jaw on his left side or the way his breathing was still a bit labored, even though he'd been sitting now for more than a minute.

"Have you eaten dinner?"

"Nah, too early for that. I will in an hour or so."

"Well" — I stood and dumped my purse onto the sofa — "I can go in there and make you something and at the same time check out the pantry and see what groceries you might need. I can go shopping in the morning before I go to work."

He struggled to push himself up as if he was going to follow behind me. "No, baby girl, you sit here. I don't need anything."

I ignored him, already heading toward the dining room, which separated the kitchen from the rest of the house. But when I made that right turn, my steps slowed as I approached the kitchen. My mouth opened wide as I took in the dishes that were piled high in the sink, then the two pots and frying pan that sat on the stove and were still filled with food — one, burned rice; the other, soggy beans. And the frying pan had remnants of scrambled eggs.

I stepped onto the linoleum and tried to do a slow three-sixty spin, but my foot kept sticking to something on the floor. This place looked like it hadn't been cleaned in a month — but I'd been here Thursday, before I went into my office. I'd left this house looking as if a Merry Maids team had paid an all-day visit. Which meant that all of this had accumulated in only four days.

"I was just about to come in here and clean up."

His voice floated over my shoulder, and I turned to face my father as he pushed his way through the dining room.

It must have been the way I crossed my arms and stared at him that made him stop and steady himself before he released one hand from his walker and held it up. "Don't start," he told me.

"Daddy, you can't —"

"I can."

"Stay here by yourself," I finished. My shoulders sagged as I said, "You would be so much more comfortable someplace where you could have help."

"No!" He was so pissed, his anger shifted from his tone to his short staccato steps as he rolled toward me. "How many times do I have to tell you. I don't need to go no place. I don't need no assistance in living. I can live all by myself."

His walker got awfully close, and I jumped back before he rolled over my toes, assaulting me on purpose, I was sure. He charged toward the sink, then turned on the faucet full blast, splashing water all over the dishes, all over the counter, all over us.

"And when I need help," he grumbled as he lifted a pan and slammed it onto the counter, "I got help. I got you."

I moaned.

He kept on, "So don't be talking to me about moving out of my home. Where I have lived all of my life. Coming all up in here telling me what to do."

Taking a breath, I shifted my tone and my attitude. "Okay, Daddy. Okay," I said, returning to the sweet daughter who had no opinion and who just did what her father told her to do. "We won't talk about that. Just let me do this." I put my hands on his shoulders, trying to direct him away. "I'll clean up."

"You don't have to; I can do it myself."

"I know I don't have to, Daddy — I want to. So you go on back into the living room, I'll bring you something to drink, then by the time you finish yelling at those people on MSNBC" — I paused, then breathed, grateful that the ends of his lips quivered into a smile — "I'll come back in there and we can talk before I go home."

That little smile of his disappeared as quickly as he'd given it to me. "As long as we don't talk about me leaving my home." Pushing himself away, he mumbled, "I'm not leaving my house. No matter what some snot-nosed kid says to me."

My eyebrows rose all the way to the ceiling. Was he talking about me? Right before he disappeared into the living room, I said, "I love you."

A grunt was his response, and that made me smile. Because there really was so much love inside that little sound.

But then I turned back to the sink and blew out a long breath. There were times when I thought my father was getting better, but even if he was, I couldn't deny that he wasn't well enough or strong enough to take care of himself and his home.

He was right: he did have me. But taking care of him was a lot. Between his doctor visits, keeping his house clean, grocery shopping, paying his bills, going through his mail, and checking the records on the barbershop that he still half owned, I wasn't sure that I was doing a good enough job of handling it all. My father may not have needed help, but I sure did.

The tap was still running, and I stacked the dishes to the side, filling the sink with sudsy water. Then I stood and stared out into the thickness of the trees in the backyard, the natural boundaries to my father's property.

After all the things I'd ticked off in my head about what I did for my dad, my greatest responsibility was just making sure he was safe. And since he was never going to leave this house, that would have to become my primary responsibility. The thoughts I had about needing to change my own life would have to be put aside for a while. I had no plans to move back home, but short of living here, I'd just have to make sure that my dad never faced any harm. Those phone calls when he told me I couldn't come by were over.

As I washed the dishes and scrubbed the pots, I tried to figure out a good schedule. At least that was the one thing about my career choice — I pretty much set my schedule, so I'd just figure out a way to be here every day, even if only for an hour.

By the time I'd put everything away, cleaned the counters and the stove, and mopped the floor, a couple of hours had passed. I was too tired to do any cooking, but I'd run out to get him something for dinner. Returning to the living room, I paused as I took in the sight of my father, leaned back in the recliner, feet up, eyes closed. What was best was that there was a smile on his face, as if he knew that all was right with his world because I was here.

If that was his thought, he was correct. My job was to make sure there were plenty more smiles to come in all the days left in front of him.

9

If yesterday had been a long day, there wasn't a word to describe today. I felt like I'd been awake for a week since I'd started at six, wanting to make sure that I took care of my father before I came into the office. I'd gone shopping, made his breakfast, then while he ate, I made a bologna sandwich and salad for his lunch, then baked a chicken and mashed some potatoes for his dinner.

All of that done before the clock even struck nine. I hadn't made it into the office, though, until a bit after ten, but even here, I hadn't had a moment to breathe. Between meetings and reports that were due, there was only one time when I'd taken a bit of a break.

I'd been standing at the elevator, about to run down to Starbucks to grab something that looked close to lunch when my cell phone rang. At first, I'd smiled, thinking that it was Stephon telling me how much he'd missed me this morning since I'd left so early. Then I'd frowned because I didn't recognize the 305 area code. But I was in sales — that meant every call was answered. I was still frowning a bit as I recalled the conversation . . .

"This is Zuri Maxwell," I said, once I answered the phone.

"Hello, beautiful." The lines in my forehead had to be much deeper now, and my hesitation made the man on the other end of the line say, "This is Julian. Julian Stone."

"Oh," I said, surprised that he'd addressed me that way. We'd just met, just yesterday, and he felt it was okay to speak to a business associate like that? "Hello." I kept my voice steady and stern.

"I hope you're having a wonderful day."

"I am," I said, maintaining my professionalism. "Busy, but I'm sure it'll be an amazing day."

"And it's about to get better," he said. "I'm looking forward to our dinner tonight."

It wasn't that I had forgotten; it was more like I hadn't really remembered with all that had been on my plate in between the hour when Julian and I had met and now.

He kept on, "I wanted to let you know about our reservation. Tonight. At eight."

"Eight?"

"Yeah, is there a problem?"

"I was just expecting us to get together a bit earlier. I was hoping around six or so. I should've told you that."

"Ah, nah," he said. "I was lucky to get us in there at eight."

What he said . . . was true . . . I guessed. Georgia's, with its popularity, was always so crowded that without a reservation it was impossible to get a table.

He said, "I hope this isn't a problem. I've been thinking about you all day."

My eyes narrowed. Had this man mistaken the reason why I'd accepted his invitation? "Julian, I just want to make sure we're on the same page; this is about business."

"Oh, yeah. Yeah, definitely. I'm sorry, you must've misunderstood me; I've been thinking of all the questions I wanted to ask you all day. So, eight? You good?"

Leaning back in my chair now, I released a sigh as I remembered how we'd ended that call. I'd told him that I *was* good because I'd been so embarrassed with how I'd interpreted (and mistaken) his friendliness.

We agreed to meet at Georgia's, even though he'd offered to pick me up so that we could ride together.

But now as I glanced at the clock on my desk — it was just a little before seven — his words — *Hello, beautiful . . . I've been thinking about you all day* — played again in my mind. I know what Julian had said he meant, but I also knew what I felt. And I was a woman who listened to her intuition.

But this was a potential new account, so I couldn't cancel. And we were going to be in a public place, and I was driving myself, so everything would be fine.

My phone startled me out of my thoughts, and my smile was instant when I glanced down at the pulsing heart on my cell's screen.

"Hey, babe," I answered.

"What's up? I thought you'd be home by now."

"You've finished painting for the day?" That was surprising to me. Most nights, Stephon painted until almost midnight.

"Yeah, I could have gone a few more hours, but what I couldn't go a few more hours without is you. You left so early this morning, and I want to make up for that tonight."

I released a long sigh. His love never

stopped, and right then, I said a quick prayer that it never would. "Awww, babe."

"So come home. Let's go out to dinner."

I sat up in my chair. "Really?" If he had Georgia's on his mind . . .

"Yeah, let's go out instead of doing a takeout. Let's eat *at* Big Daddy's."

He said that as if Big Daddy's was a big thing, and for a moment, I was kinda frozen. Now, I couldn't be mad — to my man, his invitation was a big deal. To me . . .

I said, "You forgot I have a business dinner tonight."

"Yeah . . . I did. Are you there now?" Before I could answer, he said, "I'm so sorry, babe. I hope I didn't disturb you in the middle of it."

"No, I haven't even left the office. We're not meeting at the restaurant until eight."

"Oh, that's kind of late."

"I know," I said, so glad that I'd already told Stephon about this meeting. The only thing — I hadn't mentioned that it was with a man, one man, not a group . . . at Georgia's. Because if Stephon knew that, an eight o'clock dinner would take on a whole 'nother meaning. I said, "I'm not happy about it being so late. But I'm really hoping this may turn into a new account, and —"

"Hey, babe, slow your roll. You don't have

to explain anything to me. I'm excited for you. Just get your hustle on, boo, and I'll see you when you get home. I'll be here."

"I love you."

He said, "Beyond infinity," before I clicked off the phone.

It was amazing; Stephon didn't even know it, but he'd made me feel better about this dinner. I was doing this for me, for my career, but for us, too. Just like Ms. Viv told me on Friday, I needed to be open to new possibilities. And meeting Julian right after she said that was one of them.

Grabbing my purse, I stuffed the few folders I'd need before I'd come into the office tomorrow into my tote, then bounced out of my chair.

I was ready to take care of business.

This restaurant could have easily been called Top of the World, or at least Top of Atlanta, because that was how I felt the moment I stepped off the elevator and took in the 360-degree circular view of the city from the thirty-fifth floor of the Cortland Hotel in downtown.

Atlanta's skyline glimmered bright from the city's lights. This was a postcard-worthy view, and I wanted to take it all in. I had time; I was a little less than fifteen minutes early.

Before I stepped to the hostess's station, my glance scanned the restaurant. Even from where I stood, this place was thick with elegance. It was in the way tables were draped with golden cloths and brass candelabra as centerpieces. And the way the waitstaff were dressed. Even the servers wore dresses or skirts and the men, sports jackets. It was in the light that was dim, but not dark. Far from one-hundred-watt lighting, but enough so I didn't have to squint.

Approaching the hostess, I gave her my name along with Julian's.

"But I'm a bit early," I said, glancing at my watch. I expected her to ask me to step to the side (or maybe to the bar) and wait.

But then she said, "Mr. Stone has already been seated."

That made me raise an eyebrow. I wasn't used to anyone beating me anywhere — the Virgo was strong in me.

"You can follow me."

The sights had overwhelmed my senses when I first entered Georgia's. Now, it was the sounds that engulfed me, but not in an ordinary way. Even though the dozens and dozens of tables in the circular space were filled with patrons, it was . . . quiet. Not silent, but quiet. Just a soft din of chatter and clatter, a sophisticated sound, if that could be a description, where even the laughter was polite, refined. I guessed that was just the ambience of a five-star restaurant . . . and its patrons.

As we approached one of the tables alongside the glass panels, Julian stood. I couldn't help but smile. He'd copped one of the best tables in the place. I was surprised, but then, not surprised. Julian Stone seemed like that kind of guy.

It was a bit too dim for me to appraise his suit to determine the designer, but I could tell it was gray and expensive, the type of wool blend that didn't wrinkle no matter what you did to it.

He nodded to the hostess, as if he were thanking her for delivering me, then he held out my chair. "Good evening," he said rather than hello.

I said the same to him and added, "This is beautiful." I leaned a bit so that I could see just how high we were. But there was a ledge blocking the view all the way down — built that way on purpose, I supposed.

Julian said, "So, no fear of heights?" Before I could answer, he added, "I guess I should have asked you that before I had them sit us here."

I laughed. "No fear, and I guess that's a good thing in this place." Turning, I scanned the space. "Wow."

"So you've never been here before?" There was surprise in his tone.

I shook my head. "No, it's been on my list."

"Well, then I'm glad we were able to schedule this *business*" — he paused as if he wanted me to notice that word — "dinner here. Thank you for joining me. I know the time was a bit later than you wanted."

I held up my hand. "No, this is fine." And it really was. Just being in this restaurant, surrounded by all of this, and the way Julian greeted me, had put me at ease.

Then he asked, "So, should we order a bottle of wine?" And he hardly took another breath before he added, "But only if that's appropriate for a business meeting."

I gave him a teasing smirk. "Wine would be fine. Wine would be nice."

His smile seemed brighter over the flicker of the candle's light and we agreed on a pinot noir. Before the waiter returned with our glasses, we chatted about all things that weren't important: the beauty of the beginning of spring in Atlanta, how he was staying at the Ritz (here in downtown) but preferred the one in Buckhead, and how we were both children of the South.

Once we had our drinks and then gave the waiter our entrée orders (there had been so much to select from, but I'd chosen the lobster gratin, while Julian chose the filet of Martin's Angus prime beef, with potatoes, of course), we chatted about the company that had brought him to Atlanta.

"It really is quite a concept," he said as he sipped his wine. "A personal assistant app that is Siri and Alexa on steroids. In your phone, with whatever information you want the app to have, it will be able to research and then make hotel and flight arrangements, secure dinner reservations, buy movie tickets, pay parking tickets, debate issues with you."

I raised my hand. "I need that app, stat."

He laughed. "That's what I'm hoping for — about five million people just like you." He shook his head. "Artificial intelligence is no joke, and this is a group of four young African American men who have designed this thing. I'm just happy to be down with the brothers, supporting them. I was glad they chose my company as consultants. Always support black businesses."

I had to take a moment before I spoke, because this wine — it was the smoothest I'd ever tasted. Then I said, "I'm with you on that. I was raised by an entrepreneur." When he glanced at me with a question in his eyes, I explained, "My dad has owned a barbershop all his adult life. So I know the work that goes into the business beyond cutting hair, shaving beards, and clipping mustaches. It's what's done in the back room, the part of the business that people never see; that's the hard work, the important work."

"Preach," he said, and I laughed. "Seems like your dad has taught you a lot."

"He has. I was raised by my father, so he means everything to me. From my name to . . ."

Just then, the waiter returned with our entrées, and after blessing the food, we returned to our conversation. "So, your dad gave you your name?"

"He did. He said he saw the name in an *Ebony* magazine article before I was even thought about, and he knew that's what he wanted to name his daughter if he ever had one. When my mom got pregnant, he hoped for a girl the whole time. So when I was born, he named me Zuri Hope Maxwell."

He nodded. "Great story. Sounds like a great guy."

"He really is. I know everyone says that about their dad, especially girls. But everything that I have a love for, I got from him. Like music. I may have been born in the eighties, but give me some good ole music from the sixties and seventies . . ."

"Hold up. What you know about ole-school?" He gave me a side glance that told me he didn't believe me.

And then it was on.

Over our meal — which, by the way, pleased my palate more than any food that had ever touched my tongue — we debated who was the best. From Marvin Gaye to Stevie Wonder and all the rest:

"I learned how to spell R-E-S-P-E-C-T before I could spell my name," I told him.

"And I learned about the ecology and my responsibility to that from Marvin Gaye."

We bumped fists when Julian said that.

Julian said, "And there was nothing better than 'A Change Is Gonna Come.' "

"Oh, see, now you going *way* back." I laughed. "Sam Cooke."

"So, let me ask you this." He paused so dramatically, I wondered what was coming. "Are you a movie connoisseur, too?"

"I am." Using my napkin, I wiped the corners of my lips. "Really, I don't think you can love one without the other."

He bobbed his head a little as if he were trying to decide if he agreed. "You may be right. One of the reasons I've probably seen *Titanic* fourteen times is because I love the soundtrack." And then he held his hand up as if it were a stop sign. "Do not ever tell anyone I said that. I will deny it."

"Okay." I laughed. "But I think everyone else in the world has seen it fifteen times."

Like music, our taste in movies were the same. Of course, we enjoyed the ones from our childhood: *Boyz n the Hood* and *Love & Basketball,* then the biopics *Malcolm X* and *Ray,* and when the busboy came to clear our table, I was sure he thought we'd lost our minds when we gave him the Wakanda salute.

By the end of my second glass of the smoothest wine with the longest finish I'd ever sipped, it was hard to remember when I'd enjoyed dinner so much. When the check came, there was no way for me to see it, but I knew Julian was about to drop way over one hundred dollars.

But all he did was glance down, pull out his gold card, and pay the bill with as much concern as I had when I bought a bottle of water.

"Shall we?" he said when he finally signed the check, then stood and pulled out my chair.

We strode through the restaurant that was

still filled with patrons even though the hour was approaching eleven. I took my time, wanting to soak up the elegance since I wasn't sure when I'd have a chance to visit a place like this again.

At the elevator, I sighed — oh, to eat at restaurants like this all the time. But I pulled back my desire and focused instead on just being grateful for this dinner.

It wasn't until we were inside the elevator that I remembered. "Wait, we barely discussed your business," I said, turning to him.

"I know," he said, though he didn't seem concerned. "We'll just have to do this again."

He said those words as the elevator doors parted and we stepped into the grand lobby of the Cortland. By the way Julian strolled by my side, I could tell he wasn't affected by the surroundings.

But I was. This was the closest I'd ever been to hotel rooms that were six and seven hundred dollars a night. Just like upstairs, I wanted to soak in the opulence, which was so far from my ordinary life. I tried not to slow down and gawk at the oversize crystal chandeliers or stand in awe of the marble floors.

Outside, it wasn't much better. The cars

parked along the hotel's circular driveway were Bentleys and Ferraris and Lamborghinis. I held my breath as I handed the valet my ticket, hoping that he wouldn't laugh out loud at my nine-year-old Chrysler 300.

But the valet said nothing, Julian paid for my parking (which I thanked him for), and we chatted again about things that would never matter.

When my car arrived first, Julian waved the valet away, then held the door open for me.

"Thank you again," I said. "The dinner was great. I'm just sorry we didn't get to really brainstorm on the business."

"Like I said, we'll just have to do it again."

The smile that I gave him was meant to neither confirm nor give my regrets. I just got into the car, closed the door, and sped off without looking back. I had a man I hadn't seen all day who I couldn't wait to kiss.

But before I exited the hotel's driveway and turned onto Peachtree, I did glance back . . . through the mirror. And I saw Julian still standing there. Would he call me again for dinner? Then I wondered, if he did, would I say yes?

I wasn't sure why I asked myself that question when I already knew the answer.

10

It wasn't supposed to be like this.

I wasn't supposed to smile whenever I saw Julian's number on my cell. But that was what had been happening for the week he had been in Atlanta — whenever he called, I smiled.

What was so bad about that (or maybe it was a good thing): the smile wasn't about Julian. As fine as that man was, he couldn't stand next to Stephon without being embarrassed.

But what Julian could do was take me to these restaurants that I'd only imagined. Georgia's had been the beginning, and then Julian had taken me to two more of the best. Two nights after Georgia's we'd gone to Southern Star, and then this past Monday it had been the Carriage House.

Now Julian was ringing my phone once again as I lined up my car with the curb in front of my father's house and turned off the ignition. Then I accepted his call.

"Hey, Julian," I said, always very careful to keep our conversation on a friendly but mostly business level.

"What's up?" Clearly, Julian's assessment of our conversations was the opposite.

"I'm just going to check on my father before I head to the office."

"My mother always told me I could tell a good woman by the way she treated her father."

I left his words hanging in the air because they had nothing to do with me. Not that I wasn't a good woman, but I was Stephon's good thing.

Julian said, "So, I was calling to see if we could have dinner tonight."

And there was my smile again. Without even knowing what restaurant he was talking about, I was ready to go.

But I couldn't. And I wouldn't. Not that I didn't want to — I still wished there was a way for me to pitch my agency for this account. All I could think about was how I was going to increase my commission check. But as we'd discussed the company, it'd become clear to me that Julian's only interest was in getting information. That was cool; he'd been up front about it. He'd approached me to help him, and that was what

115

I'd done. And anyway, I didn't want to be beholden to anyone for anything. That was not the way I did business.

So I said, "Come on. We've been out three times already."

"Not out," he corrected me. " 'Out' implies something else, and we have had business dinners."

That was true; after our first dinner, we'd always talked business, though the discussions never seemed very deep to me. Julian had asked just very surface questions: What kind of advertising would I suggest? Are social media formats good for advertising? I had wanted to do more of an assessment of the company, their budget, their needs, understanding their market before I made recommendations. But I let Julian lead, and I answered his questions.

I said, "Yes, it's been all business, and now that business is over."

"Nope," he said as if his word were final. "Just one more dinner, and it has to be tonight, because I'm leaving on an afternoon flight tomorrow."

My eyebrows came together, and I did a quick calculation in my head — I'd met Julian ten days ago. "I thought you were here for a month."

"I was supposed to be, but my business

wrapped up early, and you had a lot to do with it. When I made my presentation to the partners yesterday, they loved my plan, accepted it, and we're just putting finishing touches on it today and they'll be almost ready to roll."

"Wow." I hoped he didn't hear my disappointment, and even I wondered what that was about. But I didn't have to dig too deeply emotionally — this just meant going to all these restaurants was over, and I couldn't help but mourn them already.

"So, can we do dinner? One last time?"

"You just told me you gave your presentation. So there's no more business between us."

"Ah, not so fast," he said. "This *is* going to be a business dinner."

"How can you justify that?" I chuckled.

He said, "There is still the business of pitching your company as an advertising agency they should use."

That made me sit up straight in the car. I pressed my hand against my chest, wondering what had changed. But I didn't ask; what he'd just said was better than good news.

He explained, "I told them if they wanted to get the most out of their marketing plan, they really did need to have a partner, an ad agency. So before I leave tomorrow, I want to put in your name, your company's name, and —"

I stopped him. "You don't have to tell me any more. Where should I meet you?"

He chuckled. "A woman who's about her business."

"All day long," I said.

"So, have you been to Xavier's?"

Oh my God! I mouthed those words and gripped the steering wheel. Xavier's was the most expensive restaurant in Atlanta. I took two deep breaths before I let out a "No" in a tone that belied my excitement. I was going to Xavier's, *and* I was going to pick up a new account — I wanted to turn on the radio in this car, blast some music, and dance.

We agreed to meet tonight, and we agreed to meet at eight — his preferred time for dinner. I hated the late reservations because even though it was business (and that was what I told Stephon every time), on Monday night, my boyfriend had started looking at me cross-eyed. Like how many of these late-night dinners was I going to have?

But tonight would be no problem. He was at an all-day meeting, an opportunity for a showing at a new art gallery opening in Midtown right next door to the Four Sea-

118

sons Hotel. This evening, he was meeting with the two owners, who wanted to get to know him, first at the gallery's location, and then they were taking Stephon out to dinner.

So, I wouldn't have to give him another twisted-truth explanation.

I clicked off from Julian, hopped out of my car, then did a little cha-cha up the walkway to my dad's front door.

"Hey, Zuri," Mrs. Lewis called out.

I was so happy about going to Xavier's tonight, I even gave Mrs. Lewis a little wave instead of my normal scowl.

When I got to my father's front door, though, it was already opened, and my father was right there, balancing himself on his walker.

"Hey, Daddy. What're you doing?" I asked before I kissed his cheek.

"I was just standing here seeing how long you were going to sit out there in front of my house like a drug dealer."

"A drug dealer?" I chuckled.

He grinned. "Only drug dealers sit in their cars and talk on the phone. You ain't never done that before. Always coming up in here talking all kinds of business or talking to Stephon." He backed his walker up so that I could close the door. As he rolled toward the sofa, he said, "So, who didn't you want me to hear you talking to? Stephon?"

"No, it wasn't Stephon."

The way my father stopped moving so suddenly, at first I thought something was wrong. But when he looked back at me over his shoulder, his eyes were clear, though his glare was hard.

I said, "What? It wasn't Stephon. I was on a business call."

He shook his head, and in that gesture it almost felt like he was calling me a liar. With three jerky movements, he shifted his walker so that he faced me. "That was no business call," he said, as if he'd heard my conversation and now he was scolding me. "You just be careful, Zuri." He lifted his hand from his walker and pointed his finger at me. "Be very careful."

And then he pushed his walker, not toward the living room, but to the back, as if he wanted to get away from me.

I stood there with my mouth open, not having any clue what had just gone down. What was he talking about?

After a few more moments, I shrugged and dropped my purse onto the sofa before I went into the kitchen to check on what food my father needed. By the time I got back to the kitchen, I wasn't worrying about my dad — he was just talking. And I had way too much to do to try to figure out an old man's code language.

11

I wasn't sure what pleased me more — the antique mirror leaning against the corner wall that I'd found for beyond a steal at an estate sale or the red flounce dress that I was modeling in front of the mirror.

Actually, I was more than modeling it — I was getting ready to step out in it.

That thought made me grin. Today had been a day I hadn't experienced too many times as an adult — I'd played hooky. It definitely hadn't been planned, but had been precipitated by Julian's call this morning. This was the last time I was going to see him, so I wanted to do something special.

Correction: this was the last time I'd be going to one of these restaurants for a while. Now that I had a little taste of that life, though, I wanted more. So I was going to work and Stephon was going to work, and we were going to live that life.

And this dress — this was my first step. For the first time since I'd been trying to be more responsible with my money (the last three years to be exact, which directly coincided with meeting Stephon), I'd made a purchase on a whim. I'd paid more than eighty dollars.

And I couldn't afford it.

But it didn't matter.

Tonight, when I walked into Xavier's, I wanted to feel like I belonged there. I wanted to feel like Julian's equal in every way. Okay, he would probably still be wearing one of his thousand-dollar suits, and he'd be the one paying for this dinner. But still . . .

I twisted and turned in the mirror, watching the red hem rise high above my knees as I swung to the left and then to the right.

"She's a brick . . . house," I sang. I closed my eyes and danced, holding my hands high above my head. "She's mighty, mighty, just letting it all hang out."

"Wow!"

My eyes popped open and fixed on the reflection in the mirror. Then, spinning around, I faced Stephon. "Babe."

"What has you singing?" He grinned.

"And what has you home?" I rushed to him and wrapped my arms around him.

He pressed his lips against mine, a slow, full kiss. Then he stepped away with a sigh and loosened his tie. "I met with the gallery owners for a couple of hours, and I asked if it was okay if I skipped dinner."

"Oh, no," I said and eased down onto the bed. "It didn't go well."

"Nah . . ." He grinned. "It was perfect. They want to do the show with me. There's one other artist they're interviewing, but I'm pretty confident. I'll be doing the show."

"Oh my God." I jumped back up and once again into his arms. "Babe, congratulations. I'm so proud of you. This is huge."

"Yeah, it's pretty cool, huh? I'll have to come up with about a dozen new paintings."

"Wow, that's a lot."

"It is, but imagine the exposure and the money we'll make if I sold even just half of those." He shook his head. "You're right; this is a big deal."

I clapped my hands. "But wait. So why didn't you go out to dinner with them?"

"Once they told me it was pretty much a done deal, I asked if it would be okay if I left." I tilted my head and he explained, "I told them I wanted to come home and celebrate with you." He stepped back and his eyes took an appreciative stroll, starting at the red stilettos I wore, rising up and up, pausing a few times at his favorite parts of my body.

When he finally got to my eyes, he said, "I'm not even gonna ask where you got that dress, 'cause whatever you had to do for it, it was worth it." He laughed. "You're ready to go." He glanced down at his gray tailored shirt and black slacks. "And I'm ready, too. So let's get it, and I'm not talking about burgers. Let's go someplace special."

"Oh, no," I said.

"What?" He backed up with a frown.

"I didn't think you were going to be home tonight, so I have a business dinner."

"Another one?"

His tone had a little bit of an edge, and so I nodded quickly. "I know. But remember the tech company I've been helping?" That was the twisting of the truth that I'd told Stephon. That it was a tech company and not Julian.

It was his turn to nod.

I said, "Well, the person who is making the decision wants to have one last meeting tonight, and there's such a good chance I'll walk away with this account."

His shoulders slumped, his disappointment palpable.

"I'm so sorry, babe," I said. "I really want to celebrate with you, and we can go tomorrow, right? It's Friday, and it'll be better."

"Yeah, I guess." He shook his head as if he were shaking his disappointment off. "But it's no big deal. I need to get on a painting schedule now that will keep me tethered to that easel."

For a moment, I wondered if I should cancel with Julian. But this really was about business. "I wish I could cancel. If they weren't making the decision right now, I would."

"No, go." He waved my words away. "You've been working hard on this; you deserve this win."

"Are you sure?"

My tone made him turn back to me, and he held me in his arms once again. "Babe, you're doing your thing. I'm doing mine. We're doing this together. You go. Have a great dinner; turn it out."

"Okay, and even if we don't go out, I promise you a dinner this weekend that will begin with breakfast and last all day if you let me."

Still holding me, he leaned away and tilted his head upward as if he was giving my words a lot of thought. "I just might have to take you up on that."

My kiss was my promissory note. When he stepped away from me, he whipped his tie off all the way.

"You better get out of here, babe, before I rip that beautiful dress off that brick-house body. Go on. I'll be here waiting for you."

I laughed, but he didn't, and I had a feeling he wasn't kidding. So I grabbed my purse and the wrap I'd laid out on our bed.

I gave him another kiss, this one quick. "I love you."

"Beyond. Infinity."

And I sighed. Because the way Stephon said that, I knew he meant it.

12

I was smiling when I left the apartment, but once I got inside the car, the image in my mind was not of Stephon smiling. Instead, what I saw, what I remembered, was the disappointment that had been in his tone.

Yes, this was business, and I knew that my boyfriend understood. But it hurt me to disappoint him because that was one thing I could say about Stephon — he never disappointed me.

Then my sorrow deepened when I thought about the lie I'd told, though it wasn't a lie — not really. Julian *was* working for the tech company, and today *was* the last time I had to make an impression to get that account.

Still, it bothered me that I hadn't been able to tell Stephon the unfiltered truth. It was just that I didn't want any drama, and I didn't know how I'd be able to convince Stephon that it was really okay.

So I'd twisted the truth, and that made guilt swell in my heart. But the good thing was that tonight would be it. I'd either have the account or I wouldn't, and all of this would be over.

By the time I gave the keys to the Xavier's valet, I was feeling a bit better. I wanted to give my best pitch, and so I needed my mind in this game.

I was used to the ambience now, and so when I walked into Xavier's, I wasn't as impressed as I'd been when I'd walked into the last three restaurants.

Like the three times before, Julian was already inside the restaurant, already waiting at one of the best tables, and for the first time, I wondered — how did he always get a reservation and such great placement? Who did he know?

But once I sat down and he poured a glass of wine from the bottle that he already had waiting (he knew my taste now), that thought left my mind. I waited until we'd given our entrée orders before I led the way into the reason for this dinner:

"So, is there anything in particular you want to know about me or my company?"

"How long have you been there?"

I went into my spiel of how I'd been with the Silver Sky Agency for more than a year now and was one of the top salespeople. "It's a difficult industry," I told him. "Like everyone else, advertising has been affected by the digital market. But I've quickly adjusted, I know the markets, I know the best formats, and I'd be an asset to their team."

"Wow, too bad I can't hire you."

I laughed. "I just want you to know that you'd be leaving your client in good hands."

"Oh, I have no doubt about that."

Over the rest of our dinner, I gave Julian the stats about the company: its thirty-seven-year history and how it had evolved with the changing world. I told him how the company had adjusted to the mobile, data-driven "microwave market" where advertising had to be delivered in much smaller, quicker, more consistent bites.

By the time our plates were taken away, all Julian could say was, "You really know your stuff."

"I really want this account."

He nodded. "And they really need you."

If I'd thought we were more friends than business associates, I would have applauded. But all I did was give him a smile and a nod and ask, "So, what are the next steps?"

"Well, I'm going to go back to the office in the morning, tell them everything you've told me, and then they'll give you a call. I have your number."

"You do," I said. "But I want this to be a little bit more professional than that, so I want to give you this." Reaching into my tote, I handed him a prepared folder with all of the information I'd just shared. "My card is in there," I told him. "This way, if they lose the piece of paper you give them, they'll have all of my information in one place."

He laughed. "I like your professionalism."

I nodded, but my professionalism should have been expected if he was about to recommend me.

"Well, since we're exchanging gifts, I have something for you."

I tilted my head.

"I've had such a great time with you, Zuri. And I appreciate you not deserting me. I would have been a lonely man in this big city if you hadn't said yes when we met in Starbucks."

I laughed. "I doubt that. This is Atlanta."

"Yeah, but you have to be careful. You really do. In today's times, you almost want someone to vet women for you."

"Ouch," I said. "You walked up to me, remember?"

"No." He held up his hands. "I don't

131

mean anything by this. It's just that when you're successful, you have to be careful with whom you keep company, even if it's casual or business meetings."

"I guess . . . that's true," I said, then added, "I feel the same way about the men I meet. You never know."

"Exactly. So I'm grateful that I met you, and I just want to say . . ." Leaning over, he lifted something from the chair next to him — a box, it looked like. "Thank you."

I stared at the square box. No, that was the wrong description. It was a square *blue* box. No, *blue* wasn't the right word either, even though everyone called this familiar box blue, but it was really a special shade of blue — Tiffany blue.

I guessed because I was frozen, not moving at all, Julian said, "Please take it."

I did what he said, not because I was actually going to take whatever was inside, but because shock and curiosity were a brain-numbing combination. So I held the box between my hands for a moment, and when I lifted the cover, I gasped. And then I breathed just so I could take in enough air to gasp again. "What is this?"

"I think you know," he said with a smile.

Or at least I imagined a smile because there was one in his tone. But I didn't know for sure because my eyes couldn't leave the box and the bracelet.

He finished with, "It's one of Tiffany's signature . . ."

"Charm bracelets," I breathed out the words, finishing his sentence.

This was one of the bracelets I'd always wanted, that I'd dreamed that I would one day, perhaps, somehow, maybe have a chance to own since there wasn't a comma in the price. But still, it was too much, and I looked up and into Julian's eyes. What was this?

As if he heard the question in my mind, he said, "It's a gift. For you. I wanted to say thank you."

"For what?" I asked, not being able to imagine what he thought I'd done to deserve a gift from one of my favorite stores.

"For spending time with me. For brainstorming with me about the business."

I shook my head. "I can't accept this for doing that."

"Why not? You earned it."

I flinched, I frowned, I said, "What?"

"No, I don't mean it that way." He held up his hands as if he'd figured out that his words were a bit . . . off-putting. "I mean, you've *really* helped me. I told you, I would've been sitting in my hotel doing nothing, and you made my time in Atlanta more than enjoyable *and* you helped me with the business. Please, let me just say thank you."

Slowly, my glance moved from Julian back to the box. And the bracelet, which shined in its sterling silver beauty.

"It's just a little gift," he repeated.

"No," I said. "It's not. A little gift would have been a twenty-five-dollar gift card to Amazon."

"Well, I can get you that, too." He chuckled. "Maybe *little* is the wrong word, but the right words are — I wanted to do something nice for you." When I shook my head, he continued, "I hope you're not about to block my blessings. I told you, I love doing acts of kindness."

"This . . . this is not kind. This is . . ."

"My way of saying thank you," he repeated, and then he looked up as the waiter returned with our check.

As Julian studied the check, then slipped his credit card into the billfold, I studied the bracelet. It wasn't one of Tiffany's diamonds, but it was a bracelet that I'd coveted for so long.

Why shouldn't I have something as nice as this?

But as quickly as that thought came to

me, I tossed it aside. No! I couldn't take a gift like this from Julian. What would it mean?

It wouldn't mean anything, because I was never going to see him again.

That was a reason why I couldn't take this; a gift like this should come from someone who meant something to me.

"I didn't mean to make you sad." Julian broke through my mental self-debate. "I thought you would like this."

"*Sad* is not the word and neither is *like*. It's just that . . ."

"Please, Zuri, don't overthink this. How can you deny someone giving you a gift?"

The warring thoughts in my head became silent, and with an effort that didn't come from me, I felt myself nod. And then with a more supernatural effort to say, "Thank you. Thank you very much."

With those words, Julian lifted the bracelet from the box and held it up. It still took a moment for me to hold out my wrist so he could clasp the bracelet on.

The moment he hooked it to me, I sighed, but only on the inside. My entire arm looked more beautiful with this bracelet . . . and I didn't have any other way to explain it except that it felt like I was home.

Julian and I didn't exchange any more

words — what else was there to say after a Tiffany bracelet had been given? At the valet, he did what he always did — he took my ticket, paid the fee, and then we stood until my car arrived.

This time, I hesitated . . . What was I supposed to do with a man who had just given me such a gift?

Julian led me to the car the same way he'd been doing, but this time before I got inside, he hugged me.

"It's been a real pleasure, Zuri."

And then he stepped back and I slid inside.

That was it.

He closed my door, and muscle memory helped me put my foot on the accelerator and speed away. This Buckhead restaurant was about fifteen miles away from my home, which was a blessing, because any longer and I may not have made it. The entire time, my shock remained. Even when I pulled into my parking space in front of my apartment, I could hardly move because I needed a functioning brain to make that happen.

I'd left my apartment tonight with the hopes of gaining a new account. I had returned home with the account (I was sure of it) and a bracelet from Tiffany. It still took a few minutes for the fog to clear, but right when I got ready to open the car's door, I paused.

And unclasped the bracelet.

And dumped it into my purse.

Then, with a deep breath, I got out of the car, and, still moving like a zombie, I went into my apartment, where my boyfriend was waiting for me.

13

This was no ordinary Saturday for so many extraordinary reasons.

There was no music playing in our apartment, and Stephon wasn't at his easel in the living room. He'd awakened me an hour ago and said he had errands to run. When I asked if he wanted me to join him, he'd just shaken his head.

That wasn't a good sign — Stephon and I went everywhere together.

Plus, what kind of errands did he have to run? Just two days ago the art gallery had all but told him they wanted him for their opening on the Fourth of July; he had to get ready for that, and he didn't have too much time.

Something was up; I just didn't know if something was wrong.

Rolling over, I faced Stephon's side of the bed. His music dock was on his nightstand, cued up, I was sure, to Strauss's Voices of

Spring, his preferred music to wake up to over the last few days.

But that music wasn't playing; our apartment was silent.

I turned over again, now facing the window where the sun beamed as if it were proud of the day that was to come. Ordinarily, I would have closed my eyes and snuggled more into the pillow. But there was no way I could go back to sleep.

All because of Thursday.

Thursday.

Tossing the duvet aside, my feet hit the cool floor, and I scampered to the closet. Pushing my way to the back, I crouched down and found the small shopping bag that I'd tucked away behind boxes of shoes.

Inside the bag, I found the box and lifted out the bracelet. Even in the darkness of the closet, the sterling silver shined. I folded the bracelet into my hand and made my way back to the bedroom. Climbing up, I sat on the edge of the bed and stared at the bracelet.

I'd owned this elegant piece of jewelry for about thirty-six hours now, and still, I could not get used to the idea that something this exquisite belonged to me. The question remained — why? Why had Julian given this to me?

But the other side of my brain continued to ask the other side of that question: Why not? Why shouldn't he have given it to me?

Still, I couldn't help feeling like . . . this was wrong. I was hoping that by now I would've made my way over to the feeling that this was all right.

The ringing of my cell startled me. Made me press my hand against my chest and then . . . breathe. Glancing at the screen, I smiled.

"Good morning, Ms. Viv. How are you?"

"I'm good, dear, because this is a day that the Lord has made. Let us both be glad and rejoice in this. Amen?" she said.

I hesitated for a moment and said, "Yes. Amen."

"Good. Well, I was calling to not only check on you, but to give you an update. I haven't found a young lady to match with you yet."

"Oh, I was hoping . . ."

"Now, that doesn't mean that I won't find someone. There are so many young girls out here who need mentoring, and I know that God will set it up so that you'll be connected to the right girl. Just be patient."

"Okay, I will."

"But just because I don't have a mentee for you yet, doesn't mean that you and I shouldn't stay in touch. I really enjoyed our time and would love for this to be more than a business relationship. I'd love to develop a friendship."

"That would be nice," I said, thinking about how I had enjoyed my time with Ms. Viv, too.

"You know, I'm not as young as I used to be, and I don't have any children, so it's always nice when someone new comes into my life."

"Well, Ms. Viv, I want you to know that if you ever need me for anything or if you just want to call to chat, I'm here for you, okay?"

"Yes," she said with a sigh that sounded like relief. "I'm so glad to hear you say that. Thank you. So, you've been doing well since our meeting?"

"Yeah, I have been," I told her. "Just a little busy."

"With work?" she asked.

For a moment, I paused and glanced down at the bracelet. This would be the kind of situation a daughter could take to her mother for advice, right? I said, "Ms. Viv . . ."

"Yes?"

I paused, pondered, and wondered. I said, "Yes, I've been busy with work . . . and other things."

"Other things?" The way she said that, I could imagine her eyes widening, her brows rising. "You sound secretive. Anything you want to share?"

Again, I paused, then shook my head. "No, nothing secretive. Just . . ." And I left it there.

Ms. Viv accepted that as a full thought. "Okay, dear. And your dad . . . How is he?"

"He's fine." This time, I was the one who breathed a bit of relief, grateful that the subject had rolled into a new one. "I've started stopping by to see him every day, just to make sure he's good, and thank God, he's been great."

"Sounds like that's a lot on you, especially for someone your age."

It was the first time anyone had ever really acknowledged that. "It *is* a lot. But you know what? He's my dad, and I'd do this and much more. Anything to take care of and love him the way he's done for me my whole life."

"Oh, I know, dear. But for caregivers, it's extremely important they have support and take care of themselves, too. You have to keep your life balanced."

"I'm not at the caregiver stage yet. My father can do so much for himself. But whatever he can't do, I'm on it."

"You are a caregiver, but I won't debate that with you. I just want you to know you can call on me for anything. Or" — she paused — "you can talk to me about everything. You know what the book of Proverbs says — 'he who walks with the wise becomes wise.' " She paused. "It's always good to seek godly counsel."

I squeezed the bracelet in my hand. "I appreciate that, Ms. Viv."

"What I want you to understand, Zuri, is that you can appreciate yourself as well. Just listening to all that you're doing for your father and how you're working so hard at your job — I'm concerned. I hope in between all of this, you can take some time to appreciate your life."

She made me smile, and we ended the call with me promising I'd stay in touch and her promising that she would continue to search for a mentee for me, but most important, that she would pray for me as she'd been doing every day since we'd met.

Hanging up, I felt so much better. Ms. Viv had been like a refresher, a splash of water on my soul. Now, looking at the bracelet, I saw it in a different light. Whether it was official or not, I *had* done a bit of consulting for Julian. And Julian appreciated my time and my life, even if I hadn't been doing that.

"Hey, babe."

The shock of Stephon's voice sent me flying into the air — literally. I leaped from the bed, and my feet and the bracelet hit the floor at the same time. My heart was pounding when I turned and faced him standing in the doorway.

His face was bright with a grin that faded when he saw my expression. "I didn't mean to scare you."

"Oh, no," I said, pressing my hand against my chest and forcing my eyes to stay on him and not drift to the floor. "I had just hung up the phone and didn't hear you come in."

"I'm sorry."

When he moved toward me, I scurried toward him, wanting to keep him away from my side of the bed. "Are you finished with your errands?"

"Yeah, and I thought you'd be up, dressed, and ready by now."

I tilted my head. "Ready? What's going on?"

A voice from our living room shouted, "I'm going on."

"Daddy?" I said, even though I was looking at Stephon.

My boyfriend's grin was back as he took my hand and led me to the living room.

My father stood next to Stephon's easel,

balancing himself on his walker, wearing a sharp navy velour jogging suit that I hadn't seen before. As I stared at him, he took in the sight of me in my oversize Spelman T-shirt and growled, "You're not dressed yet?"

I didn't know how he did it, but my dad was the only person who could growl with a grin. And that made me laugh.

"What are you doing here?" I pulled him into a hug.

"What do you think? Stephon and I came here to pick you up, though I told him that it should just be the men hanging out." He sighed. "But he insisted that he wanted you along." My father tried some more but couldn't hide his grin. A moment later, though, he was right back to his growl. "So come on. Get dressed. I never get out of the house, and I'm ready to go."

My glance moved from my father to my boyfriend. I knew how much work Stephon had to do. I knew how much this art gallery show meant to him, yet he was taking this time out for me and my dad.

"Okay," I said to both of them. "Take Dad back out to the car," I told Stephon. "And give me fifteen."

Doing an about-face, I rushed a few feet, then stopped, pivoted, and wrapped my arms around Stephon's neck. My kiss was my thank-you before I turned back and dashed into the bedroom. I was heading straight to the bathroom when I paused and remembered.

Looking over my shoulder, I made sure Stephon was occupied with my dad before I tiptoed to my bracelet. With an exhale, I picked it up, then tucked it back into the box and shopping bag before I stuffed it behind my stack of shoes.

I was going to have to explain this to Stephon soon, I really wanted to. Not only because I wanted to wear the bracelet, but because I didn't want to keep anything from my boyfriend — not even in a twisted truth sort of way.

Once the bracelet was secure in its place, I jumped into the shower, feeling better than I'd felt since Thursday.

The sound of my father chatting, almost with glee, from the passenger seat of Stephon's Ford pickup made me want to do a group hug with him and Stephon. I was so happy that my man had thought about this, and I wondered, why hadn't I?

I guessed my focus was different, always on taking care of my father's needs — his food and shelter, his overall care. I did get him out of the house — to doctors' visits and to the barbershop when I could (he hated going there on the weekends), but I did forget about his need to get out beyond that; I did forget about his socialization.

We were twenty minutes away from one of my dad's favorite places, and when Stephon pulled up to the no-parking zone on the side of the building, it looked like my father was about to applaud. Stephon had barely put the car in park before my father was out of his seat belt and opening the truck's door.

"Hold on a second there, partner," Stephon told my father before he jumped out on his side, then grabbed Daddy's walker from the bed of the truck.

After helping my father out and making sure he was standing straight and strong, Stephon gave me a quick kiss and left us on the curb as he went to park the car in one of the lots surrounding Centennial Park.

As Stephon did that, I put my hand on my father's shoulder, and we began our stroll around the perimeter, past the flags, where my father paused every few steps to look up at each. Then, when Stephon joined us, he and I sat on the bench, while my father continued rolling through the park. He made a couple of friends, young boys around eight or nine who were walking through the park with their parents. The sight of my father interacting with the boys, his walker no deterrent, made me feel like I was dancing on the sun. It was more than his face — it was his countenance. My father was recovering, and it wasn't just his health. At fifty-eight, he was looking forward to his next phase — life after a stroke.

I leaned back into Stephon's arms, taking in the sights, then I closed my eyes and reveled in the sounds. After a moment, I said, "Thank you so much for doing this."

Stephon kissed the top of my head. "You've been at it so hard, all of those late working dinners."

Slowly, my eyes opened, but it took everything within me to make sure that was the only part of my body that moved. I didn't want to cringe in Stephon's arms and give myself away.

"And yesterday," Stephon continued, "you seemed totally out of it. Came right home and went to sleep."

I nodded, though if Stephon was waiting for an explanation, I wasn't going to offer him one. I did have a good reason — sleep was my way of not having to think about the bracelet.

"So I was thinking about your dad, concerned about you. And I wanted to do something for both of you."

Sitting up, I faced my boyfriend. "This is pretty darn special."

"And it's about to get better."

He kissed my forehead before he jogged to the other side of the Fountain of Rings, and right away, I knew where he was going — Googie Burger. I laughed and shook my head. Yes, this burger place was an award-winning establishment, but even if it weren't world-renowned, it would have been a winner with Stephon. It was a burger, wasn't it?

Making sure my dad was still occupied with the boys, I jogged to the restaurant, which looked like a spaceship to me, and stood with Stephon at the window, then helped him carry back the three classic burgers and three vanilla shakes.

One shout to my father, one glance over his shoulder, one raise of the large milk-shake, and my dad was pushing his walker and dragging that left leg at a one-hundred-yard-dash-winning speed.

Stephon and I returned to the bench, and my father used the padded seat on his walker. Then the three of us savored the Saturday afternoon, chomping on burgers, sipping on shakes, watching the Fountain of Rings show, and talking about people (mostly tourists) who passed us by. (That was mostly Stephon and Daddy — like I said, men could dish it better than any woman.) We stayed that way until the day began to cool and my father began to yawn.

By the time we got my dad back to his house, he was "Tuckered out," as he told us, and after we made sure he was settled inside, I kissed him good night.

On the ride to our apartment, there was only one way to describe what I felt — I was content. It was mostly because of the man behind the wheel of this truck.

I leaned back, closed my eyes, and listened to the music from the Bose speakers Stephon had installed in his truck. My man didn't like spending a lot of money — except for when it came to his music and his art.

It was with good reason, though. This love song — Rachmaninov's Piano Concerto No. 2 — floated through the speakers like it possessed some type of melodic magic, and the slow movement of the piano and then the strings that followed almost lulled me to sleep.

My eyes were still closed when I reached for Stephon's hand, and once I touched him, he held mine and squeezed my fingers.

He said, "Did you have a good day?"

Opening my eyes, I said, "The best."

"That was my intent." He nodded.

The smile that filled my face went all the way to my heart.

He gave me a quick glance, then, with his own sly smile, he asked, "What are you thinking?"

I didn't respond right away because there was so much in my mind. So much that I wanted to say. Was it time? And then, when he tilted his head as if he were waiting, as if he were curious, I decided that no time would be more perfect than this.

"It's time," I said. "I'm thinking that it's time."

He gave me a stare that took his eyes off the road for too many seconds, but then he nodded. He needed no clarification; he knew what my words meant — we were in sync always.

"You think it's time?"

"I do." I paused. "Do you?"

He didn't even take a second to respond. "Babe, for me, it's been time. All we have to do is set a date."

He lifted my hand to his lips, kissed my palm, then took his eyes back to the road. And as Piano Concerto No. 2 continued its serenade to the two of us, I sighed.

I'd just asked Stephon to marry me, he'd

just said yes, and now I could say it — I couldn't wait to become Mrs. Stephon Smith.

14

Sundays were the only days when I was the one to lean over and kiss Stephon good-bye. Like most Sunday mornings, his eyes didn't open when my lips connected with his; he just stretched a bit in his sleep. This was what he called his day (it was really just a morning) of rest.

Still, I paused, hoping this would be the morning when he'd rise and say, *You know what, babe? We just got engaged yesterday, so I'm going to church with you.*

But all he did was roll over, so I grabbed my purse and scurried from our apartment, already leaving more than ten minutes later than I wanted to. I'd probably still get there in time to sit in my regular spot at First Greater Hope, but the parking lot? That was going to be a situation; I'd be in the overflow lot for sure now.

I wasn't that far (about ten miles or so) from the church in Greenbriar, and once I rolled my car onto the interstate, my thoughts settled back to Stephon — at home, in bed.

This was the only part of our relationship (which was now an engagement) that challenged me — I couldn't get him to go to church.

My mother did that her whole life, and what did she get out of it?

Even when I asked Stephon to explain, he never gave me a good answer. His mother was alive, healthy, married now, and even though raising her sons had been so much of a struggle they'd often had to move in with Stephon's grandmother, his story really wasn't all that different from just about everyone I knew: raised by a single parent, who worked at least two jobs to provide for the basics of food and shelter, and even with multiple jobs, the money never stretched to the end of the month. It wasn't until I met Audra at Spelman that I'd come in contact with a black person who wasn't living a lower-middle-class existence (which to me was just a couple of dollars above poverty). So, Stephon's words weren't clarification for why he stayed in bed on Sundays.

Often, though, I wished I'd stayed with him. It was hard sitting in the pews when Pastor Lee preached about the sin that I lived. Just last Sunday, his sermon was all about fornication. But now that would be different, wouldn't it? Now that we were engaged it would be semifornication, right?

That made me half smile, though I was sure, if God was looking down right now, He was not pleased. Stephon and I were about to fix this, though, and I was so happy. I couldn't believe that I was finally ready to take this step. Not that I'd ever had any real hesitation — how could I? Stephon loved me, he wanted to take care of me, he was faithful. The only stop sign — I felt that I'd be stifled financially with Stephon. But I wasn't going to let money stop me from a love that God was trying to give me.

I was excited and couldn't wait to tell my dad, and Audra, and the world so that we could have a big celebration. But I knew Stephon wouldn't want me to do that; not just yet. Not until he could put a ring on it. I didn't know when that would be, but it didn't matter. We'd taken the first step toward the jump over the broom, and I knew our official engagement would come soon enough.

That was my thought as I swerved into the church's overflow parking lot, and now I was glad that I was here. Yeah, I still wished that Stephon was with me, but at the end of the service, I was going up for prayer. I was going to take our engagement to the altar.

Inside the church, the vestibule was Sunday-morning lit — at least that was what I called it when forty-year-old women wearing hats that hid their faces air-kissed teens with purple and pink shoulder-length locks who sported hip-hugging skinny jeans. The chatter was mixed with laughter as folks hugged and shared short testimonies of how God had been good to them this week.

I hugged the usher (I'd never known her name) who handed me a church bulletin every Sunday, then hurried down the carpeted aisle on the left side of the church, hoping that my normal seat (or one in the vicinity) was still available.

Just as I placed my Bible on the seat, the minister of music clapped, and praise and worship was on. First Greater Hope's praise team (there were no choirs here) was an award-winning aggregation of the most talented people in America who didn't have music contracts. On Sunday mornings, we didn't sing, we sang. We didn't just praise, we danced. It was a Christian club where someone at any time might yell out, *Party over here!* and all they would mean was that corner of the church was rocking and celebrating the Lord.

This Sunday was no different as we sang and danced and gave God all the glory. But what was equally so amazing was that when Pastor Lee hit the pulpit, the atmosphere shifted. Oh, the praising was still going on, but now instead of lifting our voices, we raised our minds and opened our hearts to hear a good word.

Pastor Lee began, "Beware!"

That was when I knew this was going to be one of those serious messages. Because he didn't have any kind of prologue; he was getting straight to the Word.

"Beware of . . ." He stopped there.

And many in the congregation finished for Pastor Lee, "False prophets."

Pastor Lee opened his hand in a drop-the-mic motion, and "Amen" rang through the sanctuary.

"But it's not false prophets alone of which I speak. I'm talking about what the false prophets will say to you and what they will offer you. Oh, this message is for somebody," Pastor Lee sang in that voice that could have garnered him awards as a gospel singer. He pointed to the congregation. "Somebody," he said, "needs to know about false prophets stepping into their lives, and somebody needs to pick up their Bible and go straight to the Sermon on the Mount. Somebody needs to understand what Matthew six, verse twenty-four really means." He opened his Bible, his signal that we should do the same. Pastor Lee read, " 'No one can serve two masters: for either he will hate the one, and love the other; or else he will hold to the one, and despise the other. You cannot serve God and money.' " He paused. "Whew! Praise Him."

"Amen."

"Let's break this down in the way that we do here at First Greater Hope."

I had my tablet open, ready to take notes that I didn't ever read, though my hope was that one day I would.

"Now, let me get this out of the way first — money and having money is not bad."

"Amen!"

"Money does not go against anything that is of Christ. This Scripture is not a call for the renunciation of all wealth."

"Praise Him."

A few chuckles rose from the congregation.

"But!" Pastor Lee roared, and that stopped all laughter. "Money and the pursuit of it can never be above God and the pursuit to serve Him." He stopped, and this time there was silence. "This Scripture is about idolization of the pursuit of money, of the pursuit of riches, of the pursuit of wealth, of the pursuit of material gain. When all of that goes above and ahead of God, when you find yourself in pursuit of anything — money or man — that pushes God to the side, then you are more than out of order, you are out of your mind, because now you are out of fellowship with Christ."

There were no shout-outs, no chuckles this time.

He said, "And when that happens, when something takes you out of fellowship with Christ, then you will lose. You will always lose. You will lose your connection to righteousness, you will lose your connection to true happiness, you will lose your connection to all that is important, all that matters, because you will not be connected to Christ."

"You better preach."

"This is what I know," Pastor Lee said. "I know you. Maybe not each and every one of you personally, but if you have been sitting under my tutelage for any amount of time, I know you know the Word, and with the Holy Spirit inside of you, you know the way!"

"Hallelujah."

As Pastor Lee continued to preach to the over four thousand of us in the sanctuary, I pressed back in my seat as if I wanted to get away from Pastor Lee's words. For a moment, it felt like Pastor Lee's message was just for me. Because sometimes, I did feel like I was so focused on money. But I was focused on money because I didn't have any . . . Well, I shouldn't say that. I had a roof over my head and food to eat . . . and I had a job, and I was always grateful for that.

I shook my head. No, this wasn't for me. I didn't have enough money to be putting anything ahead of God. I released a long exhale, feeling a bit relieved. Maybe this message was for me, but it was for a day that was far in the future. One day, I would have money, and I would have to remember that God always came first. But right now, with the way my life was set up, my desire for money was not overriding my love for God. I was good.

I closed my eyes and said a prayer, thanking God that I was on the right track and asking Him to always keep me there.

Just as I opened my eyes, Pastor Lee held up both of his hands, the sign that his sermon was complete. But while others stood around me, clapping, raising more praises to God, I stayed in my seat.

I felt agitated all the way down to my spirit, though I didn't know why. For the rest of the service, I crossed my arms and hugged myself, rocking back and forth, trying to settle my soul. But no matter how much I prayed, I still felt flustered, and now even a little flushed. It was getting hot in the sanctuary, so I did something that I had never done before. When one of the deacons stood at the podium and asked first-time visitors to stand, I stood — and headed toward the church's door.

My plan to go up to the altar for prayer for me and Stephon would just have to wait until next week. Because today I had to get away. I didn't know why, but I needed to get outside to breathe.

15

It had taken me just about all week to rid myself of that feeling from church on Sunday. I couldn't remember another time in my life when I'd left First Greater Hope unsettled rather than uplifted. But I'd finally tucked Pastor Lee's message into a corner of my mind. I would save it for the day when I received a commission check that was life-changing. I'd remember then that I always have to put God first.

That was my thought as I rolled my car into the parking lot of Lenox Square for my Thursday-afternoon stroll. I turned off the ignition, then pulled out my cell phone. It had been a week since I'd had dinner with Julian, and I hadn't heard from him or anyone from the tech company. I'd promised myself to give it a whole week and not call until tomorrow. But I couldn't wait. I wanted to see what Julian had to say about my chances of getting this account.

I scrolled through my phone, found the last time Julian called me, and clicked on his number. Right away, through the speakers in my car, I heard three familiar tones, then:

"The number you've dialed is not a working number. Please check the number and dial again."

I frowned and tried the number again . . . then again . . . and one last time. Shaking my head, I whispered, "I can't believe this," as I pressed END and then deleted Julian's number from my cell phone.

What was that about?

This was a big disappointment. I didn't even know the name of the company (or the name of the app) to follow up with the owners myself.

I shrugged, then slid out of my car and crossed the parking lot, entering Lenox Square on the Neiman Marcus side. But thoughts of the call I'd just made were still on my mind. It was just odd that his phone was disconnected, but now I guessed I could absolve myself from any guilt with this bracelet. I glanced down at it on my wrist. For the last week it had felt more like torture than a gift. I couldn't wear it, not on the regular. Only at times like this, when I was alone. And I certainly didn't wear it every day, never wanting to take the chance of getting so used to it that one day I'd forget it was there and Stephon would see it.

I jiggled my hand a bit and tossed the last of my thoughts about Julian out of my mind. He was gone; clearly the opportunity for a new account had left with him, and I needed to move on, even from obsessing about this bracelet.

All I wanted to do now was enjoy my regular late-afternoon Thursday stroll before I set out to my dad's. I hadn't taken this walk in two weeks because the last two Thursdays had been filled with Julian.

I turned my attention to my task. Lenox Square wasn't as upscale as Phipps Plaza, yet I could still smell the wealth in the air. Like at Phipps, I had a normal path in Lenox Square, passing some of my favorite places: Stuart Weitzman, St. John, and Louis Vuitton, which is where I paused, my attention captured by the black hobo bag in the window display.

I'd been salivating over this bag for more than three years now . . . yeah, three years. It was ridiculous. They'd updated the bag about a dozen times for each of the seasons that had passed since the first time I saw this purse. But I had a feeling the seasons would change a dozen times a dozen times a dozen times more before I'd be able to buy something this expensive. Especially since now Stephon and I were getting married. And his idea of saving money wouldn't line up with my idea of buying this bag.

Stephon and I hadn't set a date, nor had he purchased a ring. But that didn't matter. I had the man, and we'd decided to think about all of that after Stephon's art show in July. He hadn't yet heard if he was going to be the featured artist, but I didn't need to wait for a call to know that this blessing was his. He was the best in Atlanta; I knew he'd be selected. So once his show passed, we'd be able to focus on us.

"Do I know you?"

I turned to the voice, then my eyebrows rose. The voice — what I assumed was British — didn't match the package: a black man, well over six feet tall.

"I think I know you," he said, changing his line around a little.

It was a bit surprising that this man recognized me — or rather, Thelma Evans. Of course, he thought I was the actress, but before I told him that, I did my usual assessment, and the first word that came to me as I studied him was . . . *interesting.* He wasn't dressed in one of those expensive

Italian suits that revealed a man with money, but still, I could tell he had it, if I was judging the measure of this man's wallet by what he wore.

He was casual, only wearing sweatpants and a matching crew-neck top — except both pieces were cashmere. It was a collection that I'd seen last Christmas and had so wanted to buy for Stephon. Finally, I said, "No, I don't think we've ever met."

He shook his head. "We have. I know you." There was so much certainty in his tone. After a moment, he snapped his fingers.

And then as he pointed his forefinger at me, I did the same to him, and together we said, "Thelma from *Good Times.*"

He chuckled. "I guess you hear that a lot."

I nodded, then extended my hand. "I'm Zuri Maxwell."

"Aha! I knew it. It was much more than Thelma."

I frowned. "So . . . we *have* met?" As I asked the question, I scrolled through my memory, wondering how I'd forgotten someone like him. He should have been memorable, if only for his height.

He chuckled as he shook my hand. "No, I'm teasing you. But this meeting is more than a coincidence. It has to be some kind of cosmic thing."

"You've lost me."

"I'm sorry, let me explain. You have two first names and so do I." He smiled. "I'm Alexander Gayle." He reached into the pocket of the Louis messenger bag that he carried and handed me a card.

"Alexander Gayle," I read.

"Since my mother birthed me." He laughed.

From the red-and-white embossed card, I read, " 'Abbey Global Developers. Offices in San Francisco, New York' " — I paused and looked up at him — " 'London.' That explains the accent."

He nodded. "Yes, I'm a proud Brit. Didn't Idris make us sexy to you American women?"

I didn't want to tell him just *how* sexy Idris had made the Brits, though this man was representing his country well, too. He had the coloring of Idris and he carried the same kind of mystery in his eyes, along with his closely shaved beard and blemish-free skin.

But it was his laugh that I liked the most; it was a sophisticated belly chuckle, if there was such a thing. And it was comfortable, making me feel as if we were (almost) already friends.

"I'm based out of London," he continued. "Just here in Atlanta for a month to complete a real estate project. Lofts downtown."

I moved to the side as a squealing woman jumped beside me and dragged a man to the window. Her waist-long blond hair bounced as she tapped her finger against the glass and pointed to the purse I'd been coveting.

She'd been so rude, both Alexander and I looked at the couple for a moment.

The woman said, "There it is, baby. That's the one I want for my birthday."

The man's eyes were on his phone; he never looked up. In a tone that told us how bored he was, he said, "Let's just get it now; I'll get you something else for your birthday."

She shrieked, grabbed his hand, and dragged him into the store.

Alexander's and my eyes followed them, and when he turned back to me, he shook his head.

I shrugged. "There goes my purse."

"Were you about to buy that? I'm sure they have more than one."

Waving my hand, I said, "No, no, just a bit out of my budget . . . but anyway, you said you're here in Atlanta building lofts."

He shook his head. "No, they're already

built. The Enclave on Peachtree."

"Oh, wow. I'll have to check them out."

"You're in the market for a new home?"

"No, I just love looking at model apartments. I've always had a passion for interior design, and checking out model apartments and homes is one way I study."

"Blimey, look at that." He shook his head as if my words were unbelievable, though his words were not understandable to me. "You are not going to believe this." He didn't give me room to ask him what he was talking about. He continued, "I'm actually here looking for a firm to decorate our apartments. That's the only reason I'm in Atlanta."

A spark of excitement shot through me.

He said, "So who are you with?"

"What?"

"Your firm? What design company do you work with?"

And just like that, he extinguished all the excitement I'd had.

"Oh, no, I don't work for anyone. I don't even work as an interior designer. It's just a hobby that I love."

He shrugged as if that didn't matter. "Do you have a portfolio?"

I didn't; I didn't really know what a portfolio for a designer consisted of, but it couldn't have been more than a few pictures. So I twisted the truth. "I do," I said, thinking of Audra's home. I could definitely take pictures of that and also Stephon's and my bedroom. There would be enough to put a portfolio together.

"I'd love to see it," he said. "Now, this is only a short-term project — a couple of weeks — but if this is a hobby for you now, this could be a stepping-stone that'll take you where you want to go."

"Oh my gosh; that would be so cool. So . . ."

He said, "Well, you have my card. Why don't you text me your number, because I don't answer numbers that I don't know . . ."

I chuckled, understanding that.

"And then we'll set up something." He glanced at his watch. "I'm on my way to have dinner with a mate, but you have no idea. I hate when I have to spend time interviewing firm after firm. This could be great for both of us. So, you'll text me?"

"As soon as I get in the car."

He gave me a thumbs-up, then rushed off the other way, and I stayed there watching him until he rounded the corner.

"Wow." I did a slow spin until I faced the store's window again. And that purse. That

I'd been looking at for a dozen seasons. There might be hope for me and this purse after all.

16

I made the turn off the exit ramp of I-285, and as I waited at the light, I hummed. It was no tune in particular; I was just happy and humming. What a difference two weeks could make. That was how long it had been since I'd felt this little shift in my life. Since I'd first met Julian and now Alexander. When Ms. Viv had told me to open myself to new experiences, I was sure she didn't have any idea how she had spoken these experiences into my life.

I'd almost told Stephon about Alexander's offer last night, but changed my mind. Tonight would be better. I could make him a wonderful dinner and we'd be able to relax and celebrate with wine (and other things), and I wouldn't have to worry about getting up for work in the morning.

But before I did that, I wanted to check in on my dad since I'd missed seeing him yesterday. After talking to Alexander, I'd changed my plans. Instead of stopping by Dad's, I'd driven downtown to get a peek at the property that Alexander had mentioned.

I'd parked across the street and had done more than just thought out how I would decorate the interior of the units; I'd imagined Stephon and me living in a place like that. All the glass on the outside made me only wonder what the inside looked like. I really wanted this opportunity with Alexander, and I was going to do whatever I had to do to get it.

As I rounded the corner onto the block where I'd grown up, my cell phone rang. Glancing at the screen, my eyes widened just a little — I had locked Alexander's number into my phone yesterday right after I left the mall.

"Hello?" I said, sorry that I sounded tentative. I'd just been thinking about this man and now he called? Was this call about taking everything that I imagined away? Was this going to be like another Julian thing?

"This is Alexander Gayle," he said, sounding so professional. "How are you?"

"I'm great?" And then I banged my hand against the steering wheel for again sounding as if I weren't sure. Who would want to hire someone who answered every question with a question when a question wasn't the answer?

He said, "Listen, I just had an appointment cancel and I was wondering if you and I could get together now for an early dinner."

As I eased my car into my father's driveway, I said, "Oh, I haven't had time to put together my portfolio. I'll have it done this weekend."

"No, no. I know that. As long as I have that by Monday, we'll be fine. But I really believe you'll be able to handle this project, since it's just four floor units. So I'd like to get to know you and go over what this will entail and answer any questions you may have."

I turned off my car, thinking about my father and Stephon. I really didn't want anything to get in the way of tonight.

"I hope you don't have other plans," he said. "I'd really like to meet with you so we can get this project moving."

Glancing at my dad's house, I wondered if he'd already seen me. And then, with just a little shift of my eyes, I saw Mrs. Lewis standing on her porch, peering at me like she really was the director of Homeland Security.

Through my silence, Alexander said, "If

you're not too far, we can meet at Del Rey's . . ."

My eyes and my mouth both opened. He had to be kidding. Del Rey's was another top restaurant that I'd been dying to visit.

"If you can do it now, we can meet early . . . say, five?"

I glanced at the clock on the dash, wondered if I could make it to downtown in forty-five minutes in Friday-evening traffic, then said, "Okay," as I revved up the engine. Backing out of the driveway, I told him that I would be there by five.

"Bloody fantastic. See you then."

I clicked off my phone and glanced in the rearview mirror. Mrs. Lewis was still there, still watching. Ugh! Why didn't she just go back into her house? I hoped she didn't say anything to my father.

But I couldn't think about that right now. I was about to visit another great restaurant and meet about another great business opportunity. I cranked up the volume in my car as one of my favorite old-school songs punched through the speakers.

" 'Betcha by golly, wow,' " I sang along with the Stylistics. " 'You're the one that I've been waiting for forever . . .' "

I sang and thought about Stephon all the way on the ride to downtown.

■ ■ ■ ■

It was amazing how quickly I had become used to being in these kinds of restaurants. I was used to the ambience, the highbrow staff and patrons, the quietness even though the spaces were always filled with dozens and dozens of people.

I was now used to the smooth European wines rather than the store brands Stephon and I could afford, and entrées that cost upward of forty, fifty, sixty dollars each.

But even though I was used to all of this now, it still felt like the first time every time I stepped into a place like Del Rey's.

"So, what do you think about all of this?" Alexander asked me.

I hesitated for a moment, not sure what to say. Everything that Alexander had just told me about the Enclave on Peachtree was exciting if not a bit overwhelming — I'd be decorating four loft apartments that would serve as models and then be sold after the other fourteen units were off the market. The models would be offered fully furnished, so I had to think beyond design; I'd have to think about function for the families who would finally call the model lofts home.

This was exactly what I wanted to do.

I said, "It's perfect. I told you, my major concern had been how I would do this and still keep my job. But if you're convinced that I can do it on the weekends . . ."

"And a few evenings," he added. "Whenever you're needed."

I nodded. "Then, if you like my portfolio, I will give it my all."

His face filled with a grin, though it wasn't really his whole face. He grinned with half of his mouth. I'd never seen anyone smile so brightly that way.

"Bloody fantastic," he said.

I just loved his voice — I was beginning to get used to his accent and his phrases. "Now, I'll still need to see your portfolio."

"Definitely."

"And you'll have to sign a confidentiality agreement."

"Okay," I said, wondering what he'd want me to keep confidential. Not that I was going to tell anyone about this gig. Well, no one except for Stephon . . . and my dad . . . and Audra. That would be it. But now that I knew I'd have to sign an agreement, I'd tell them now . . . before I signed anything.

"I have to run this by my business partner, but he's a good bloke, and he'll be happy if I'm happy. I have a lot of faith in you, Zuri. You've impressed me." He paused. "Now, there's one thing we haven't talked about — salary."

I inhaled. I had no idea how much an interior designer made. I mean, I'd only had one real paying job — Audra had paid me two thousand dollars, but I figured that was because she was my friend and was just looking for a way to give me some money.

"Abbey Global doesn't pay by the hour, just by the project," Alexander explained, "which to be honest, will give you a bit more money."

"Okay." I nodded.

"So you'll receive five thousand for the whole project. If it takes longer than a month, we'll renegotiate. You'll get half once we sign the contract, then the balance will be divided over the four weeks. Is that satisfactory?"

Satisfactory? He wanted to pay me five thousand dollars for going shopping for designer furniture? And then to decorate? If I didn't have a fiancé at home, I would have jumped up, sat on that man's lap, and given him a kiss. Five thousand dollars would mean everything to me and Stephon right now. This would be the seed money for our wedding.

"Yes," I said, trying to keep the giddiness from my voice. "That will be fine." I was amazed at the way I sounded — like five thousand dollars wasn't really all that big of a deal when it was actually life-changing for me.

As the waiter brought the check and Alexander slipped his credit card (his was platinum) into the billfold, he told me that I'd start a week from tomorrow if all went well.

"I'm very excited about this. Thank you for the opportunity."

He nodded before he said, "There is one more thing. You'll receive a company credit card."

That made sense to me. I'd used Audra's credit card to purchase all of her furniture.

"Of course," I said. "That will make it easier for you to keep all the records from my purchases."

He held up his hand as if he were about to correct me. "Oh, no, I'm not talking about the furniture. You'll have accounts at all of the major showrooms to make it easier for you and everyone. But you will be representing Abbey Global."

I nodded, though I didn't understand.

He said, "The card will be for you to pick up a few suits and some dresses, if you wish."

"What?"

"In this business, shopping at some very high-end places is part of your responsibility."

"Yeah, I get that."

"And these accounts, you'll be visiting as *our* representative. So, it's important that . . ."

My eyes narrowed a bit. Was this man saying that he didn't like the way I dressed?

"I don't mean this as any kind of insult." He shook his head. "Believe me, for certain meetings and circumstances, I have to dress a certain way. Our company wants to portray a look that goes all the way to our designer."

"Hmmm," I hummed, mostly because I wasn't sure how to take this.

He said, "You look bloody fabulous right now." Leaning closer to me, he said, "But what would be wrong with a designer dress or two? Or three or seven?"

"Nothing, I guess." My voice was soft, and my words were slow. "I've just never heard of a job doing something like this."

"Really?" He tilted his head as if now my words surprised him. "Lots of companies have uniforms."

I guessed what he was saying was true — lots of companies did tell their employees how to dress. I just never expected it at a company like this . . . *and* they were paying for it.

Alexander signed the check (which I was sure was close to two hundred dollars in this place), then led me from Del Rey's. Like Julian, he paid for my valet, and when my Chrysler arrived, he held my car door open and told me that he was really looking forward to working with me.

"Get that portfolio to me as soon as you can," he said before he closed the door and waved me away. "And we'll have dinner next week."

It was a good thing that my car pretty much rolled forward on its own. Because it was hard to do anything except play over all the thoughts in my mind: five thousand dollars, new clothes — no . . . new *designer* clothes. Alexander had specifically mentioned designer. All of this, and I'd be doing the one thing that I loved.

It really was true — I had opened my mind and my heart to the prospect of new possibilities, and they were coming my way.

Glancing at the clock, I saw that it was right before eight — later than I wanted it to be. I thought Alexander and I would have been finished by seven, giving me time to see my dad before going home. That extra hour had made a difference. If I stopped by my dad's now, there was no telling what time I'd get home to Stephon. Maybe I could see my dad tomorrow. But that thought lasted just a moment. I loved my man, but I was going to see my daddy.

So I turned my car onto the freeway and headed toward Stone Mountain, reveling in all that had just happened. When I pulled into my dad's driveway, I saw the flicker of the television's light through the curtains. Good, he was still awake. Wait until he heard this news!

Jumping from my car, I rang the doorbell, and then I did what I always did — I asked myself, why in the world was I not using my key? But my dad's house, his rules, so I played his game.

After more than a minute of waiting, I peeked through the window to see if maybe my dad had fallen asleep in his chair. But beyond the TV's light, I couldn't make out much more. Still, I rang the bell again, though this time, I didn't wait.

I couldn't . . . My heart was already pounding.

I pushed the door open and called out, "Daddy?"

My eyes scanned the living room. Nothing was out of place — yes, the TV was on and in front of his recliner, a tray table sat with a plate covered with bald chicken bones. His dinner, I was thinking.

"Daddy?" I shouted.

My steps couldn't keep up with the pace of my heart as I rushed to the hallway. I got to his bedroom first.

Nothing.

Then the bathroom, and I gasped.

"Daddy!"

He was sprawled on the floor, his body twisted in a way that let me know . . . he'd had another stroke.

"Daddy," I whimpered as I knelt next to him.

I breathed a little easier when I saw his chest rise and fall — the sign of life. But once I pressed my fingers against his neck for his pulse, my fear intensified — it was so faint.

"Oh my God," I said, fumbling in my purse. But I couldn't get to my phone; my hands were shaking. "Oh my God. Please, Lord, help me."

"Zuri?"

Mrs. Lewis!

I screamed out her name and heard her footsteps rushing toward me. Her voice came into the bathroom before she did. "I saw you come in, and you didn't close the door," she said. And then she stood in the doorway. "Oscar!" she exclaimed.

"Mrs. Lewis. Please." I handed her my purse. "My phone is in there, and . . ."

In the first second, she grabbed my purse; in the next one, she pulled out my phone; and before I had the chance to inhale twice, she was on the line with 911, giving them the information and then barking out orders for them to get to my dad's house now.

If tears hadn't been flooding from my eyes, if my heart hadn't been pounding with such fear, I probably would have smiled. For the first time in my life, I was grateful for the director of Homeland Security. Because of Mrs. Lewis, I could focus on my dad.

"Daddy," I whispered, holding one of my father's hands and stroking his hair with my other. "Daddy, please hold on. Just please, please hold on."

17

I should have been there. I was supposed to
have been there.

When I'd been sitting in my father's
driveway talking to Alexander, had my
father been inside then? Had he been on
the floor crying out for me?

"Oh, God." I sank into the hard chair in
the waiting room of Grady Memorial and
covered my face with my hands. There
would be no way for me to survive if I lost
my father. If he was going to die, then I'd
have to die, too.

"Zuri."

I leaped from the chair and jumped into
my boyfriend's arms. The moment he pulled
me into his chest, I wept. I mean, I really
cried, as if I knew that now it was safe to
release all of my sorrow.

"It's my fault," I cried.

"No, baby, no," he said as he held me
tighter. "This isn't your fault."

But it was — Stephon just didn't know yet.

When I'd squeezed every tear from inside of me, Stephon led me back to one of the chairs. Still he held my hand as he sat next to me.

"What happened?" he asked.

Stephon had to ask because he had no idea. When the EMTs had arrived, Mrs. Lewis had helped me from the floor and reminded me to call Stephon. She'd pressed his name on my cell for me and then when he'd answered, all I'd said to him was, "Baby . . . Daddy."

That was all I could get out, and Mrs. Lewis had taken over before she walked me to the ambulance and made sure I got into the back with my father.

"Can you talk about it yet?" he asked as he squeezed my hand. "You don't have to."

"No." I shook my head. "I'm fine." I looked over Stephon's shoulder, hoping to see a doctor or a nurse, someone to tell me my father was going to be all right.

Turning my glance back to Stephon, I said, "When I got to Daddy's, I found him on the floor in the bathroom."

"Oh my God." He pulled me into his arms. "I can't believe you had to go through that." He paused, then leaned back, confusion contorting his face. "So what happened? You got there around four, right?"

I'd forgotten I'd called Stephon as I'd left my office. "No, I didn't go there then. I mean, I was on my way to Daddy's, and then I got a call . . ."

"Ms. Maxwell?"

Stephon and I jumped from our chairs at the same time and rushed to the door, where a black man in scrubs stood holding a tablet. The first thing I noticed about him was he looked like Martin Luther King Jr. Seriously. Like the image of every picture that I'd ever seen of the man was standing before me right now. But I refused to say anything, knowing how looking like Thelma had affected my life. Still, his physicality, his bearing — I liked this man already.

He said, "I'm Dr. Mills. Your father is Oscar Maxwell?"

Stephon and I nodded.

He tapped his tablet. "Your father is going to be fine."

"Oh my God."

Now I *loved* this man.

Before this moment, I'd been sure every tear had been drained from me, but I was wrong. Stephon had to hold me again.

"I was so scared," I sobbed, then got myself together enough to ask, "He had another stroke, didn't he?"

"No." The doctor said with a frown and shook his head as if he wondered where I'd gotten that idea. "He was severely dehydrated, though, and his blood pressure had actually dropped, gotten too low."

"Really?" I looked from the doctor to Stephon and back. "I saw him Wednesday, and he was fine."

"That happens. We have to keep him hydrated, may have to look at his medication and make sure he's taking everything properly." He paused. "Does your father live alone?"

"Yes, he has been," I said. "Though I get by there to see him every day . . . just about every day."

He nodded. "Well, it may be time to think about alternative care, but I'll have someone talk to you about that."

"Okay," I breathed. "Can I see him?"

"Yes. We're going to admit him; I want him under observation for the next day, maybe two. He'll be moved from the emergency room to a room of his own. It may be an hour or so."

"An hour before I can see him?"

"Oh, no, I meant it'll probably be an hour before he'll get a room. But you can go in. The nurse is in there making sure your father is comfortable. But no worries." The doctor paused and looked at me and Stephon. "He'll be fine."

After Stephon shook the doctor's hand, Dr. Mills led us through the double doors and then pointed to the last curtained area in the space. I tiptoed over, then pushed the curtain aside to step in.

For a moment, I just stayed there, studying my father lying in the small bed (though he looked smaller), the rails raised. A nurse stood over him, adjusting two tubes that were pinched into my father's veins. And then there were the machines. One high above the bed, with dozens of numbers in a rainbow of colors. Then, on the side of the bed, another machine, another monitor, this one with tubes that led to my father.

I pressed my hand against my lips, hoping to push back the sobs that were trying to rise within me. It was only because Stephon put his arm around my shoulders that I was able to conjure up enough strength to move toward the bed.

My father's eyes were closed, but then, as if he knew I was near, his eyelids fluttered, then parted.

"Hey, Daddy," I whispered.

It took him a moment to turn his head and focus on me. But when his glance settled and he looked at me with eyes so clear, I wanted to drop to my knees and give thanks to God. "Hey, baby girl," he croaked.

Leaning over the rail, I took his hand. "How are you feeling?"

His chin bowed to his chest as if he was trying to nod.

"You scared me, you know."

When Stephon stepped beside me, my dad smiled. "I must . . . be sick . . . if you stopped painting." His voice was raspy but clear.

Stephon and I laughed a little.

"You know this is the only place I'd be," my man said to my father. "You're my family."

Though Daddy moved like it took all kinds of effort, he raised his hand and reached toward Stephon. He took my father's hand, and my dad nodded. "You take good care of her," he said in a tone that made me panic.

"Daddy!" I exclaimed. "Don't say that. You're going to be fine. Nothing's going to happen to you."

He shook his head a little, swallowed, then said, "What are you talking about, baby girl? I know nothing's gonna happen to me. I told him to take care of you tonight 'cause I'm . . . sleepy. I wanna go to sleep. And I want him to take you home."

Stephon and the nurse laughed, though all I could do was breathe with relief. I guessed it was true: my dad was going to be fine.

"Well," the nurse said, "your dad is right. He's probably very sleepy. We gave him something to help him rest comfortably."

"Okay," I said and watched my father's eyes flutter closed. "But I thought he was going to get a room."

"He will," the nurse said. "But he doesn't have to walk; we'll roll him up there."

Now my dad's eyes were closed, almost sealed, as if just that fast he'd fallen into a deep sleep.

Stephon said, "Well, if he's going to sleep, we should go home."

I shook my head. "I'm not leaving him."

"I think he'd want you to go home, babe. Get some rest so you can be strong for him tomorrow."

"No," I said, wrapping my fingers around the bed rail as if I were preparing for a war — I was going to stay.

"And where're you going to sleep?" the nurse asked as she secured one of my father's tubes. "I agree with your husband. You'll be better for your father if you get some rest."

"That's right," Stephon whispered into my ear, "listen to your husband."

Tears burned behind my eyes again, though I wasn't sure why. Did I want to cry for my daddy, the relief I felt that he would be fine? Were my tears for my boyfriend, the man who stood with me now and who I couldn't wait to marry? Or did I want to cry because I feared the future? Dr. Mills said my dad shouldn't be living alone. What was that going to look like?

"You ready, babe?" Stephon asked and squeezed my shoulder.

My eyes were still on my daddy as I nodded. Stepping away from Stephon, I leaned closer to my father. "Good night, Daddy," I whispered before I kissed his forehead.

I stayed hovering over him until Stephon took my hand and led me from the room, though I kept my eyes on my father until we stepped outside of the curtain. If Stephon hadn't been there, I was convinced I would never have made it home. He had to help me into the car, then he drove with one hand while he held me with the other. Stephon showed me, without saying a word, all the reasons why I was so grateful that God had chosen him to be the man I would marry.

When I saw our bed, the exhaustion I felt

was like a burden that I just wanted to lay down. So I stripped, leaving every piece of clothing and underwear right where they dropped, and I climbed into the bed. But once my head rested on the pillow, my eyes stayed opened wide.

It was only when Stephon put his arms around me and pulled me into him that my thoughts settled, my anxiety waned. I lay there, just breathing, just thinking.

Until Stephon said, "Babe?"

"Hmmm."

"So, what happened? Why weren't you with your dad this afternoon?"

I sighed, having forgotten all about that. Having forgotten that Stephon and I had been interrupted earlier when I'd been ready to tell him all that had happened.

But right now, the truth felt like a bag of coal too heavy for me to hold. I'd need too many words to explain. So I said, "I was on my way and got a call about work." That was true. "A new account." Another truth. "So I went to that meeting, and then after, I headed back to Dad's." The whole twisted truth.

When I finished, Stephon pulled me so close, it seemed like he was trying to make us one.

"Don't worry about anything," he said. "I

193

got you, babe. I got you all the way."

I blinked back tears because I was just too tired to cry. I held on to my man. I'd figure out how to untwist this truth with him in the morning.

18

All I wanted to do was lower my head and massage my temples. It wasn't that I had a headache, but I was preparing to do that as a preemptive measure because surely, one was not far away.

But then the hospital's social worker repeated, "We can only release your father to a safe environment," and that made me fold my arms against her words. She'd already said that, so why did she feel the need to reiterate that to me?

Since she was standing and I was still sitting beside my father's bed, I had to look up to look straight into her eyes. I narrowed mine and told her, "I understand that. I will always make sure my father is safe."

When she nodded, her ponytail bounced, and once again, I wondered if she had just graduated from college. I'd thought she was a nurse's aide when she first walked into my father's room asking if I was Zuri

Maxwell. She'd introduced herself as Ms. Cobb and then gone straight into her spiel about my father's care and safety.

"Of course." Her tone seemed like she wanted to de-escalate the tension inside our discussion. She was probably used to dealing with hyped-up loved ones. "We just want to work with you. Your father's been living alone, correct?"

My arms were still folded, my tone still sharp, my nerves still shot. I glanced over the rail of his bed, and wondered if he was asleep or just keeping his eyes closed. I said, "He's been living alone because that's what he wanted." I paused and asked, "Should we really be having this discussion here?"

"It's fine." She gave me another ponytail-bouncing nod. "If he were awake, I would include him in this. In fact, I would like to speak with him as well because I understand his desire to live on his own. As we age, no one wants to lose their independence. But now, because of his stroke and this incident, we're going to have to take more than just what he wants into consideration."

I tightened my arms across my chest — my protection, I guessed, against her words. It's not that I wanted to have an attitude with Ms. Cobb. It was just that I was already stressed out about this. Last night, I'd watched the clock tick by every hour, waiting for the decent time when I could jump out of bed and shake Stephon awake to take me to the hospital.

But my insomnia wasn't just from wanting to rise and rush to see my dad; I couldn't sleep because of all the questions in my mind, the same questions the social worker was addressing now.

She said, "I know this is a very trying time. It always is for a family when tough decisions have to be made. But you have to understand . . ."

"I do." I stood up from the chair so fast, it tilted over. "I have some things to work out, and I'll get back to you."

Ms. Cobb's eyes widened a bit, but she accepted my words as her dismissal. She gave me her card, told me she'd be in touch, and then I plopped back down into the chair once she left me alone.

As I stared at my father resting in the bed, it was hard to believe that last week at this time, we were getting ready to go to Centennial Park. The park was just a little over a mile from the hospital, but it seemed light-years away.

Leaning back in the chair, I shifted, trying to find comfort in the uncomfortable seat. When my phone vibrated, I slid to the edge

of the chair, read my text, and smiled —
this was my real comfort.

Just checking, babe. You good?

This was the first time I'd smiled for real
since I'd found my dad last night:

Yes. No change. Stay focused, keep
painting, I'll let you know.

A second ticked by, then:

K. I'll be back in a couple of hours. I'll
bring you something to eat. I love you.

My fingers couldn't type the words fast
enough:

Beyond infinity.

I leaned back in the chair and wondered if
I should have told Stephon about the discussion I'd just had with Ms. Cobb. But no —
I really wanted him to focus on his work,
and I needed to digest all the information
myself first. My thoughts returned to Ms.
Cobb and the conversation, which had left
nothing but weight on my heart. What was I
going to do? There really weren't many options, especially not in Georgia. We could

find some kind of assisted living facility, but my dad would have to sell his home, and not only would that be traumatic for him, but even after the sale, would that be enough money? How long would that money last? My father was still a relatively young man.

And then the other option . . .

I could move home; I could take care of him. But what would that mean? And what would that mean for me and Stephon? I couldn't ask him to move in with my dad. And how would my dad and I even live if I gave up my job?

My job.

Alexander.

I sat up straight in the chair. I guessed I'd pushed him out of my mind, but now, remembering him made tears burn behind my eyes. Pushing myself up, I moved around the machine and kissed my dad's forehead. "I'll be right back."

The moment I stepped out of the room, I released a long stream of air as if I'd been holding my breath the whole time I'd been inside. Passing the nurses' station, I walked down the long hall, keeping my eyes away from other patients' rooms until I found the fourth-floor waiting room.

It was small, with about ten or twelve

chairs, but it was fine because it was empty. Finding the remote, I lowered the volume on the television, then slumped into another uncomfortable chair.

I stared at my cell, really wishing I didn't have to do this, but for me, my father had to come before everything.

It still took another moment before I opened my text app:

Alexander, I want to thank you so much for the opportunity. It meant so much to me. But I won't be able to accept the position of designer.

I paused and wondered if I should just leave it there or explain. After a moment, I continued:

My father was rushed to the hospital last night, and though he's going to be fine, my focus has to be on him for a little while.

Another pause. This was a text, not an email, but there was one more thing I wanted to say:

Please keep me in mind if you're ever in Atlanta again and a job like this comes up. Again, thank you so much. Best, Zuri Maxwell.

I reread my text, and then my finger hovered over the SEND button until I pressed it. I really wanted to cry, but I didn't because it didn't matter what I wanted. The only one who mattered was my dad. No one would be able to take care of him better than me.

Still, I stared at the text and wondered what this was all going to mean. I'd have to talk to Stephon, but I wanted to go to him with a plan so he wouldn't feel obligated to move in with me and my dad. Stephon doing that was not realistic. He was already busting out of our apartment. The living room was his studio, and I spent most of my time in our bedroom because of that — there was no way he'd be able to do that to Daddy's living room, that we'd be able to live that way at Daddy's house.

My ringing cell phone took me away from these thoughts, and the name on the screen surprised me. "Ms. Viv," I said the moment I answered.

"Zuri, dear, how are you? How is your father?"

Now I frowned. "How did you know?"

"Oh, there are so many people in so many places, but none of that matters, dear; I'm really concerned about you. How are you?"

I sighed . . . and then I did something I

201

didn't expect — I cried. "I don't know why I'm upset right now," I said. "Daddy's going to be fine, and for that I am forever grateful."

"Thank God for that. You're probably just relieved."

"I'm relieved, and I'm a little scared. I have so many decisions to make that will be life-changing for him and for me."

"Like what?"

"He can't live alone any longer, though I don't know why I'm upset; I've known this was coming for a long time. I've been trying to talk to my father about it. And really" — I sighed — "I shouldn't have let him live by himself after his stroke. But he insisted."

"Oh, I know. It's hard for parents to switch roles with their children."

"I get that. But now he won't have any choice," I said.

"So what are your plans?"

"I've been asking myself that; I think I'll move in with him and give him the care he needs until we can figure this all out."

"Oh, no," she said. "I think that will be too much on your plate. You're already doing so much."

"I know, but what else am I supposed to do? I'm his daughter, and I have to take care of him."

"I understand, and I may have a solution." She paused for a moment. "I may know someone who can help."

She had hardly finished her sentence before I began shaking my head. "My dad and I can't afford to have someone come in with him. That was the first option I looked into, but the cost of in-home care . . ." I stopped right there. That was enough. She could figure out the rest.

"When is your father going to be released?" Ms Viv asked as if she hadn't heard (or was ignoring) what I said.

"I don't know yet. I was thinking today, but the way he's sleeping, maybe tomorrow or the next day."

"Well, you keep me posted, and I'll see what I can do."

"Ms. Viv . . ."

"Zuri, don't worry about anything. You take care of your father, and I'll do my best to take care of you. Just remember to pray over him, Exodus 23:25." She paused, and I wondered if she was searching for the Bible or just trying to remember the Scripture. Then she said, " 'Worship the Lord your God, and His blessing will be on your food and water. He will take away sickness from among you.' And that is a promise, Zuri. I'll check in with you tomorrow."

She clicked off before I could say good-bye . . . or maybe she just didn't want to hear me protest anymore. Looking down at my phone, I realized this was the first time since I'd met her that Ms. Viv hadn't made me feel better.

In fact, I felt a little worse because her words added weight to my burden. Did she think I wouldn't be able to take care of my father? I'd show her. I'd show everyone.

With a new determination, I stood up and marched up to the nurses' station.

The nurse who was on duty for my father looked up from the computer, where she'd been tapping on keys like she was writing a novel or something.

I said, "I need to speak to Ms. Cobb, the social worker."

The nurse nodded. "Okay, when she comes back up on the floor, I'll tell her to stop by your dad's room."

I added, "That's fine, but if you can reach out to her, that may work better. Because I need to speak to her as soon as possible so I can know when my father and I are going home."

Then I did an about-face and marched right into my father's room because the one thing that Ms. Viv had told me to do, I was going to do: I stood at my father's bedside, opened the Bible on my phone, and prayed Exodus 23:25 over and over again.

19

It almost felt like a party, the way we were piled into my father's bedroom. It was only me, Stephon, Audra, and Joseph — but then, there was my father, and he filled up the bedroom with his presence.

"I don't know why y'all think I need to be in bed in the middle of a Monday afternoon," my father groaned and grumbled.

"Because you need to rest," Stephon said.

"Rest is for the tired," he said as Stephon and Joseph got him into the bed. "And I've been in that hospital, lying around for two days. How am I gonna be tired?"

But when he lay back on the pillows that Audra plumped up for him, he grinned and I laughed. My father loved all of this attention.

I opened the blinds to allow a little sunshine in and behind me, my dad was still mumbling, "So if I'm not tired, you know I'm not sleepy."

"Daddy," I said turning to him, "we can either do this here, or we can take you back to Grady Memorial."

"I ain't going back to Shady Grady!"

Stephon, Audra, and Joseph laughed while I exclaimed, "Daddy! Stop it."

"You know I ain't neva lied. Shady for real."

I gave my man and my friends a side eye, especially Joseph. He was a doctor at Emory. Wasn't laughing at that kinda like letting someone talk about your sibling? "Don't encourage him," I scolded them, then I peered at my daddy, and when he blew me a kiss, I laughed, too.

"Well, since y'all did all of this, you might as well let a man rest. You say you want me to sleep and then you have a party in my room. Get on out of here."

Audra kissed him good-bye, and then Joseph and Stephon gave him what I called the bruh-man handshake and hug. Even stretched out on his back, my dad was a full-fledged black man.

I stayed until the others stepped out, and as I leaned over to kiss him, my father patted the side of the bed. "Sit down for a moment," he said. When I was settled, he began, "Zuri, I know what you told that social worker, but you can't stay here with me." All signs of his teasing grumbling were gone.

I shook my head. "I don't want to talk about that right now, Daddy. Get some rest." I tucked the cover up closer to his chin.

"No. I mean, I'm gonna rest. I was just kidding when I said I wasn't tired. Moving from the hospital to home really did tucker me out, but I've *got* to talk to you about this, baby girl. I can't let you do this. I can't let you give up your life to take care of me."

"Why not? You took care of me."

He shook his head. "That's different. I was supposed to."

"And I'm supposed to do this. But not only supposed to, I really *want* to, Daddy."

His face bunched into a frown, and he squirmed beneath the covers like he was uncomfortable, agitated.

"Okay, Daddy," I said, not wanting to upset him further. "Let's talk about this later."

My words seemed enough to calm him, and when he nodded, then closed his eyes, I kissed his forehead before I joined the others in the living room. The TV was on, though the volume was low and Joseph and Audra stood by the door.

"Are you leaving?" I asked.

Joseph said, "Yeah, I gotta get over to the hospital by two."

"Thank you so much for being here for me and my dad."

"Always," Joseph said. "You're fam." He shook Stephon's hand, then kissed Audra good-bye. To Stephon, Joseph said, "Check out the Uber driver before my wife gets in the car, will you?"

We laughed, but then Stephon said, "Always, you're fam," repeating Joseph's words.

When Joseph left us alone, Stephon and I settled on the sofa, while Audra took over my dad's recliner.

"I know you've got to be exhausted," Audra said, "but have you two had time to make any decisions?"

Glancing over my shoulder at Stephon, I sighed before I told Audra, "Well, they released him to my care after I told the social worker I'd be the one responsible; I told her I'd be staying with him."

"Stay? Like move in here?" Audra's eyes darted between me and Stephon.

"For now."

She wagged her finger back and forth between me and Stephon. "So, how is that gonna work?"

Stephon shrugged. "We're gonna find a way to make it work. Like Joe just said, this is my fam. And this lady right here" — he pulled me back into his chest — "she's the most important person in my life."

Audra pressed both hands over her heart, and I rested my head on his shoulder for a moment.

But then I lifted up and said to Audra, "So, what we're going to do for now is I'm going to ask my boss for family leave for thirty days and then try to work out the whole plan during that time."

Stephon nodded, and then he picked up the story, filling Audra in on what we'd decided over the weekend. "I'm gonna research just how much Dad could get for selling this place and check into some assisted living and long-term-care facilities."

"I can help with that," Audra said. "Joseph may be able to give us some leads, too. My only concern is . . . your dad is still so young."

"That's one of our concerns," I said. "We could sell this house, but even with the little bit of money he gets from the barbershop and social security, I doubt if it's going to be enough to pay for his care, since I would want him in one of the best facilities."

"Wow," Audra said.

And then, after a moment of silence, I said, "It's just hard. You don't want to get old and you don't want to get sick in this country."

Audra leaned back. "Well, while you're figuring this out, maybe we can all do some kind of schedule and you can keep working. I'd help out with that," she said. "I mean, yeah, take family leave if they give it to you, but if it's not paid . . ."

Stephon moved to the edge of the sofa. "That's what I was thinking," he said, though he hadn't said that to me. "I'm home during the day, and if you're willing to help . . ." he said to Audra.

"I am!" My best friend shot up in the chair. "You can take a couple of days and then I can take the others." Then, looking straight at me, she said, "And you can go to work and take over in the evenings."

Then the two of them grinned at me as if they had just worked it all out, and though I laughed, I felt so blessed.

But still, I had to break it down to them. To Stephon, I said, "Really? So how are you going to get ready for your show in July?"

Audra leaned forward again. "You have a show?"

"Yes," I answered before he could. "It got lost in all of this stuff going on with Dad, but he just found out on Saturday that it's a definite. A new art gallery in Midtown wants to present him as the featured artist when they open. And he has just three months to get ready, so" — turning back to him — "how are you going to have all of those paintings if half the time you're here? It's not like you can just pick up and paint anywhere."

He shrugged. "We'll figure it out."

"And what about you?" I faced Audra. "You have two children."

"And an au pair. Abagail is wonderful with Lyle and Lily."

"*And* you're a stay-at-home mom because you don't want to miss anything with your children. You told me you wanted to be present for everything."

Just like Stephon, she shrugged and said, "We'll figure it out."

When the two of them bumped fists, I sighed. Reaching for their hands, I held them both as I said, "No one on Earth is more blessed than I am to have you. I so appreciate all that you want to do. But this is my dad."

"So what're you going to do?" Audra asked.

"I'm going to do what any daughter who loves her father would do. I'm gonna work it out. And I have every confidence that I will."

■ ■ ■ ■

I was grateful for the hours Audra had spent with me. We didn't get a lot of time like this, and even though much of the last five hours had been focused on cooking and cleaning up a little, it was girlfriend time well spent.

"Thank you so much for everything," I said, hugging her when she came out of my dad's bedroom after telling him good-bye.

"No thanks are ever needed for fam, right? Is the Uber here?"

"It is, and Stephon has already checked out the driver." I hugged her again at the front door, but when I opened it, we both got a surprise.

"Oh!" the young woman on the other side exclaimed as if she were a little bewildered, too. "I'm sorry." She stepped back a bit. "I'm looking for Zuri Maxwell."

I did my usual — a quick assessment of the woman who was probably five five (I knew this because we were eye to eye) and thinner than me (like a size four to my size eight), and she was younger than me, too . . . college age, I guessed, though I wasn't sure because she was dressed in the blue nurses' scrubs.

Was she here from Grady?

"I'm Zuri," I told her.

When she smiled, I thought she could have been a toothpaste model, and the enthusiasm that bubbled out of her made her fit to lead her college cheerleading team. "I'm Brenda Reed," she said and held out her hand to me as if I was supposed to know her.

Audra waved and pointed to the car that waited at the curb. I nodded, but my attention was all on this woman.

After shaking Brenda's hand, I said, "Are you from Grady?"

"No, Ms. Viv asked me to stop by. Viv Matthews."

That took my smile away, and in an instant I sized up and summed up the situation.

She said, "Is this a good time?"

The only reason I didn't tell this woman no and just send her on her way was because unless she lived right around the corner, she had probably made quite a drive — that's just how it was in Georgia. So the least I could do was not send her back out in rush-hour traffic. I could offer her a seat, a moment's reprieve from I-285, and something to drink.

I motioned for her to come inside, then gestured toward the sofa, but before she could sit, I said, "I'm sorry, Ms. Viv didn't tell me she was sending anyone by. What's this about?" Although I already knew.

Brenda tilted her head. "Really? She told me she had spoken to you."

Just as she said that, Stephon came from the kitchen and I introduced the two. As I settled in the recliner and Stephon sat on the arm of the chair, Brenda made herself comfortable, facing us from the sofa.

"Ms. Viv said you were looking for a home healthcare aide. Here are my credentials, my licenses, as well as a dozen references, including one, of course, from Ms. Viv," she said as she passed me a folder.

I pressed my lips together, though I tried to keep a smile. It was official — Ms. Viv was going places where she had no business. Our friendship was going to have to end.

"Ms. Viv?" Stephon asked, and I tapped his leg, my signal that I'd explain later.

I said, "Well, she knew my father was in the hospital, but I told her we weren't going to be using an aide."

Brenda gave me another one of those bewildered expressions. "Oh, really? I was sure . . ."

I shook my head, and before she could finish, I said, "No. An aide is not something we can afford." And then I added, "Although I'm sure you're very good."

"Oh." She said that word with understanding. But her smile remained when she added, "I guess Ms. Viv didn't tell you that you were covered."

"What?" Stephon said.

"Covered by what?" I asked.

"It's part of a Girls First initiative she has, I believe," Brenda said. "I don't know how it works with everyone, but I know how it works with me. She helps young women getting started in their careers. I really want to be a nurse, but I need to earn some money, so this is" — she paused — "one of the ways I'm doing it with Ms. Viv."

"Okay, so if you're trying to earn money, then I would have to pay you."

She shook her head. "No. You're not my first client, but all of the clients have been covered, and I get paid by Ms. Viv."

"Wow," Stephon said as if we'd just won the lottery.

But I knew that we hadn't. First, this didn't make much sense to me. My father had always taught me that if it glittered, you better take that gold and have it appraised because it probably wasn't real.

Stephon said, "So let me get this straight . . . you would work here . . ."

216

"Well, it wouldn't be me alone. Usually, for someone who needs the full-time care that your father may require, there would be two of us on staff, switching off hours and days. But after assessing your father, I would be the primary caregiver."

"And we wouldn't have to pay the second aide either?" Stephon asked.

When she shook her head, I could feel the warmth of Stephon's grin.

Stephon said "Wow" again, and I folded my arms, annoyed that he couldn't see that something was wrong with this picture.

So I made it clear to both of them. "Even though this all sounds wonderful, I don't think it would work."

"Why not?" Stephon said.

This was not something I wanted to talk about in front of Brenda, but my man wasn't leaving me a choice. "You know how my dad is," I said, even though that was only part of my concern. I passed Brenda an I'm-so-sorry smile. "He doesn't want anyone in his home. He thinks he can take care of himself."

Brenda laughed — no, she giggled — as if my words tickled her. "I've had that happen before."

"You've never met anyone like Oscar Maxwell," I said, trying to shut her down so

217

that I could get her out of here. "There is no way my father would agree to this."

"No way your father would agree to what?"

All three of us jumped up when we heard my father's voice, and when I rushed to my father's side, Brenda did, too. That annoyed me — and pleased me at the same time.

"Daddy, what are you doing up?"

My father paused, glanced up at Brenda, and when she gave him that toothpaste smile, he grinned.

Oh, lawd!

"And who is this beautiful young lady?"

"Did you hear what I asked you?" I said to him, though he wasn't looking at me.

"You think you can distract me by answering my question with a question that has nothing to do with my question?"

"I'm Brenda Reed," she said, and then she held his elbow as he pushed his walker toward the sofa. He accepted her aid, something he would never do with me.

When he settled onto the couch, Brenda asked, "Are you comfortable?"

"Who are you?" he growled with a grin.

And that only made Brenda smile some more. "I'm your new aide, if" — she paused — "that's all right with you."

"My aide?" My father looked at me, his

face creased with his confusion.

Oh, yeah, my dad was about to shut this all the way down.

But then . . . he grinned . . . and said, "Wow, you work fast, baby girl."

No, no, no! I said, but only on the inside.

To Brenda, he said, "How much is this gonna cost me? Am I gonna have to sell my house?"

She laughed. "No, not at all. You're gonna get to keep your house and your money. I'm just going to be here to make sure that all of your needs are met."

And then my father, who, nine months before, had had a stroke, who, three days before, had collapsed and been found unconscious on the bathroom floor . . . that man had the audacity to say, "*All* of my needs?"

"Daddy!"

"Dad!"

"Mr. Maxwell!"

Stephon, Brenda, and I exclaimed at the same time.

"What?" He looked at each of us with innocence in his eyes. "I wanna make sure that if Ms. Brenda is gonna be here that she knows how to cook and clean . . . do all the things that you've been doing, baby girl." He shook his head. "Y'all need to get your minds straight," he growled. Then, with a grin, he said, "So when do you start?"

And when three pairs of eyes turned and stared at me, I lowered myself back onto the chair and just shrugged.

20

I waited until Brenda left with her promise to return first thing in the morning (that meant eight o'clock to her) with her bag for her first week of work with my father.

I waited until Stephon had helped my father get settled in bed and we made sure he'd taken all of his medicine.

Then I waited until Stephon and I walked to his car and he kissed me with a passion that let me know he was going to miss me — this first night that we wouldn't sleep in the same bed since he'd moved in a year ago.

I waited until his car was down the block, out of my sight, then I ran into the house, checked on my dad again (he was asleep), and slipped back outside onto the porch. I left the door a bit ajar, and I did something that I made a point never to do when it was not that many minutes away from the midnight hour.

I never called anyone after ten — something I'd learned from my father, I guessed. A call after ten meant trouble.

Well, this call I was about to make . . . was trouble.

With my finger, I punched on Ms. Viv's name in my contact list, then pressed the phone to my ear, already pacing the length of the porch. I was ready to go in, and when she answered on the first ring, I exclaimed, "Ms. Viv!"

"Zuri, dear." She called my name with so much concern in her tone. "How are you? How is your father? I've been praying and praying, and I know that the Lord has heard our cries."

Just like that, she'd poured water on the three-alarm fire that had been raging inside of me. Still, a few flickering flames remained. "My dad is fine. We got him home today."

"That's great."

I paused from my pacing. "But you already knew that."

I could feel her smile before I heard her chuckle. "Yes, I did. So that means you met Brenda."

"I did, but I have a feeling you knew that already, too."

"Of course. She had to call me. She told

you she works for me."

"But you never mentioned that you owned a home healthcare business."

"I *did* tell you. I may not have been specific, but I told you I've been an entrepreneur with several enterprises. This is just one of the things that I do, and it is part of my Girls First program. There was just no need to explain all of that to you until now."

My eyes narrowed as I stared out onto the darkened street. "It just seems weird . . . that I would need this and then suddenly you come to my rescue."

"What's weird about it?" she said. But before I could answer, she continued. "Zuri," she said with a sternness in her tone that I hadn't heard before, "I'm only trying to help you. This is a blessing that the Lord has sent your way. Now, you've met Brenda, you've seen her credentials . . ."

"Yes, all of that is fine. That's not the problem I have with this."

"So, what is your problem?"

"I told you I couldn't afford an aide."

Ms. Viv sighed as if my words not only annoyed her but weighed her down. "I know Brenda explained that to you; this is all part of my business."

"I just have never felt good taking things from people. Everything in this world costs something."

"That's what's bothering you? That you don't have to pay for this?" Again, her question was rhetorical, because she continued, "This program is based on need. People receive the services based on that."

Even though she couldn't see me, I shook my head.

"So based on what you told me, I thought your father needed these services, and now he has them." She released another sigh. "I was only trying to help you, and believe me, helping you is important to me."

This was the part that I just couldn't figure out. Ms. Viv liked me — I knew that. But why was she willing to help me like this? Why was she willing to do this for me financially? And then I had other questions — like how could she afford to give away these services for free? But even though I wanted to know, that question (asking about her finances) felt a bit invasive to me. Was I supposed to just come right out and ask her how much she had in her bank account? Even if I had that kind of guts, I knew her well enough to know she wouldn't answer my question.

She broke through my thoughts with, "Is that what's really bothering you, Zuri? You feel you should pay for an aide?"

"Yes," I said. "And that's why I . . ."

"Five hundred dollars," she interrupted me.

"What?"

"If you want your father to have an aide, it will cost you five hundred dollars a month."

I froze. Stephon and I didn't have a spare five hundred dollars sitting around, but still I said, "Okay." I nodded. "Okay." Paying made me feel a bit better about this offer.

"Finally," she said like she was a bit exhausted. "I'm glad that's out of the way."

I hadn't meant to take Ms. Viv through all of that, and I didn't want to seem ungrateful, so I said, "Thank you, Ms. Viv."

"You're welcome. I'm just glad I'm in the position to do this for you and your dad. And now you'll be able to get back to work, right? Get back to your life?"

That was an odd question, since today was the only day that I'd missed. But still I said, "Yes."

"Great. Well, you have a good night, dear. And I'll check in with you again."

"Good night," I said. "And thank you so much. I don't want you to think I don't appreciate this. I really do, and I appreciate you."

"Well, we all have so much to be grateful

for. Let's just all count our blessings. And the five hundred dollars?"

"Yes?"

"Drop the check in the mail to me . . . tomorrow." Then she clicked off the phone before I could say anything.

I stared at my cell for a moment and chuckled. Be careful what you ask for, right? But still I felt better — it seemed like it was all legit . . . strange but legit.

The five hundred dollars was going to be a stretch. We had it in our account now, but who knew what next month would bring? I didn't want this to fall too much on Stephon. We were in this together, yes, but Oscar Maxwell was still my dad.

Then I remembered the bracelet. That Tiffany bracelet. Maybe I could take it back or maybe pawn it. I didn't know how much I would get, but since it was brand-new . . .

And then . . .

Oh, my goodness.

Stepping back inside my father's house, I bolted the door and wondered if it was too late. It was just minutes before midnight now — could I reach out to Alexander?

I had to. I couldn't let more time go by.

I opened my messages and typed the text:

This might be the most unprofessional

thing I've ever done — texting someone so late — but I hope you'll understand. This is what this opportunity means to me. It turns out my father is fine, and I'll be able to work on the Enclave if that is still available. I will send you my portfolio . . .

I paused. I hadn't taken a single picture.

tomorrow evening. Please let me know. Thank you, have a good evening, and I apologize for reaching out so late.

As I flopped onto the couch, I tried to work this all out in my mind. I'd taken off work today; surely one more day wouldn't be a problem, especially since my plan had been to take off a month and I'd already told my boss about my dad.

So as soon as Brenda arrived in the morning, I'd get over to Audra's and help her straighten up so that I could take photos of her place. Then she and I would put my portfolio together.

Glancing down at my phone once again, I saw it was now a new day. But I had to do it — I had to make another call. Audra might be asleep, but she'd be thrilled when I woke her with news of this gig.

Before I dialed her number, I looked up

to the ceiling and imagined heaven. "Thank you so much, Father. Thank you so much for working this out, for answering prayers spoken and the ones in my heart."

And then, as I dialed Audra's number, I smirked and said, "And thank you, too, Ms. Viv."

21

This had been a whirlwind . . . no, that wasn't the right word. This had been three weeks that had moved at supersonic speed. That was the only way that I could describe this time — supersonic and spectacular.

It was still difficult to believe that this was *my* best life.

If my life were a puzzle, every single piece had found its place and was now part of a divine design. First there was my father. And Brenda. And Ebony, my dad's weekend aide. For a man who never wanted anyone in his house, Oscar Maxwell was suddenly fine with these women inside his home.

It seemed that Brenda was beyond competent — she was intuitive. She knew how to read my father, so besides taking care of his needs: his food, his medicine, and making sure he rested when he was supposed to — she spent time with him when he wanted company, and she made herself scarce when she sensed he did not.

Every morning, when I dropped by (because he was still my daddy), I found him up, dressed, at the *dining room* table (no more eating from a tray in front of the TV), scarfing down the type of breakfast that would be sure to pack on some pounds.

But he was happy. And healthy. And he was safe.

So with my father taken care of, I could focus on my work — which was also a blessing. I'd picked up a new account at the ad agency (though I had never heard from Julian or the business he'd been working with), so more billable hours and a higher quarterly commission were on the way, I hoped.

And then . . . there was this . . .

I did a three-sixty spin, taking in all the corners and angles of the living room in the largest loft model in the Enclave on Peachtree. Less than one hour ago, the last of the furniture had been placed in all four units, and I'd done a walk-through, finding just little things — adjusting the toaster in the kitchen, wiping a smudge off the mirror in the bathroom, smoothing out a bump on the silver-colored duvet in the master bedroom.

It was all in place: perfection. And it was

ready a week early.

I couldn't believe I'd done it so quickly, but the thing about working with Abbey Global was that I really had a team. The assistant who worked on the site did all the administrative work for me as well. And I came to understand that the name of Abbey Global carried weight. It was probably because of the billions the land developer spent around the world, because people asked me, *How high?* before I even asked them to jump.

Still, while it had been fabulous, it had been work. Way more hours than I'd expected, spending ten hours and more on Saturdays and missing church on Sundays, going from showroom to showroom, discussing my ideas with every store designer, learning so much about square footage, room measurements, and furniture dimensions. It was a learn-by-fire project; I'd jumped in, gotten a bit scorched, but come out of it without even the hint of smoke on me.

Walking across the polished concrete (yes, concrete — my idea) floors, I moved to the windows. These lofts had so many amazing features and amenities, but there was nothing that would top all of this glass — there were far more windows than walls (though the brick walls in these lofts were everything).

Looking out onto the courtyard, I gave thanks once again for that call I'd received from Alexander three weeks ago. He'd reached out to me the next day to say he still wanted to see my portfolio. Audra and I had taken dozens of pictures of every room, then chosen the best and sent them in a presentation that Audra had put together at lightning speed.

We'd only had to wait a little more than twenty minutes when I received Alexander's text:

You got it, now work it.

That was exactly what I'd done — I'd worked it.

As I shifted, I could see a bit of my reflection in the window, and I turned to the dining room area, where one of the walls was mirrored. When my image came into view, I shimmied a bit — I couldn't help it. This cream-colored, formfitting sleeveless sheath with the knee-length flounce hem was made for me to dance. And dance was what I did, every time I passed a mirror. It was the first St. John piece I had ever owned, and there were six more designer outfits just like this at home in my closet.

My cell phone rang, and I turned to find my purse. Just about every call had been about business these last few weeks, so I didn't want to miss anything.

But the pounding heart GIF on my screen made me smile.

"Hey, babe," I said when I clicked AC-CEPT.

"Has *he* seen it yet?"

I ignored the way my fiancé referred to my boss. "No, Alexander is on his way, but I'm ready for him. The models are spotless and look spectacular. Ready for showing. They'll sell out, I have no doubt. Probably in record time."

"That's great." There was no real enthusiasm in his voice when he said that, but there was nothing but love in his tone when he added, "I'm so proud of you."

"Thank you."

"So, after Alexander sees the models, you think you'll be home tonight?"

"You say that like there have been nights when I didn't come home."

"Let me rephrase . . . You think you'll be home before midnight?"

Indeed, that had become something of the norm in the last three weeks. Alexander always wanted to talk business — he wanted to know what designers I'd settled on and the color schemes, how I had found working with the salespeople in the showrooms, and, of course, he kept his eyes on the budget. So I'd spent many hours with him talking business over dinner. And if I thought Julian had been something, Alexander Gayle was Julian Stone on steroids. The restaurants he took me to were even more exclusive, more expensive — many (like the Galaxy, which was my favorite so far) didn't even have prices on the menu, so I knew what that meant.

But although it was always business and a lifestyle that I just adored, my boyfriend wasn't here for any of it.

I said, "I hope to be home right after Alexander takes the tour," and then I prayed that in an hour I wouldn't have to send him a text; I'd done that too often since I'd started this project.

"You hope," Stephon said, "but you don't know."

"Babe," I said, thinking it would be best to take another approach. "Look at it this way. This coming weekend will be my last weekend."

"I thought it was all done today." I heard his frown.

"I am, but just because I finished early

doesn't mean he'll let me go. And I won't leave if it means missing out on getting the final payment of this five thousand."

I said the dollar amount as a reminder to Stephon what this was all about — our money.

But he said, "You don't have to stay for that. You've been paid half and for the three weeks you've been there already. You've done your job."

"But I haven't completed the contract," I said, and then, just because I didn't like the way this conversation was going, I added, "Oh, babe, I gotta go. Someone's coming."

"Okay, call me when you can."

"Love you," I said.

"Beyond infinity, baby. Beyond infinity."

I clicked off my phone and sighed. I loved that man so much, and Stephon had always supported me. He'd been so excited at first, when I'd come home on the night I'd officially been given this gig and told him about meeting Alexander and having the opportunity to do something that I had always wanted to do. Stephon had been so pleased, he'd gone to Big Daddy Burgers, bought a bottle of wine from Target, and then we had celebrated all . . . night . . . long.

But his passion for my passion had wavered when he found out about my clothes . . . especially the dress that I was wearing now. I sighed as I remembered . . .

Maybe this hadn't been such a good idea, I thought as Stephon stared at me like I'd grown two heads and both of them were speaking languages he didn't understand. I had just stepped out of the dressing room to show him this fly St. John. He laughed as I danced, but then as he came close to me, he caught a glimpse of the tag.

His eyes got wide. "Babe, I love this, but we can't afford it. Eleven hundred dollars for one dress?"

Ugh! I wondered how he had peeped the tag like that. Dang, I should have known — Stephon was always checking about the money. "We don't have to worry about it," I said, stepping aside so that no one coming out of the Neiman Marcus dressing room would overhear us. "Alexander gave me a credit card to buy clothes."

"You wanna roll that back and tell me that again?"

The only reason I'd asked Stephon to come shopping with me was because I'd wanted to be open about everything with this gig. I'd hidden so much from him about Julian — but with this, I'd wanted

Stephon to know it all and be a part of it. That didn't seem like such a good idea right now.

"It doesn't make sense that some dude is giving my woman a credit card to buy whatever she wants."

"He's not some dude — he's Alexander Gayle, my boss. And he didn't give your woman a credit card to buy whatever I wanted — he gave one of his employees a credit card, and this is just like purchasing a company uniform," I said, giving him the explanation that Alexander had given to me. "Look at the credit card." I searched inside my purse that I'd left outside with Stephon as I'd gone into the dressing room. When I fished it out of my wallet, I held the credit card up.

I hadn't expected Stephon to take it from my hand, but he did. And he turned it over like he thought it held a secret or a lie. Giving it back to me, he shrugged. "I still don't feel comfortable with this."

He stood there, shaking his head, like he wanted me to agree. But there was no way I was going to let Stephon talk me out of buying a brand-new . . . designer . . . wardrobe. Nuh-uh. Not with the way I'd been shopping — one item at a time, looking for sales at Marshalls. And that was crazy — who looked for sales when everything was already on sale?

"You know, they're only paying me five thousand dollars for the gig," I said, trying to make it sound like it wasn't very much money when that was at the top of the scale for designers — I'd googled it. "So," I continued, "he has to make up my pay in some kind of way. And you know it's all a write-off for them."

"I guess," Stephon said. "I should've known something was up when you went into Neiman Marcus. But I thought they were having a sale . . ."

That was the last decent conversation we'd had about Alexander Gayle and the Enclave on Peachtree. It was a good thing this project was wrapping up so that we could get back to our lives, where I was home most nights before Stephon was ready for dinner.

But for me?

Walking back over to the windows, I sighed. I loved living this way — the restaurants, the wine, the clothes, the credit card with no limit, the life that was filled with something to do every night, if that was what I wanted.

There was nothing wrong with wanting

this life, right? Nothing at all wrong with living a fabulous life.

"Wow!"

The sound of the voice made me spin away from the windows, and then I smiled when I saw the approval that already shined on Alexander's face. And he hadn't yet entered the loft; he was still standing in the threshold.

I stayed still as he first studied me with appreciation and then turned his glance to the massive space. This model was called the White House because that was the color of everything — some shade of off-white: pearl, ivory, eggshell. And the dress I wore made me seem like another accessory.

He didn't speak a word as he took his own tour. The heels of his shoes clicked against the floor of the open plan as he walked through the grand room, dining room, and kitchen, which had a separate breakfast area. Then he checked out the two rooms with doors on this level: the bathroom and the room I'd decorated as a study.

I didn't move; there was no need for me to follow him through the unit as he walked up the wrought-iron spiral staircase that led to the master bedroom, which was complete with a sitting area, a faux fireplace, and of course a master bath the size of a small apartment. My work would do the speaking for me.

When he came back downstairs, though, the smile that he'd worn was gone and his face was blank. No, that was the wrong word — it was like he'd seen a ghost or something. What happened? What had gone wrong?

His steps were slow as he approached me, his face holding that same expression. My heart began to pound.

Then he said, "I'm just . . . blown away," and I released a long breath of relief. "I told you to work it, and you did. You not only worked it, but you nailed it."

I gave him a nod to show my appreciation for his compliment and because I couldn't yet speak, he had scared me so much.

He paused and did a slow turn, taking in the grand room once again. "I'm just chuffed about all of this. Amazing job. You truly are a corker."

I laughed. "Can you speak English?" I asked, something that I often had to say to Alexander.

He held up his hand as if he were apologizing. "Sorry. In English . . . as you say" — he smirked — "I was saying that I love this and you are a standout." He shook his head. "And to think you did this in a little more than a fortnight." Looking at me, he added, "We got you for a steal. I'm going to have to pay you a bonus."

A bonus. I clapped at that, but only in my mind. I stayed in my professional mode and asked, "Do you want me to take you through the other units?"

He nodded, and I did just that — we walked through the other three, or rather Alexander did. I wanted him to see the lofts without me hovering by his side. But each time, his reaction was the same — he'd return to where he left me and call me a corker.

When we returned to the first unit, he said, "Zuri, I truly am so pleased."

"I'm glad."

"Well, you finished early, but I would still like you here this weekend in case there are any last-minute adjustments we may have to make before we open for showing next week."

"Of course, I'll be here. You have me for a month, remember?"

"Well . . . I'm hoping . . ."

I tilted my head as he paused.

He said, "I'm hoping I can get you for one week past a month."

"What do you mean?"

"Not for the whole week; I'm sure you

want to get back to your life." He paused as if he was waiting for me to agree; I didn't. He continued, "But I'd need you for next Saturday, the nineteenth."

"Okay," I said, and in my mind the wheels turned. What else would he need me for — was there an extra loft somewhere?

Then he explained, "I've been invited to a little gathering."

I frowned. What did that have to do with me?

"With Usher."

I tried to stop myself, but my eyes widened.

"And I'd like you to go with me."

Now my mouth matched my eyes.

I didn't say a word as he explained that this was a private party, a red-tie affair, where Usher was introducing a new singer to about two hundred of his closest friends.

"So, do you think you might be able to make a way to go with me?"

Alexander had no idea — he had me at "with Usher."

I guess because I hadn't said a word, Alexander continued, "I really hope you'll say yes, and of course, I'll pay for your gown and accessories."

More shopping? An event with Usher?

He said, "So what do you say? Next Saturday?"

"Yes, I'd love to go," I said, not able to get the words out of my mouth fast enough. "I can't wait."

He smiled and said thank you, and I was grateful when he didn't say he wanted us to go to dinner, though that was a first. I scampered out of there before he changed his mind and jumped into my car. But before I took off, I covered my mouth with my hands and released a scream. If I'd had any room, I would've kicked up my heels.

This was going to be ah-may-zing.

There was only one challenge — how would I ever get out of the house on a Saturday night looking like Cinderella going to the ball? From his call today, I knew Stephon was teetering on the edge, and telling him that I was going out to an Usher party with Alexander would push him over.

But I'd have to figure it out, and I'd have a week and a half to do that. I wasn't about to miss this.

No way. Because this was the life.

22

This had taken so much planning. Twelve days to be exact — since the day that Alexander had invited me to the event.

For twelve days, my focus had been on Stephon. I had done everything short of inviting him to go to work with me. He'd even followed me over to my dad's a few mornings, and we'd had breakfast with him, joking about his new life, before I went to work and Stephon returned home to paint.

That was my objective — to share the same space, to breathe the same air as much as I could with Stephon. Even when he was painting, I stayed close, hanging out in the bedroom, just so he knew I was near.

It may have seemed simple, but it had been a challenging task. During these twelve days, Alexander had invited me out to dinner three times, but with the project over, I didn't understand why we needed to go out. What did we have to talk about? Though I wasn't lying to myself. Under different circumstances, not knowing what Alexander wanted to talk about wouldn't have been a concern. I would've jumped at the chance to go to dinner just to see where Alexander would have taken me.

But I'd been able to push off his invites, blaming it on my real J.O.B., but all the time assuring Alexander I would be there with him on Saturday, the nineteenth.

Saturday, the nineteenth.

Today.

It had been hard to sleep last night; a cocktail of excitement and anxiety had worked me over like caffeine, and I'd spent most hours staring at the ceiling and doing a minute-by-minute countdown.

Then this morning, I'd jumped out of bed, even before Stephon, so that I could see my father before the party tonight. It was hard not to share where I was going, but maybe one day, I'd be able to tell this story. My father wasn't an Usher fan; he was old-school to his core. But he knew who he was, so his excitement would've matched mine.

Now, as I zipped up my roller garment bag, I felt far more anxiety than excitement. This was the moment the last twelve days of spending all of my time with Stephon had been all about.

When I opened our bedroom door, Edvard Grieg's Morning Mood played through the apartment, even though it was two hours past noon. Taking a deep breath, I rolled my bag into the hallway, then paused, the way I did every Saturday, staring at the man I loved, with his muscles (that I loved, too) bulging from his bare back as he worked his canvas magic.

Today, though, I didn't stay to enjoy the view. With another breath for courage, I moved to Stephon, gave him a kiss on his head, and then moved toward the door.

Stephon glanced at me and then did a double take. "Wait, where are you going?"

I tilted my head. "I didn't want to disturb you, but remember, I'm going over to Audra's? I'm spending the night with Lyle and Lily."

"Oh" — he put his paintbrush down — "is that tonight?" He stood and frowned.

"Uh-huh," I said. "Did you forget?" And I wondered why my heart was assaulting my chest.

"Yeah, I did." He strutted to me, and for a moment, his bare chest distracted me. When he wrapped his arms around me, I dropped the suitcase. "I feel like I just got you back, and now you're leaving me again?"

"It's just for one night. And the last time, I was away with my dad. That was one night, too."

"That should be proof that one night is one too many for me."

"Me too. But you have to paint." That was the card I had to play. "You have to get ready for your show. And this will give me time with the twins and time for Audra and Joseph to get away on a night when Abagail is off."

He nodded like he agreed, though his expression told me he really didn't.

I took that as my cue — I had to leave now. "Babe, I'll see you first thing in the morning," I said. "I'll get back here before you're even awake."

That was a truth I had twisted just a bit. I *would* be back in the early hours of the morning, and he *wouldn't* be awake — not at one or two or whenever Usher's party would be over. I hadn't figured out what truth I would twist when he asked me why I was home early. But I couldn't focus on what to say when I returned, when right now I had to keep all of my attention on walking out of this door.

"Okay," he said.

I gave him a kiss that was meant to fill him with satisfaction and make him yearn for tomorrow. But when he said, "You know what?" I wanted to take that kiss back because I could tell from his tone that I *didn't* want to know what he was about to say.

"I'm going to just put all of this aside and come with you. Just give me about twenty to take a shower and . . ."

"No!" I exclaimed.

The volume and tone of my voice made his head rear back just a bit.

"I'm sorry." I held up my hands. "I just meant no, you have to paint and . . . and . . . and Evelyn's going to be there."

"You didn't tell me that."

"Yeah," I said, the lie coming to me faster now. "It's going to be a godmothers' night. So the two of us will entertain the twins, and I don't want you to feel uncomfortable . . . or for her to feel uncomfortable if you're there. You know, she's not seeing anyone right now, and I don't want her to feel like a third wheel." I was overexplaining, so I pulled him into my arms. "Just let me do this. Tonight." I pressed my lips to his forehead. "And then tomorrow" — my lips made a journey to his nose — "will be a day you'll always remember." When my lips traveled to his, my man was ready. And the kiss, which was long and loving, let me know I had won.

When we pulled apart, I pressed my forehead against his. "And you know what?" I didn't give him room to respond. "If they get home early enough, I'll come home to you. Cool?"

He nodded, and I breathed, relieved — now I'd need no explanation for coming home in the middle of the night. He kissed my cheek before he opened the door, and barefoot, bare-chested and all, he rolled my suitcase to the car for me. At first I walked behind him, all proud with the way his body was poppin' . . . until I saw the two girls, our next-door neighbors (who were sisters, I believed), standing outside their door, staring at him like he was the chicken on the bone.

Now, these women were no kind of competition for me. My man wasn't into waist-long blue-and-pink weaves (that was the tall one) nor pencil-thin blond braids that almost touched the knees (that was the other one). And he definitely wouldn't be attracted to the neck tattoo on the one with the braids or the blue contacts, which I guessed were meant to match the hair of the tall one.

Still, the way those sisters gaped at him, I almost wanted to roll my suitcase back inside so they didn't think I was leaving for good.

But, of course, I didn't do that. When Stephon dumped the bag into the trunk for me then opened my door, I wrapped my arms around him, leaned back onto the car, pulled him close, and kissed him like I was trying to get my tongue to tickle his esophagus.

When he stepped back, he was in a daze.

I smiled, and before I slid into the car, I said, "See. You. Tomorrow," making sure my words were clear and crisp and loud.

He grinned, as if he was onto my little display. He closed the door, then leaned into the window. "I hope you have lots more of that tomorrow."

"Oh, I will," I said, turning on the ignition. "I definitely will." I shifted the car into drive. "Now go on. Get back inside."

"Nah," he said. "I'm gonna just stand here and watch you drive away."

I shifted the car back into park, crossed my arms, and poked out my lips.

He laughed. "Okay, babe." Another peck on my lips. "I love you."

"Beyond infinity." I said it and meant it.

I watched him trot to our door and when

he was inside safely, I turned my gaze into a glare as I stared at the sisters, who were now staring at me. But then I shook my head and grinned. Why was I even putting any kind of brain energy into these girls? It was after two and Alexander was sending a limo to pick me up at five. That was where all of my attention needed to be.

I had to get ready to make my debut into high society.

On the entire drive to Buckhead, my anxiety had waned and my excitement was on the rise. But when I jumped out of my car, then dashed up the pathway and rang Audra's doorbell, my best friend's expression deflated every good feeling I had.

"I don't like this," Audra said without even saying hello. I stepped inside, and when she closed the door, she continued, "We're not in college anymore. We don't lie to our men and then ask our friends to cover for us."

I sighed as I followed her up the steps, while she kept on grumbling.

"It's a good thing Joseph is out of town. You know he wouldn't go along with any of this."

When we stepped into one of the guest bedrooms, it seemed like her lecture was over, so I asked, "Where are the twins?" as I dropped my garment bag onto the gray duvet on the bed.

"Don't try to change the subject." She wagged her finger the way she did when she talked to her children.

I guessed the lecture wasn't over. "I'm not. I just want to say hello to my godchildren."

"Hmmm," she hummed, and without words, she was calling me a liar. "Well, they're not here."

The way she said that, I didn't want to ask her any other questions. She stood and watched me like an overseer as I opened the garment bag and eased out the gown I'd purchased last week.

For a moment, I forgot about my friend and her judgment as I held up the red tailored dress. I sighed now, the same way I'd sighed when I first saw this designer piece: the fitted stretch-jersey bodice gave way to a sateen trumpet skirt, and the white sash at the waist gave this elegance a little flavor. Plus, it showed just enough skin — the sleeveless dress was cut deep on the shoulders — bare arms, almost bare shoulders.

It was another ensemble that cost over a thousand dollars and that after tonight would just hang in my closet, and the thought of that pushed out another sigh from me.

"Where did you get the dress?"

Dang! I really had forgotten Audra was here. She still stood as if she were in charge, glaring her disapproval.

"Audra." I bounced down on the bed. "I'm going to this party with Alexander, and I didn't tell Stephon because he would never approve. But how can I miss a party with Usher?" I whined like one of the twins.

She paused for a moment, then sat next to me. "Are you interested in Alexander?"

My frown was deep. "Are you kidding me?"

"Are you going to answer me?"

"No." And I put all of my body into that answer, shaking my head, my shoulders, and my hands. "I'm not interested in him in any way. I love Stephon, I'm clear about that. But what does love have to do with a party like this? Who wouldn't want to go?"

She raised her hand. "I wouldn't. Not if I had to lie to Joseph."

I sighed. "I just don't want the drama. It was bad enough with all the dinners I had with Alexander. Stephon had a lot of problems with that."

"And what *was* with all of those dinners?"

she asked as if she were cross-examining me for Stephon.

Pushing myself from the bed, I stood, thinking that maybe if I looked down at her, I could get her to hear me and understand. "I've told you everything, Audra. You were the one who cheered me on about working with Alexander. So you know it was all business."

She narrowed her eyes. "I *knew* it was business, but I don't know that anymore." She shook her head. "I think you're getting caught up."

"In what?"

"In this life. You've been talking about this being how you want to live for so long, and I'm afraid that you're getting carried away by it all. The dinners, this party — after tonight, your life isn't going to be enough for you."

"That's not true."

"It's not? How many times did you have a business dinner with Alexander?"

At this point, the only thing I was glad about was that I hadn't told my best friend about Julian. If she'd known about him, she'd be ready to hold some kind of intervention for me.

I said, "We had a big project to do in a

short period of time. People have meetings, Audra."

"Justify it any way you want." She stood. "I'll leave you alone to get dressed." Before she left the room, she turned back to me. "Let me know if you need any help."

"I'll need help. I'm sure of it."

"Okay, I'll be back." She paused. "I love you, Zuri. I just hope you know what you're doing."

"What I'm doing is going to a party. One party."

She nodded and left me alone. For a moment, I sat on the bed and thought about Audra's words. Why had this become an issue? Was it because I'd lied to Stephon? Maybe I shouldn't have done that, but it wasn't like I was cheating on him. If there had been any way Stephon could have gone to this event with me, right now, I'd be saying, *Alexander who?*

Glancing at my watch, I jumped up. It was already three, and though I had two hours, I wanted to take my time with everything from my shower to my makeup.

So I started in the guest bathroom, which was familiar to me, but not because I'd spent too many nights over here — I knew my way around every part of this home because it was all my design. Having two hours gave me time to linger in the shower, then I lotioned up, and by the time I returned to the bedroom, Audra was back, too.

She was in a better mood. I was glad about that, especially when she offered to do my makeup. If she hadn't become a biochemist, Audra could have easily had a career as a celebrity makeup artist, and the proof was in the results, because by the time she was done, my face was beat.

"This gown really is beautiful," Audra said as she held it for me to step into. And when she zipped it and I turned around, she gasped. "Beautiful," she repeated.

I turned to the leaning mirror to check it out for myself . . . Yeah, I'd chosen well.

"Oh," I said. There was one thing that would put an exclamation point on this outfit. I grabbed the purse I'd been carrying and dug into the side pocket. And there it was — the Tiffany bracelet. Handing it to Audra, I said, "Can you hook this on, please?"

I held out my wrist, but Audra didn't move. She just stared at the bracelet in her palm. "Where did you get this?"

If I had thought about it for one moment, just one, I wouldn't have done this. I wouldn't have put more ammunition right into Audra's hands. I said, "It was a gift."

She covered her mouth with her hand. "From Stephon?" She grinned. "Wow, it's beautiful."

I was standing on the corner of Truth and Deceit. Because the way Audra had been checking me all afternoon, I didn't want to go through this with her again. But now that she assumed this was from Stephon, I couldn't leave that out there like that.

So I made a right turn on the corner and said, "I don't want to talk about this, but I'll just tell you — it was a gift for a consulting project I did."

Her grin rolled back, and now her eyes narrowed. "What kind of consulting did you have to do to get this?"

"Didn't I just tell you I didn't want to talk about this?" I snatched the bracelet from her and hooked it on my wrist myself.

"Zuri, I'm getting worried . . ."

"Nothing to worry about." I grabbed my clutch. One glance at the clock, and I had good reason to end this conversation. "The limousine should be here by now. Would you mind putting my bag in my car, and then I can just leave when I get back?"

She folded her arms. "You're welcome to stay. You know that."

"Thank you, but I really do want to get

257

home to Stephon."

She nodded but said nothing, and that was fine with me. I moved out of the bedroom in front of her and held my gown as she followed me down the stairs. I hugged her before I stepped out of the door, and she watched me until I slid into the limousine that was waiting at the curb.

After I said hello to the driver, I turned back to the window to wave to Audra. But she had already closed her front door.

23

If I hadn't been in a gown and wearing four-inch stilettos (which were brand-new, too), I could have walked to the InterContinental Hotel. The drive was less than ten minutes, but I was grateful for it because I needed the time to shake Audra's attitude off of me.

And ten minutes was enough, because by the time my limo pulled to the opening curve of the hotel, I was back to being nothing but excited. Even though we'd arrived in that short time, it still took at least that many minutes for my limo to roll from the street to the hotel's entry.

The uniformed doormen for the InterContinental opened the limo's door, and the moment I stepped out, Alexander was there to take my hand.

"You look beautiful," he said, and gave me a hug.

"Thank you." And then I stepped back

and did my thing. I smiled with appreciation as I took in Alexander's Armani tuxedo. And the reason I knew for sure that it was Armani? I had been looking at all the Armani tuxedos for so long, waiting for the day when I could buy one for Stephon, thinking that he'd need it soon for a major art show or something even better — our wedding.

Alexander extended his arm to me, and though I hesitated for a moment, I realized that he was just being a gentleman. I held his arm as we passed through the bustling mass that jammed the hotel's entry. Of course, not everyone was here for Usher's party, but still, this was a top-shelf crowd. The men and women who milled around were all in expensive garb — casual, professional, after-five. And there was glitter everywhere: from gold that shined from watches, to platinum that sparkled from necklaces . . . and then there were diamonds, of course.

We made our way through the massive space to the Windsor ballroom, and the crowd thinned, but those who remained were dressed for the red-tie event: women in the most elegant red gowns and men wearing tuxedos with some variant of red cummerbunds and bow ties.

As we stepped into the hall that led to the ballroom, the flow slowed, but then when I saw a flash, I figured out why. There was a red carpet? And paparazzi? Of course there was; this was an Usher event.

"I'm just going to step over there," I whispered to Alexander.

"Why?" he asked. "You don't want to have your picture taken?"

No, I didn't. Not with him. I didn't want anything out there making it look like Alexander and I were a couple.

But when he said, "Ah, come on," I agreed. There was no chance of Stephon ever seeing this photo. It wasn't like Alexander was a big celebrity, and I certainly wasn't anyone that anybody would know.

So when it came to our turn, I posed as if I had a man at home. Alexander did wrap his arm around my waist, but only in the way a friend does when taking a picture with a friend. My hands were in clear view of the lenses, though.

Still, I was glad when that part was over and Alexander led me to the entrance of the ballroom. There were at least two hundred people moving through the space, stopping and chatting, grabbing flutes of champagne from waiters and hors d'oeuvres from waitresses.

But then, I saw . . . Jamie Foxx. Oh my God!

"Shall we?" Alexander motioned, and I nodded because I couldn't speak.

I could hardly breathe when Alexander shook Jamie's hand and they chatted — well, not a conversation, but they shared at least ten words before Alexander introduced me.

"Nice to meet you, Zuri," he said before he tilted his head a little. "You know who you look like?" But before he could tell me, someone tapped his shoulder and Jamie rushed off.

Of course, I knew what he was going to say. But that was the first time ever I wouldn't have been annoyed by the comparison.

Alexander led me to one of the tall white-cloth-draped tables, and it was a good thing it was only a few feet away. I leaned on the table and was so glad when Alexander stopped a waiter, who served us champagne. I had to take a breath to calm myself.

"Are you okay?" His forehead was creased with his concern.

"I am . . . I just didn't know there would be so many . . . *people* here."

"Ah, yes, people," he said. "Celebrities. But you're correct, they're people, too." He chuckled.

I nodded. "And Jamie Foxx . . . he talked to *me*. He seemed really nice, too."

"He is, and you'll find everyone you meet here tonight is just like that."

Alexander was right. After I steadied myself enough to sip the champagne, which was, like everything else in the past few weeks, the smoothest, richest bubbly I'd ever tasted, I settled down enough to mingle with the people and enjoy the ambience.

The food was never-ending, the champagne was forever flowing, there was an open bar if one fancied something other than the expensive champagne the waitstaff served, and the music . . . that was fire. But this was an event hosted by Usher, and it was known that he loved old-school jams, too.

But the best part for me — the people. Yeah, the celebrities. Alexander impressed me with how many of them he knew. He introduced me to Chris Tucker and Keyshia Cole . . . and, oh my God, when Winston Duke shook my hand, I wanted to ask him to bark at me!

I played it like I was cool and had class, though; I just said hello and sipped more champagne to keep me calm.

Meeting all of those celebrities was the

highlight, truly, but it wasn't them alone. I loved hobnobbing with the other high-powered people. No one publicly knew their names, but Charles, an entertainment attorney, kept me humored with stories about how sometimes he felt more like a babysitter than a lawyer. And Tracy, a personal stylist (she gave me her card), told me how she would love to style me because I was the perfect Coke-bottle shape. (And not one mention of Thelma.) Finally, Kathy, an art dealer, talked about how she loved discovering new artists. I so wanted to tell her about the best undiscovered talent on Earth, but how would I explain meeting her to Stephon? Still, I took her card — this was for my man; I'd figure it out.

It was hours filled with mingling and mixing and being among people and an environment that wasn't my normal but felt like it should be. Yes, this should be me all the time.

When Usher came onto the stage and introduced his new artist, Onyx, I felt like one of his friends. I applauded with the crowd, rocked as Onyx performed a couple of R & B selections he'd written, and then at the end of the evening, hugged and promised to stay in touch with a few of the people I'd connected with.

By the time Alexander opened the door of the limousine and then slid in beside me, I couldn't remember having had a better time, and that's what I told him.

"Thank you so much for this," I said.

"It was my pleasure." He patted my hand, but didn't move his away. "To have you there with me meant everything."

I nodded, then slipped my hand from his. "So, this is it, I guess."

He shook his head. "I'm hoping you have one more dinner in you."

When I got into this car, my plan was to say good night and good-bye. But just *one* more dinner? What could be the harm in that?

"That would be nice," I said.

"Great, I'll make reservations for tomorrow night . . ."

Oh, no! There would be no way I could have dinner with him tomorrow. Not after leaving Stephon tonight.

"At Pinnacle."

Pinnacle. Another place I'd always wanted to go. But still, no. At least no to tomorrow.

"I would love that, Alexander, but I just can't go tomorrow. Can we do Monday or Tuesday?"

The way he shook his head, I could tell the day was nonnegotiable. And then he told me why. "I'm leaving to return home on Monday. Flying across the pond. Going back to London."

"Oh, I didn't know."

"So tomorrow is it. And I have a surprise for you."

"What?" I asked, my eyes wide with attention now. "What's the surprise?"

He smiled. "Now, if I told you, it wouldn't be a surprise." He paused. "Just a way for me to say thank you for all you've done."

"You've already thanked me."

"How? By paying you for doing a job? By going to dinner to discuss work? Even tonight — I was there representing Abbey Global. Still all work to me. But this dinner tomorrow will be just me and you, and me saying thanks to you."

I turned to the window as the car eased onto Audra's cul-de-sac. Dinner . . . tomorrow . . . at a place I always wanted to go . . . with a surprise waiting for me. The surprise, what could it be? Alexander said that it was his personal way of saying thank you. It had to be some kind of gift.

"So . . ." Alexander said, right as the car stopped.

Just one last dinner. Just one last gift.

"Will you be able to go to dinner with me?"

Just one last time.

Another moment of hesitation, then I said, "Yes. I'll meet you there, at Pinnacle."

"Great." He smiled, then signaled for the driver to get out and open the door for me. "I'll text you with the time, okay?"

I wanted to ask him not to make it too late, but the time tomorrow really wasn't going to matter. Even if we ate dinner at noon, Stephon would not be pleased that once again, I was going to be away. But for dinner at Pinnacle *and* a surprise, I'd just have to figure it out.

24

I was old enough to remember when my relationship with Stephon was simple. I went to work in the office, he went to work in the living room, in between we took care of personal stuff, I spent time with my dad . . . and the rest of the time we came home to just us.

But somehow, life had zigzagged into a complicated ring of twisted truths, and I was now always having to come up with a plan to get away from my man. The thought of that made my heart dip a bit, especially since all I wanted to do was spend my life with Stephon. But at least this was coming to an end. After dinner tonight, I wouldn't have to do this anymore.

Just this one final dinner, and this one last . . . surprise.

I had done a good job of putting this day together and showering Stephon with all of the attention. After not going to church and serving him breakfast in bed, I tried to coax Stephon back to his painting.

"Nah, babe. I'm gonna spend the day with you; we haven't had enough of these days recently."

"What are you talking about? You act like we don't sleep in the same bed every night."

"There've been too many times when that's all we've done. Just sleep in the same bed. You've been working so hard, and I just want to spend this time with you."

When he sealed his words with a kiss, I switched to plan B and convinced Stephon to leave the house. Hanging out would feel more like quality time.

So I drove us to Centennial Park, and as the May sun heated the air to the high eighties, we strolled past the flags (Stephon loved to do that, just like Daddy), then bought hamburgers (of course) and shared a shake before we moseyed over to the National Center for Civil and Human Rights.

The sun was still high when we got back to the car, and just as I slid behind the steering wheel, my phone vibrated with a message:

Dinner at 7. Can't wait for you to see your surprise.

269

"Is everything all right?"

I must have been staring at the text longer than I meant to. "Oh, no. Just something from . . . my boss." Another twisted truth.

"On Sunday?"

"Yeah," I said, wondering if there was a way for me to prep Stephon for what was to come in a few hours. "We have a big presentation next week, and he just wanted to tell me something about it." There was no way I could call that a twisted truth. That was just a lie.

"Oh." And then Stephon held my hand after he turned up the radio to his favorite station: classical, of course.

But after one song, I tuned to V-103 just in time for one of my all-time favorites. When that beat hit, I started bobbing my head and Stephon pretended that he held drumsticks and was a master player.

"I said you wanna be starting somethin'
You gotta be starting somethin'."

At the traffic light, I raised my hands above my head and chair danced like I was in the middle of a club. Stephon hunched his shoulders up and down and came closer to me, and we danced together till the light turned green.

"Hee haw!"

We partied just like that, song after song,

and by the time we got home, I almost didn't want to go out. What was a dinner at Pinnacle when I could spend the rest of the night with this man?

But it was that surprise that was going to take me away.

"I'm gonna cue up Netflix. Anything you want to watch in particular?"

"Nah," I said, glancing at the clock in the kitchen. I was going to have to have this play out pretty quickly now, since it was just after five. Counting backward, it would take me twenty minutes to get downtown, then another twenty minutes to get dressed. So I had about an hour to cuddle with Stephon and set my plan in motion. I put my purse on the sofa and then followed Stephon into our bedroom.

But even as I lay back in Stephon's arms, my thoughts were on the clock . . . and what I would say . . . and would Stephon be too disappointed. On the sly, I kept glancing at my watch and watching the minutes tick by.

"What's up?"

I looked up at Stephon. "What?"

"You got somewhere to be? You keep checking the time."

"Oh, no, I was just wondering how much longer for this movie because there's something coming on Lifetime I wanted to see

271

tonight."

He rolled his eyes and I laughed before I said, "Oh, that's my phone."

"Huh?"

"My phone . . . is ringing."

He scrunched his forehead as if that would help him to hear better, but he shook his head.

Jumping up, I said, "I left my purse in the living room." I dashed as if I were expecting an important call that I just couldn't miss. My heart pounded as I pulled my cell from my purse, and I made sure it was off before I pressed it to my ear.

I began a conversation with nobody as I stood outside of our bedroom.

"Well, the numbers that I have are on the computer. You don't see the spreadsheet?" I paused and listened to nothing. Then, "No, those aren't the right numbers." Another pause. "Oh, I see what's wrong: you gave me the first estimates. I'd have to redo all of that."

More dead air, and now Stephon stepped into the hall with me.

"Can't we do that tomorrow?" This time, I didn't wait for too many seconds to pass before I said, "Okay, I can come in. But all I want to do is take care of this and then get back home." I looked up and at Ste-

phon. "I was spending time with my fiancé."
Another pause and I finished with, "I'll be
right there."

Stephon released a long stream of breath
as I pretended to click off.

"I'm so sorry, babe."

"I can't believe you have to go into work
again. That's all you've been doing."

"But this is my real job," I told him.
"Remember, all of the hours I've been
working were for the Enclave. This is the
one that pays the bills."

"Still . . ."

"Still what, Stephon? You've always supported me with work. We support each
other," I said and glanced to the living
room, which had once been as elaborate as
any of the lofts I'd just designed.

But now my sofa was pushed up against
the wall, covered with hefty plastic; my
tables were the same, except for my coffee
table, which was lined up against the wall
by the door. And the centerpieces of *my* life
were now *his* easel, *his* paintbrushes, *his*
tubes and jars of paint.

I'd been all in for Stephon, and I wanted
him to remember that.

"I'm sorry," he said, pulling me into his
arms. "I'm being selfish."

And now there weren't words for what I

felt. But "like crap" was pretty close.

"You're right," he said. "Go on. Take care of your business, and I'll get some painting done."

"Okay." I kissed him. "That's best anyway. I don't want anything to get in the way of your show." And I meant that.

"I'm gonna change. Even though it's Sunday, I don't want to go in like this." I glanced down at the shorts and tank top I was wearing.

He nodded, but there was a sadness in his eyes that once again made me ask myself, Was this worth it? When Stephon walked over to his easel, began his prep, and sat before his canvas, I rushed into the bedroom. My outfit was already planned; I couldn't do anything too casual — I was going to Pinnacle. But I couldn't be too dressy either — that would lead to questions.

So I put on my black halter jumpsuit and then a white blazer, so it didn't look too dressy. But I'd be able to leave the jacket in my car.

By the time I stepped into the living room, Stephon had Requiem Mass in D Minor playing, and that made me pause. I didn't understand classical music the way Stephon did, but he tried to pour into me all that he knew. And now, not only did I recognize most songs, but I knew their origins, their messages — and this last song, written by Mozart, was considered one of the saddest moments in classical music history.

It took everything in me to move toward my man, kiss his head the way I always did, and wait for him to kiss my cheek.

"I love you," I whispered and tried to put every bit of emotion inside of me into those words.

"Beyond infinity," he whispered back.

When I stood outside our apartment door, I paused, needing a moment to get myself together. This was no big deal. I was just going to this dinner. I'd get this gift. And then I would do everything I could to make this night up to Stephon.

He would never have to worry . . . This would never happen again.

Pinnacle was everything I expected it to be — just like all the other restaurants — and by the time dinner was over, it didn't feel like leaving Stephon had been worth it.

"You seem a bit gutted," Alexander said.

I tilted my head, my signal for him to speak the kind of English that I understood.

He nodded, understanding my motion, and he said, "Gutted, despondent. Like you're really upset about something."

"Oh, no. I'm just tired."

Leaning closer to me, he said, "I miss your vivaciousness."

"I'm sorry."

"Well, maybe this will cheer you up."

And then time slowed down and I had a déjà vu moment. Like Julian, Alexander leaned over to the chair beside him (like Julian, he'd arrived before me) and he lifted something — only his was much bigger than what Julian had given to me. His was in a bag. A big one. A bag that, like the blue box had, already told me what was inside.

"Oh my God," I said before I was able to even get the bag into my hands. And when I looked inside, it was exactly what I'd been coveting. "How did you know?" I said, lifting the designer purse from the Louis Vuitton shopping bag.

"You've forgotten; that's how we met. In front of the store. You were looking at the purse." He paused. "I take it you didn't purchase it yet."

"No, I didn't. I couldn't." And then I came back to my senses. "And I can't."

"What?"

I shook my head and tucked the purse back into the dust bag before I dropped it into the shopping bag. "This was so thoughtful of you, but I can't accept something so . . . expensive."

"Tosh," he exclaimed. And this time, he didn't even wait for me to ask for a translation. He said, "Nonsense. That's ridiculous. Why can't you accept this?"

"Because it's such an expensive gift."

"Well, isn't that better than a cheap one? Besides, don't look at it like a gift," he said as the waiter brought over our check. He glanced at the billfold, then said, "Think of it as the bonus I promised you."

"I thought you were kidding about a bonus."

"Well, I wasn't. Like I said before, you deserve it." He pointed to the shopping bag. "And you deserve that purse. So let's not go back and forth. I know you want it: accept it, and just say . . ." He paused and smiled.

I looked down at the bag and said, "Thank you."

He signed the check with a flourish and then stood before he held out his hand to me. As we walked through the restaurant and into the massive lobby that was the bar area, then waited outside at the valet, it took everything for me not to peek inside the shopping bag and see if I really had that designer purse.

When my car arrived, Alexander did what he always did — he waved the attendant away and stood by my door himself.

I set the shopping bag in the passenger seat, then turned to Alexander. "Thank you for everything. This has been the best experience for me."

He grinned. "And you've been the best fantasy ever."

"Fantasy?" I laughed, waiting for him to give me the translation of that word.

But his cell phone rang, and when he glanced down at the screen, he said, "I'm so sorry, but I have to take this."

I nodded, gave him a hug, then by the time I slid into my car, he was already engrossed in his conversation. I sped away, but then, right outside, I pulled over to the first space along the curb. Turning on the overhead light, I grabbed the purse out of the bag and held it to my chest.

Oh my God! I really owned this purse.

As gently as I could, I set it back in its place. A surprise, a bonus — whatever he wanted to call it, this was the best gift ever.

Driving home, I nodded. Yeah, it had been the worst to leave Stephon, but this night had turned out to be the best. And now I could go back to my life with my man, feeling just a little bit richer.

25

When Ms. Viv had called this morning, I smiled. Because I hadn't thought about her — until that moment. So right after I greeted her (and she told me how blessed she was and then recited Psalm 23), I'd told her, "We're having a barbecue at my dad's for Memorial Day, and I'd love for you to come."

There was so much quiet on the other end that at first I wondered if the call had dropped.

But then finally, "I would love to come by and meet your father, Zuri. I've heard so much about the legend. That would be wonderful. What time?"

"Well, I'm at my father's now, but we're expecting everyone here by about two."

"I'll see you then, dear."

Now I watched her sitting next to my father on the sofa, chatting as if they'd known each other for longer than just an hour. Satisfied, I bobbed my head and sang along to the music coming from the system that Stephon and I had given my dad last Christmas and that was wired through the whole house. "Joy and pain. Like sunshine and rain." I snaked my way through the living room, maneuvering through my dad's buddies from the barbershop and Mrs. Lewis, who I now considered a friend, finally making my way through the kitchen, then to the backyard.

Before I pushed open the screen door to the deck, I paused and watched Stephon and Joseph as they lorded over the two barbecue grills while Audra laid out the first pans of food.

Lyle and Lily sat at the table on the deck, eating hot dogs, though Lily ate hers without a bun. I kissed them both before I took the two steps down to the concrete slab, and right as I joined the guys at the grill, Frankie Beverly belted out the Black Backyard Barbecue National Anthem:

"You make me happy . . ."

"Uh-oh, watch out now," Joseph said as he took Audra's hand and twirled her around.

"This you can bet . . ."

I lifted my arms above my head, and two seconds later, Stephon was all over me.

"Keep this PG-rated," Joseph kidded as he and Audra did a little cha-cha. "My kids are over there."

We laughed, and the four of us grooved to the song that I was almost sure every black kid knew before they turned ten. As we danced, I took a little mental break, checking out for just a couple of seconds to revel in this moment of family and friends.

I so loved my life. I so loved this man.

Over the last week, I had put in the work to bring us all the way back to this point. Every day and night of this week, the vow I'd made to myself became true — my focus had been all on Stephon. My job? Of course, I still did that well, but it was just nine to five, and even when Stephon was painting when I got home, I was there. I was the attentive, dutiful fiancée, which is who I wanted to be.

The result: we were back to who we were before I met Alexander. No, even before then. Before I met Julian. We were back to the beginning of spring, and that was a good metaphor for us.

"Before I let you goooooooooooo . . ." the four of us sang together and then fell out laughing.

These were good times.

When Stephon and Joseph settled back in

281

front of the grill, Joseph said, "With the way you two were dancing right then, you need to be married."

Stephon wrapped his arm around my waist. "I'd marry her tomorrow, but she wants me to get the art show out of the way, and then we'll plan from there."

"That's right," I said. "I've gotta take care of my man and make sure he takes care of his business."

They all laughed.

Stephon said, "And I'm down with that, 'cause when we get married, my business is gonna be you."

When he kissed me, Audra and Joseph said, "Awww," together.

"Don't 'awww' us," Stephon said. "We're gonna be following your example. How long have you been married now?"

"Ten years," Audra said. "Can you believe it?"

I shook my head.

"I almost feel like an old lady," she said.

"Not old," Stephon said. "Not the way you guys keep the fire burning. I love that you still go out on dates and everything, even with the kids."

I stiffened and tried to think of something to say, to intervene, to stop the words that I knew were about to come.

Stephon said, "So where did you guys go last week?"

The stare that Joseph gave to Stephon was blank. The one that Audra gave to me could have sent me to my grave.

"When?" Joseph asked.

"You know, when Zuri stayed over with the twins. Well, stayed till you guys got home."

Joseph cocked his head as if he was trying to remember something that he'd forgotten. "We didn't . . ."

"Uh, babe," I said. "Uh . . . Joseph wasn't there." My eyes were stuck on Audra's. "He was away."

"Huh?" Stephon said. "I thought you took care of the twins so that Joseph and Audra could go out."

"Uh . . . I thought I was, but when I got there, I found out that Joseph was away. But Audra . . . She had to go out."

There was a too long moment of silence, and with my eyes, I pleaded with my best friend.

Audra said, "Yeah, uh . . . I needed to go out. Met up with some of my . . . sorority sisters." The stare she'd given me before would've sent me to my grave; now the glare she gave me was meant to send me straight to hell.

"You didn't tell me about that," Joseph said.

"I forgot," Audra growled, sounding just like my father.

"You better watch out, sweetheart," Joseph said. "They say the mind is the first thing to go."

Stephon and Joseph laughed; Audra and I didn't.

"As long as you're not steppin' out on me, I'm cool," Joseph said as he kissed his wife's cheek.

For some reason, the guys found that funny, and I was glad they laughed, easing some of the tension, but not enough of it, because Audra said:

"No, no worries. *I'm* not stepping out."

And then she stomped into the house, and after a moment, when it didn't seem like the guys noticed, I followed her.

Right inside the kitchen, she spun around and her finger was in my face before I had a chance to back up. "Don't you ever put me in a position again where I lie to my husband."

"I'm so sorry, Audra."

"You better be. I don't do that. I don't lie, I don't keep secrets, I don't . . ."

"I know," I said, stopping her before she went through her litany of perfection. "And you have no idea how sorry I am; it will *never* happen again."

"You damn straight it won't. This is your drama, and I'm no longer your supporting actor."

She spun back into the backyard, and it was then that I realized I hadn't breathed since Stephon had almost blown up our world without even knowing it.

But I didn't have a second to catch my breath before I heard, "Zuri, dear." Looking up, Ms. Viv stood in front of me. "Are you all right?"

"Yes."

She squinted and shook her head as if she knew I had just twisted the truth. "Seems like you and your friend were having a little . . . discussion."

"No, everything's fine. Are you okay? Do you want something? I think the chicken and ribs will be ready in a moment."

"Oh, I wish I could stay, but I have another engagement."

"I didn't realize that."

"Well, when you invited me, I wanted to come over and spend a little time with you and your dad. Your father is lovely, dear."

Lovely. That wasn't a word I'd ever heard anyone use to describe Oscar Maxwell.

"And he said everything is working out

with Brenda."

"Yes." I nodded. "Thank you again for that."

"Well, we must thank the Lord for that. But the part where I helped, you're certainly welcome. This has worked out for you *and* for me. Well" — she glanced into the back-yard — "it looks like you're going to have quite a day."

Looking over my shoulder, I checked out the scene. Audra stood behind Joseph with her arms wrapped around his waist. She laughed along with her husband and Ste-phon . . . and then her gaze met mine.

And I shuddered.

"Well, Brenda will be back tonight, so your father will be in good hands." Ms. Viv brought my attention back to her. "Don't you worry."

"I don't. Not with Brenda here. Thank you, Ms. Viv. Let me walk you out."

I followed her into the living room, then stood back as she said good-bye to my dad, Mrs. Lewis, and his friends. I didn't want to be rude, but I wanted Ms. Viv to leave. I needed to get to the backyard — to try to make things right with Audra.

When Ms. Viv and I stood outside of my dad's front door, I hugged her, so grateful for her in so many ways.

286

"Thank you for coming over."

She nodded, took one step down from the porch, then turned back around. "Oh, and dear. The five hundred dollars for this month. You'll send it soon?"

For someone who had insisted on paying, I hadn't made the payment for this month. Not that I didn't have the money; I had it from Abbey Global. But after I'd made the first payment, I was thinking that maybe Ms. Viv wouldn't expect another.

But I'd asked for this, I'd set it up this way, and now I had to pay. "I'll send it tomorrow, Ms. Viv."

Another nod before she said, "And you might as well send the money for June, too, since we're just about there."

I had a feeling she was trying to teach me a lesson — about how gifts should be gracefully and gratefully received. I was surprised she didn't have a Scripture for me with this teaching.

"Yes, ma'am."

Another nod, another step. But when she stopped again, I wondered if there would be any money left in my bank account by the time she got into her car.

She said, "Maybe next week you can stop by and we can have tea again. I truly hope to have a mentee for you sometime soon."

This time I was the one to nod, and she left with a smile. I stood on the porch until she drove away. Then I turned and stepped back into my father's house. But the moment both of my feet were over the threshold, the talking that had been going on in the front room stopped.

No one said a word, except for Frankie Beverly and his crew. "These happy feelin's, I'll spread them all over the world . . ."

But besides that, all of their eyes were trained on me.

"What?" My glance traveled from my father to Mrs. Lewis, then to his buddies, and finally back to my dad.

"How you know that woman?" my father asked.

Those words made my frown deepen. "From the mentoring program that I joined. Why?"

"I don't like her," my father said.

"Me neither," Mrs. Lewis chimed in.

Oh, Lord. What in the world happened?

And that's what I asked my father.

But all he did was cross his arms and glare out the front window, like he was looking to make sure she didn't come back. "She quotes too many Scriptures for me."

"What's wrong with that? Doesn't that mean she knows the word of God?"

"Nah," Mrs. Lewis said. "The devil quoted several Scriptures in the Bible."

"Well, she does a lot of good in the community. Remember, she's the one who found Brenda," I reminded him. As much as he liked his aide, there was no way he couldn't like the woman who had sent her.

"Brenda's cool. And Ebony is, too. But that one there" — he pointed his finger to the window — "shady lady."

Everyone in the room nodded like they were his backup performers.

Then Mrs. Lewis said, "Yeah, shady and sneaky."

And that right there sent her back to the she's-no-friend-of-mine column.

"That's it!" My father pointed at Mrs. Lewis. "Those are the words for her. She's shady, and she's sneaky." He turned his finger to me. "Don't you trust her, baby girl. Don't you trust her at all."

So I was just supposed to walk away from my new friend because my dad thought she was shady? I shook my head and moved toward the backyard but then took a detour. Inside the bathroom, I closed, then locked the door, pushed down the cover on the commode, and plopped down.

This holiday had twisted into something else real quick. First, Audra . . . there was a real chance my best friend would never speak to me again. Then Ms. Viv . . . and she wanted her money tomorrow, taking one thousand dollars from the five thousand I had locked away in the bank. And now my dad . . . who had never given me a warning like that about anybody at any time.

What was going on?

I didn't know how it had happened, but this Memorial Day had turned into a holiday that I didn't want to remember.

26

It had taken me four days. Because I wanted to give Audra time to cool down from Monday. No . . . that was a twisted truth. I really did want her to cool down; I needed her to. But the real reason I'd waited four days — I was afraid. I was afraid of my best friend.

I mean, if anything were to go down between us physically, I could probably take her, since I had a little height on Audra. But as mad as she'd been with me on Memorial Day . . . no doubt, her anger would have overcome my strength.

So instead of risking my life and saving her from catching a case, I decided to give her this time. And me too, because I had to figure out what to say.

My hands were still shaking when I finally found the courage to call her this morning. And asked her to meet me.

The blessing — not only did she not tell

me to take the shortest route to hell, but she said, "Where, what time, and you're paying."

Then, I'd scored an extra point when I told her to meet me at Pinnacle. "But not the restaurant, just the lobby, the bar," I'd said. "I can't afford one dinner there, let alone two."

"Still impressive." She'd hung up without saying good-bye, but by just agreeing to meet me, I'd jumped the first hurdle with Audra.

Now I speed-walked into the restaurant, running a bit late because I'd just come from having tea and scones with Ms. Viv. I'd owed her a visit, but didn't stay as long as I would've liked. She didn't mind, especially after I told her I was on my way to Pinnacle.

"Oh," she'd said, "I'm really glad that you're getting out."

I was glad about that, too, especially to be getting out with my best friend. The moment I stepped into the lounge area, I spotted Audra, sitting at one of the bar tables. As I approached, she stood, and when she reached out her arms to hug me, I almost wanted to cry.

"I'm sorry," I whispered.

She rubbed her hand on my back. "It's cool."

As we sat down, I said, "I'm really glad you've forgiven me."

"Well," she shrugged, "no one is as bad as the worst thing they've ever done."

I repeated those words in my mind and tucked them into my heart. My friend, full of the grace and mercy I so badly needed.

"Plus, you're paying, and you're treating me to this fabulous place." She held out her arms like she was that model on *Wheel of Fortune*. "I've been dying for Joseph to bring me here, and when you said . . ."

Audra stopped midsentence and noticed my purse hooked on the back of my chair. "What in the entire world?" She motioned with her hands for me to pass her the purse, and when she held it, she turned it from one side to the other, and right before she turned it upside down, I snatched it from her grasp.

"Really?"

"I'm just . . ." She leaned forward as if she had to be careful that what she was about to say would only be heard by us. "Where did you get that bag?"

She'd caught me off guard with my bracelet, but I was ready for this. "From the store . . . Where do you think?"

"You know what I'm asking."

"No, really. I got it from Lenox Square. I used some of the money I earned from my interior decorating gig."

Before I got the last word out, Audra was already shaking her head. Leaning back, she crossed her arms. "No, you did not take that much money from what you earned to buy this purse. No," she said again.

Dang. Audra knew me too well. That explanation had worked on Stephon. Of course, my man knew me, too, but what my best friend knew was me *and* the price of this purse. It would never occur to Stephon that anyone would carry anything that cost three thousand dollars.

Now, Audra rocked her body toward me. "What's going on, Z? I mean, first the bracelet, and now this purse. Together, do you know how much money this is? What have you gotten yourself into?"

Her eyes were so full of concern, but she was serious, too. Like she was ready to call the police to get my confession if I didn't fess up to her. I had no choice. All I could do was share the last two months of my life with her. It would stay between us — that I knew for sure. She was that kind of best friend. "Okay, well . . . a couple of months ago, I met this guy . . ."

"Wait" — she held up her hand and motioned to the waiter — "I have a feeling I'm going to need my first drink for this."

Once we gave our drink and appetizer orders to the young man, I continued with my story. "I met him . . . Julian . . . in Starbucks, actually. The Starbucks near my office."

Then I went on to tell Audra all that had happened to me with Julian — the consulting I'd really done for him, and the wonderful restaurants he'd taken me to.

"And since I wasn't charging him for the consultations, he bought me that bracelet. But it wasn't like it was diamonds or anything."

Cue up the waiter, who returned with our drinks just in time for Audra to take the biggest gulp of her wine.

I kept on. "Julian left, and then right after that, I met Alexander. You know that whole story, and a couple of weeks ago, before he went back to London, he bought me this purse."

"The purse that you've wanted for so long," Audra said with all kinds of skepticism in her tone.

"I know, it seems crazy, right? But that was where I met him. In the mall, in front of the Louis store. So he knew."

She took another gulp and her head went back to shaking. "This doesn't add up. Two guys? Both of them buy you expensive gifts?"

"That part is just a coincidence, I think. That there were two."

"No, there are no coincidences in life like that," Audra said. "Men don't spend that kind of money on you just because . . . and you found two?"

"See, I don't agree. Look, you've been out of the dating game since college, and really, you can't even count college because you met Joseph the first week we were there. So you haven't been single since, what? High school? And me, until I met Stephon, or rather reunited with him, I'd been dating nothing but scrubs. This is just a world you and I never knew existed. This is a world where men treat their women with appreciation."

"Their women?" She crossed her arms again.

"Wrong choice of words. I mean women — any kind of women. But when you think about it, it's not all that much. The Tiffany bracelet is very nice, but not expensive, and every dime that Alexander spent on me was a write-off since I worked for his company."

She did a slow nod as if my words made

sense to her.

"Plus" — I held up my hands — "you don't have to worry about this anymore. It's over. I don't care if a man walks up and offers me a million dollars, all I'm going to focus on right now is Stephon, his show, my work, and, once his show is over, our wedding, because we're finally going to get married."

She raised her glass to the waiter, her signal that she needed another. After he took her order, she said, "I hope you're serious about that."

"I really am. And anyway, one part of what you said is probably true — what are the chances of me meeting two men like that? Certainly, there will never be a third."

I saw the concern folded in the creases of her forehead.

"Look, there's nothing for you to worry about. I'm going to take these gifts as the blessings they are and just keep it moving from here."

"I'm glad, Zuri, because honestly, I don't have the same feeling you have about this. It creeps me out."

I had no idea how a bracelet and a purse could do that to anyone, but I left it alone. I'd already made the promise this was the end, and that promise was the truth.

I shrugged as I stuffed a fork filled with a crab cake into my mouth and then pressed my fingers over my lips as the personification of tall, chocolate, fine, yet stately man did a slow stroll toward our table. He did a little stutter step right before he got to where we were, which slowed him down a bit. Then he nodded at me, and I did the same to him. As he passed by, it took everything in me not to turn around and follow him with my gaze. It was something I had done a million times when I was out with Audra. I always told her I was involved, not dead, and my friend knew I loved studying a well-dressed man.

But because of what I'd just told her and everything that had unfolded in the last few weeks, I kept my eyes focused on Audra.

"So the only good thing about meeting Alexander was that you did get to decorate the Enclave, and" — she paused — "I went by there on Tuesday to check them out."

I waved my napkin at her. "Why didn't you tell me?"

"Because I wasn't speaking to you."

I laughed and then heard a voice behind me say, "No, I flew Emirates. You know that's the only way to fly to Dubai." He chuckled and I twisted in my seat to get a glimpse of whomever was speaking about my dream vacation.

It was him. Mr. Stately.

I had enough of a view to do what I did best: I checked him out. And he kept on talking about Dubai.

"Isn't that just rude?" Audra said. "So loud."

When I turned around, I realized I'd done what I wanted without her realizing it. "Yeah, extremely rude."

"Anyway, you did a fabulous job on the models. Oh, my goodness. I was telling everyone in there that my best friend, even though I wasn't speaking to you, was the decorator."

We laughed, and then we just sat and chatted, or rather, Audra chatted while I listened. Her voice mixed with the man's behind us, and though I loved my friend, I gave more attention to him. My eyes stayed on Audra, but my ears — all on Mr. Dubai. (I had changed up his name already.)

I so wished Audra and I could switch seats — that would have made my eavesdropping much easier.

As my friend chatted about the Enclave and how beautiful the units were and what was I going to do next with my interior designing (which was nothing unless another gig like the Enclave dropped into my

299

lap), I listened to the man talk about his adventures. In the last months, it seemed he'd been to Dubai, Dublin, and Durango.

I had three questions about that: Who was he? Was he traveling the world in alphabetical order? And where in the world was Durango?

"Oh, my goodness!" Audra exclaimed.

I blinked and brought all of my attention back to her. "What?"

"The time. I promised the twins I'd watch a movie with them tonight since Joseph is out of town again."

"Oh, well, you go on." I waved her away. "This is my treat, so I'll take care of the bill."

As she gathered her purse and bolero jacket, she said, "Too bad I'm in a rush or you'd be paying for my parking, too." She grinned.

I reached into my wallet, pulled out a twenty, and then I shouted, "Hey," when she snatched the money from my hand. "That was just a joke."

"That'll pay for half," she said before she leaned over to hug me.

Shaking my head, I watched her rush out of the restaurant. And then with Mr. Dubai's voice still in my ears, I slid over to where Audra had been sitting.

Now I had the perfect view. I could check him out without him noticing, since the chair in front of him kinda blocked me.

But then, I guessed the chair in front of him didn't give me enough cover, because he glanced up and our eyes locked.

Dang! That was embarrassing. I lowered my eyes as quickly as I could, reached back into my wallet for my credit card, then signaled to the waiter. Now I wanted to just get out of here. I didn't want this dude thinking I was some chick he could pick up.

I paid the bill, then, as I stood and checked to make sure I didn't leave anything behind, I felt his eyes. I guessed I deserved the scrutiny since I'd done the same to him. As I passed his table, I gave him the same nod that he'd given to me, but he held up his hand. "John, I gotta go. The most beautiful lady just walked by."

Then, in one motion that felt like it took one second, he clicked off the phone, stood, and held out his hand to me. "And I meant that," he said. "Harrison Wellington."

When I reached for his hand, I peeped the diamond watch on his wrist. "Wow, that's a mouthful." And as soon as I said that, I wished I'd chosen different words.

But then when he smiled, my thoughts were taken away. Because I wondered which was brighter — his teeth or the diamond stud in his ear.

He said, "I introduced myself, but you haven't told me your name."

That was true — that had always been my modus operandi: to never give out my name. Until I met Julian and Alexander. Now I was committed to going back to who I used to be.

He didn't seem to notice that I hadn't responded to his statement. He said, "I hope I wasn't speaking too loudly. I've been told my voice carries, but I was so excited to share my experiences in Dubai with a friend. Even though I own a travel business, that was my first time to the United Arab Emirates."

"That's someplace I've always wanted to go," I told him.

"Really? Well, you should, and I'd love to tell you all about it."

As the chatter and the clatter continued all around me, I hesitated, thinking about the vow I'd *just* made.

He said, "If you have room for one more drink, I'd love to tell you all about Dubai and the many other places I've been."

From the way he'd been talking, sharing with me all the places he'd been would take a lot longer than one drink. But surely, he

302

could tell me about Dubai over a single glass of wine. And it was just one glass, just one conversation.

I held out my hand. "I'm Zuri Maxwell." And then I sat down.

27

Just as I eased my car into my parking space, my phone beeped with a text notification. I didn't even turn off the engine, I just grabbed the phone and smiled as the image popped up on my screen. It was just a picture, although I shouldn't say "just." It was another picture from Harrison. Of Dubai. This time, he had shared pictures from the world's largest mall.

Oh, the damage I could do in a place like that.

If I could get there.

If I had money.

I sighed, turned off the engine, then tossed my phone into my purse. For the four days since we'd met, Harrison and I had been texting — it was casual, completely friendly, though he had asked me a few times to have dinner with him. I told him no, having dinner with him was not a possibility, and that was the truth. I think one of the reasons why I'd gotten a little caught up — as Audra explained it — with Julian and Alexander was because from the beginning, I knew I'd only go out to dinner with them a time or two. Of course, it turned out to be a time or ten, but they had both left Atlanta, returning to their homes, and I'd returned to my life.

But Harrison lived right here in the ATL. There was no need to start something I didn't want to finish. So after that text where I told him that going out with him would not happen, from that point I'd only responded to the texts that spoke about Dubai and not dinner.

But with every picture he sent, my desire to take a trip grew. Wouldn't it be amazing if Stephon and I could go to Dubai for our honeymoon? Then, because I didn't want to get too carried away, I asked myself — wouldn't it be great if we could get on a plane to go anywhere? Seriously, I would take a plane to nowhere and back. That was my thought as I stepped into our apartment and heard Stephon's voice.

"All right, Ray."

I tilted my head, trying to make sense of the conversation before I heard anymore. Ray . . . his stepfather — although Stephon didn't consider Ray much of a father to him since they'd never lived in the same home. He'd married Stephon's mother years after Stephon had left home.

I gave Stephon a peck on the lips, then stood back, and he kept nodding. He didn't look pressed or stressed, and if he was nodding, then whatever news Ray was sharing had to be mostly good.

And then he said, "Okay, I'll talk it over with Zuri and get back to you."

My frown deepened when he said that. He clicked off the phone, and I spoke before he could tell me anything. "What's up with Ray?"

When he sighed before he spoke, I became a bit concerned. "It's not Ray; it's my mom, she's in the hospital."

"What?" I pressed my fingers against my lips.

Stephon held up his hands. "No worries. She's okay. I mean, they think she's gonna be okay." He sighed. "I'd never heard of this, but seems she has adult-onset asthma." The question in my eyes made him continue, "She had trouble breathing this morning, and first, they thought she was having some kind of heart attack, but when they got her to the hospital and did the tests — at least they found out it wasn't heart failure."

When he shook his head slightly, I knew what he was thinking. His grandmother, who had often taken Stephon, his mother, and his brother in when life became a struggle, had died of heart failure.

Moving to him, I said, "It sounds like your mom is gonna be okay; it didn't have anything to do with her heart."

"I know," he whispered.

"So that's a good thing, right?" At least it seemed like it was to me, and I wanted him to believe that, too.

"Yeah, it is," he said, though his tone didn't sound as if he believed his words.

"What? What's bothering you?"

He shrugged. "I don't know exactly. I'm just thinking it's been a while since I've seen my mom, and maybe this might be a good time to get out there."

That made me raise my eyebrows. Stephon's mother and Ray had moved to Portland a week before I hooked up with Stephon. And in the three years we'd been together, he'd never taken a trip to Portland, even though I'd tried to encourage him to visit her.

But Stephon wouldn't be moved. It wasn't that he was stubborn about it, he just didn't see any need to go. And it wasn't that he had any hate for his mother, it was just that it didn't seem like he had a bunch of love for her either.

But I guessed there was nothing like a parent going into the hospital to gain a new perspective. After all that I'd been through with my father, I understood.

I said, "Well, that'll be good."

"You think I should go?" His tone was tentative.

"I think you should go if you feel like you should."

He nodded. "Yeah." He paused, and then with a bit more strength, he said, "Yeah, definitely, I think I do wanna go. I mean, I know it's not surgery or anything, but . . ."

"She's your mom, and she's in the hospital."

"She is, and . . ."

"You want to be there. Go, babe," I encouraged. "It'll be good for you to see your mom."

He nodded again. "Okay, yeah." But then he paused, and the way he squinted, I could tell that his mind filled with a new thought. "My only concern . . . What will the cost of the ticket be? Last-minute? Across the country like this?"

"It doesn't matter; we have the money. This is what a little cushion is for. You taught me that."

"But that cushion? That's your money."

I leaned back as if I were trying to see him better. "Since we've been together, we've never done that. Never separated our money."

"Yeah, but you worked so hard, and I don't want to . . ."

I kissed him before he could finish, hoping this made the decision for him. When I moved away from him, I said, "Now, I'm taking over from here. You get back to work. I'm going to check for flights, make your reservations, then pack for you. You're doing the right thing."

"I wish you could go with me."

"I will if you want me to."

He blew out a long breath. "But the price of two tickets . . ."

"We have the money."

"I don't want to spend all of the money you earned that way." He shook his head. "No, I'll go. Like you said, she's going to be fine, and I want our first time on a plane together to be for something else, something special. Not this." This time when he paused, whatever thoughts filled his mind brought a smile to his face. "We'll take a flight somewhere for our honeymoon."

"I like the way you think. So let me get

working on this. When do you want to leave?"

"Tomorrow." He stopped. "Or Thursday, whichever is . . ."

"Cheaper?" I shook my head. Would there ever be a time when he wasn't adding up dollars?

He gave me a smirk. "Not as expensive," he clarified. "And then I'll come back on Sunday. That'll give me either four or five days out there." He nodded as if he was really beginning to feel this idea. "Yeah, she'll be home and I'll get to spend some time with her away from the hospital."

"You got it. I'm on it."

He pulled me into a hug, and I rested my head against his chest. "Do you know how much I love you?" he whispered.

"Yes, I know." I kept my voice as soft as Stephon's. "It's the way I love you, and it has something to do with infinity."

28

I really did believe in signs, though I wasn't one of those people who went overboard and saw signs in everything. But this . . . this was a sign.

Because why would I have just received this text from Harrison the moment I dropped Stephon off? I hadn't even pulled away from the departures curb at Hartsfield–Jackson, still jammed in, unable to move, surrounded by cabs, Ubers, and passenger cars, each dropping someone off for an airline departure.

That was the only reason why I had time to study this text.

It wasn't like Harrison knew Stephon was going out of town; it wasn't like Harrison even knew about Stephon at all. And even if he did, the only people who knew Stephon was leaving Atlanta were my father, Audra, and Ms. Viv, but only because she'd called to check on me this morning.

Harrison was blind to all of that, so when he just sent this text:

> I'm having dinner with a few friends tonight and I'd like you to join us . . .

I knew that was a sign.

Because this was the first time that Harrison had asked me to go to dinner when accepting was a possibility. By the time the dinner hour hit Atlanta, Stephon would be more than twenty-five hundred miles away from home. Not that I was doing anything behind his back — but with him away, I could hang out with a new friend and his friends without Stephon thinking there was more to it. Plus, it was *his friends* that made the difference. This dinner with Harrison wouldn't be about *me.* This was a gathering — small, I guessed, though he hadn't said how many would be there. Seven, eight, maybe nine people. I didn't think it would be any more than that because of the last part of the text — the part of the text that was the winner to me:

> Dinner at Polaris, for the opening. My treat for everyone.

Polaris!

312

The hottest new restaurant on the scene in Atlanta, on the rooftop of the Carriage House. It was right around the corner from the Enclave, and everyone had been talking about it because it was a partnership endeavor among several of the Housewives of Atlanta. The waiting list for a table was supposedly over two months, and Harrison was getting in on opening night? And getting in not only for himself, but for a few of his friends? Who did he know?

It didn't matter; I was so there.

Glancing at the clock, I saw it was almost noon, but now there would be no way for me to go into work. How could I? I had a special dinner that I had to attend.

Yes, this was a sign, because the timing couldn't have been any better.

There was very little difference between this event and Usher's party. Except there may have been even more celebrities here. I couldn't believe I was milling around in a crowd with everyone from the mayor (yes, Keisha!) to Monica. There was no red carpet tonight, but what there *was* was a whole lot of security.

At the checkpoint, I was asked for my ID. Right as I handed it to one of the young women behind the desk (who all wore black tuxedos), I said, "Zuri Maxwell, a guest of Harrison Wellington."

After a quick check and a nod, I was passed off to a tuxedoed gentleman and led to the rooftop. I paused at the opening and took in the sight — it looked like heaven. From the carpet to the cloths that covered the tables to the waitstaff's tuxedos, everything was white. There were hundreds — no, thousands of little lights draped around the perimeter and on every table, and each light twinkled like a star.

As my escort led me inside and toward the back (which I guessed would serve as the front because a small stage was set up), Harrison came into my view. He stood, holding a glass filled with a clear liquid (I couldn't tell if it was water or vodka), and he was talking to what looked like an older white couple; I couldn't tell for sure since their backs were to me. The only one I could see clearly was Harrison.

I would never have thought it was possible, but he looked better today than when I'd met him a week ago. *Classy* was the word to describe his look, in the classic tuxedo he wore. There was no flair added; this was strictly the elegance that was the simplicity of black tie. Harrison could have been the model for *Sophisticated GQ*. That wasn't even a magazine, but it should have been, just so Harrison could have been on the cover.

I hadn't bought an outfit for this occasion, deciding to recycle the red flounce dress I'd bought to have dinner with Julian, but with the Tiffany bracelet on my wrist (and a twenty-five-dollar clutch that really did look like a Neiman Marcus purchase), I felt like I fit in.

Harrison turned and spotted me. "Zuri," he said and pulled me into a hug. "Thank you for coming." Then he stepped back. "You look absolutely stunning."

"Thank you."

"Let me introduce you to my friends." He turned to the couple he'd been talking to. "Fred and Ginger, this is my friend Zuri."

Really? I held my chuckle inside, though I wanted so badly to ask if they were dancers; but since I always got the Thelma comparison, I left it alone. But my thoughts switched to another lane when Harrison motioned to the table for us to sit down.

Wait a minute . . . I felt like I was trippin' the way I was trying to get my mind to make sense of what was in front of me. The table was set for four, and when Fred held out a chair for Ginger, Harrison did the same for me.

Four? This looked like I was Harrison's date. Had I been set up?

When I sat down, I wanted to pull out my phone and scroll through my phone to reread Harrison's text. He'd said a dinner with a *few* friends.

This . . . was not . . . that.

And I was pissed.

So what was I supposed to do with my pissivity? I mean, I could get up and walk out, but what purpose would that serve? Yes, it would let Harrison know I didn't appreciate his game and that he couldn't play me. But then, I would be getting up and leaving an event that I so wanted to attend. And as twisted as his truth had been, I *wasn't* having dinner alone with Harrison.

But still . . .

"So," I began, needing to say something to Fred and Ginger, or else I just might turn to Harrison and tell him what I thought of him, "how long have you guys known each other?"

Harrison and Fred exchanged a glance before Fred said, "We've been business partners for a few years." Then he turned his attention to me. "Zuri . . . that's such a beautiful name."

"Thank you," I said. "My father named me."

316

"It means *beautiful* in Swahili," Harrison said.

I leaned back. "You speak Swahili?"

"Ndiyo, mimi, mwanamke mzuri." And then, he translated for me, "Yes, I do, beautiful lady."

"Wow," Ginger said.

"I'm impressed," I added.

The way Harrison smiled made me wonder if he knew he had just gained a much-needed point.

"I'd wanted to speak the language for so long, since I was a teen," Harrison said to us. "And so I mixed my love for traveling with my desire to learn Swahili. It's a Bantu language, so I've traveled extensively throughout Kenya, Uganda, and South Africa, mostly, to learn the language and the culture." As if he knew he had his audience enthralled, he paused for just a second before he schooled us further. "About a hundred and forty million people speak Swahili as a native or second language."

I wanted to stand up and applaud. Wait, no . . . just snap my fingers the way people did to show their appreciation to spoken-word artists because he'd taken something that I wanted to do — learn to speak Swahili — to the next level.

Another point scored.

From there, the hits just kept on coming. Harrison was like Stephen Curry: a scoring machine.

"I'm meeting with a music collector tomorrow," Harrison told us, changing the subject.

I wasn't sure what he meant, but Fred seemed to understand. "More music?"

He nodded, then turned to me. "I am an old-school connoisseur. Mostly R & B of the eighties and nineties, though I do have some disco from the seventies. But mostly I collect vinyl from those two decades."

This was crazy. I remembered how Julian had these interests, too.

We chatted some more about Harrison's travels over the appetizers of lobster deviled eggs. Then we debated about the best boy and girl groups going all the way back to the Temptations and the Supremes over our steak and lobster entrées. Between the food and the conversation, by the time the night ended, I had almost forgotten how the night had started.

Almost.

When I told them all that I was leaving, Harrison said that he would walk me out. We said good night to Fred and Ginger, leaving them on the dance floor, of course. We were silent as we made our way down in the elevator with several other partygoers, and Harrison spoke his first words when we got to the front of the hotel and saw that the valet line looked like it was a couple of miles long.

"Give me your ticket," Harrison told me.

I did what he asked, and then he led me back inside. Standing to the side, I watched as he whispered to the hostess.

"Your car won't be long now," he said when he returned to me. "A couple of minutes or so."

I nodded. "A *couple* of minutes . . . Is that like a *few* friends?"

He tilted his head as if he didn't know what I was talking about, however someone once told me that you could lie with your mouth, but not with your body and Harrison was exhibit one to that theory. The twitch at the edge of his lips told me that not only did he know what I was talking about, but he was a bit amused by it. I hoped all of that perception also let him know that this was it — he'd never see me again.

"What I promised you in the text, I delivered."

I crossed my arms. "You led me to believe there would be a few people here."

He shrugged a little. "How do you quantify a few? Plus" — he turned around and his gaze roamed over the crowded restaurant — "there were over two hundred people here."

I narrowed my eyes. "Not only do you know what I mean, but you knew what I would think, and I don't appreciate the tricks, Harrison. That, to me, is as bad as lying."

"Well, then let me ask you this — would you have come here to dinner? Just with me?"

"No."

He held up his hands. "See? You would have missed all of this. I just did what I had to do."

"Fine, and I'll do the same."

There was that little twitch at the edge of his lips again. "Does that mean you won't have dinner with me on Saturday?"

Was this dude dense? "No, and let me tell you why — I'm involved with someone."

He said, "Aren't we all?"

My rebuttal was on the tip of my tongue, but his words made me pause. Hadn't someone said those words to me? Was it . . . Julian?

"So are you saying you're asking me to go out with you even though you're involved with someone? What would that make me?"

"I never said I was involved with anyone. You inferred that from my words. What I said, what I've been saying, is that I want to have dinner with you. Just one more dinner."

"Why?"

"Because I love to eat dinner every day."

I smirked.

"And I enjoy your company. Here's the thing — I just enjoy hanging out and talking to intelligent people, and you impressed me as a woman who would want to do the same."

All I did was tighten my arms across my chest.

He said, "Let me ask you this, if I were a woman you'd met at Pinnacle and we started talking and I said we should get together some time for dinner, would you agree to meet me?"

I didn't respond.

"Exactly," he said, as if I had acceded. "So I don't understand why this is a big deal. I love my business, I love to travel, and what's even better are people who are enthusiastic about what I do. It's been quite a while since anyone has reacted to me the way you have. You want to see all my pictures, you ask me a thousand wonderful questions, you do what all of my friends used to do, but now . . ." He shrugged. "They're bored with me, and you're not." He paused. "But if you give me the chance, if you'll have dinner with me again, I promise, I'll answer every question you ever had about traveling to any part of the world. And I'll talk about it so much that you'll get bored, too. And once you reach that point, I won't ever call you again."

I had no idea why I was standing there, contemplating his words. "We just had dinner together."

"Yeah, but it was with a few friends." He paused long enough to grin. "Okay, then, let's switch it up to a lunch . . . on Saturday."

The thing about this was there was so much I wanted to know from Harrison. This was a man who had traveled to Africa just to learn a language. I was intrigued. And I was curious.

Was I curious enough to say yes?

"I have a boat . . . a small one, but we can take it out on Lake Lanier."

He . . . had . . . a . . . boat? Who had a boat in Georgia?

The valet signaled to us, and Harrison walked me to my car before I had time to give him an answer.

But when he opened my door, he said, "So I'll see you on Saturday. And if you don't have a good time, I promise I won't ever ask to see you again."

In just those few seconds ticking by, I reviewed the facts: Harrison knew that I was involved — so I'd told him the truth. Stephon was still with his mom — so there would be no explaining, no drama.

And we'd be having lunch . . . on a boat.

"Saturday at noon?" It was a question, but he nodded.

And just before I slid into the car, I said, "I'll see you then."

29

For me, all the restaurants I'd been to over the last few months had never been about the food. Truly, I wasn't much of a foodie, but what I *was* was a lover of an exciting life. The rich and famous had eaten at those restaurants and hobnobbed at the events I'd attended.

But now, as I leaned back and let the sun beam down on my face, I wondered how many of the people I'd admired in the last few weeks had actually been out on a boat on Lake Lanier, just drifting on the current.

I'd taken the almost-one-hour drive from Atlanta up to the lake by myself, even though that hadn't been Harrison's plan.

"I'll send a car for you," he'd said after I told him I wouldn't ride with him. "I don't want you alone."

But I'd told him I'd be fine, and then I'd started out the morning by stopping by my dad's and explaining I couldn't stay long because I had a work event to attend.

"Dressed like that?" my father had growled and looked at me like I was suspect.

"It's a summer outing for the employees," I said with a bit of bite in my tone. I guessed that came from not telling the truth.

My tone had not fazed my father. His eyes had narrowed and he glared at me as if he knew I was a liar.

But I'd gotten away, leaving him in the hands of Ebony, who was stuffing him with the same kind of breakfast that Brenda served him every weekday.

It wasn't my father, though, who'd made me tell Harrison I'd get there on my own (even though a limo showing up at my father's house wouldn't have been a good look). It was because for me, I didn't want this to be more than it was — just lunch on Harrison's boat.

So he'd accepted my desire to meet him at the south side of Lake Lanier, and then he'd been waiting at the marina when I arrived and led me onto what he called his forty-foot pontoon. There were other boats around; most, I noticed, were rentals. But after he'd helped me on, we took off at a comfortable speed, then settled a couple of miles from the dock.

I was a bit surprised at the number of

other boats that were out, from fishing boats to pontoons. Who knew that Georgians enjoyed the summer this way? But it made the scene all the more interesting to me. And I felt better, actually. I wasn't in the middle of some ocean alone with this man. This was as public as all the dinners and events I'd attended.

As I lay back on the cushioned lounger, Harrison laid out our lunch.

"This is going to be simple," he said. "Nothing like the food we had on Thursday. Just sandwiches."

"That's fine. Do you want any help?" I asked, sitting up.

"What I want is for you to relax and enjoy yourself. Remember, I'm trying to make an impression."

Less than ten minutes later, he had our lunch set out. *Just sandwiches* was what he had said. But what he served was a blackberry-bacon-brie grilled cheese, which I had never heard of, I had never tasted, and was the best grilled cheese sandwich in the world.

We sat at the small round table in the center of the boat and for a while, we said nothing. Just ate, sipped a fabulous German wine, and floated.

My thoughts took on the motion of the

boat, drifting, and I imagined my life like this all the time. Stephon and me on a boat, one leisurely weekend, me on one side, lying back, reading, and he, on the other side, stretched out with a paintbrush in his hand and a small canvas resting on his lap.

Oh, the paintings my man would be able to create out here instead of stuck in the middle of that little apartment. And then we could drift to one of the shores so that we'd be under the eyes of nature only as we made love for as long as we wanted.

"So, have I made up for the dinner on Thursday yet?"

When I turned toward the voice, I had to blink a few times. Not because I couldn't recall where I was, but because I'd forgotten who I was with. I was grateful for my sunglasses, which I hoped hid my blank stare. But my expression stayed that way for just a moment. Once again, I marveled at how fine Harrison was. Yes, he was fine physically, but it was more in his sophistication. He always looked like a model to me, but today, he looked like a model with money. And what was funny about that was that he was wearing the simplest of outfits: white shorts and a white golf shirt with a blue striped cardigan tied over his shoulders.

Another model, this time standing on the

highest point of his boat, holding a glass of wine, representing some yacht company. *Sophisticated GQ.* Maybe I would start that magazine and use Harrison as my only model. He'd be the only one needed.

It took me a while to finally answer his question, but I did with, "Yes. You're on your way to making Thursday up to me."

He grinned, then took a sip of his wine. "I love coming out here. Even with all of these people around us, it's so peaceful."

I took another bite of my sandwich before I asked, "You've told me all about your travels, but when did you get started? When did you open your travel business?"

"I did it straight out of Morehouse."

"Wait, you went to Morehouse? When?" I didn't give him a chance to answer. I pressed my hand across my heart. "I went to Spelman."

He didn't look moved by my words, as if he already knew that fact. Had I told him when we met at Pinnacle and just forgotten? But then he said, "I'm not surprised. All of that class, all of your independence: Spelman is written all over you."

I gave him a single nod as a thank-you and motioned for him to continue.

"I came out in two thousand three."

"Right when I was coming in," I said.

He nodded as if he had figured all of that out, too. "I majored in business administration and management, and was blessed enough to have a half dozen job offers. But as graduation got closer, I began to think about the fact that for the rest of my life, I'd be working every single day. That was too scary for me."

I chuckled because I remembered when I realized that, too.

"I wasn't ready for that, so I took some money my grandmother had left me when she passed away. She'd bought me savings bonds for my birthday and Christmas every year until I was eighteen and told me I could have that money when I graduated. Well, much to my parents' chagrin, I took that money and some money I'd saved and traveled through Europe."

"Wow." I chuckled. "I thought only white people did that."

He shook his head. "Adventure has no color. I headed to Europe — the Western part, of course. I started in Spain, actually — Madrid — then worked my way through the continent. Next were France, Italy, Germany, Belgium, and Amsterdam before the finale in the UK.

"But what was best about my travels was that I didn't hang out a lot in big cities. I didn't have a whole lot of money, and I wanted it to last, so yeah, I visited Madrid, Rome, Paris, and all the others, but I made those day trips and spent my time in the places no one ever heard of in geography class: Lyon in France, Genoa in Italy. It was a much more intimate experience. Everywhere I went, I made friends."

I sighed with longing. "What you did . . . I'd love to do that. But it's something I could only dream about."

"Not really; you could do it if you wanted to." He grinned, raised his glass of wine to me, and continued, "Eventually, I got short on money, but what I did have was a long list of contacts. Lots of the smaller hotels in the less touristy cities do what I call guerrilla marketing. They were looking to promote their businesses in all kinds of ways. And I made a deal with all of them — if I ever brought them any business, I'd get a piece of it."

I turned so I could see him more closely. "So you went over there with the idea of starting a business?" This dude just impressed me more and more.

"No, but I went over there with a business degree, and the best thing that major taught me was how to think strategically and to always keep my business eyes open. So when a guy with a little bed-and-breakfast in Toulouse gave me a card and told me he paid for referrals, especially American referrals, the money wheels in my brain churned, and I collected cards and made deals as I made my way through Europe.

"When I came home, I shared my adventures with a few people, helped them plan some trips, and had so many clients that I went back and made more deals, with not only the hotels, but I put together a discount book with restaurants, transportation services, and local attractions, and I sell that separately. So even if someone makes their own travel arrangements, I still sell the discount book. Between the discount books and my referrals for about one hundred and fifty different businesses, I hit my first million in about nine months. That was almost twelve years ago."

Well, he'd just given me a chunk of information about himself — he was a millionaire, had been one for a while. The only question I had now was how many millions. "That's fascinating. And the name of your company?"

"Travel Edge," he said with a confident smirk.

"I really like that name."

"So," he continued, "what makes you so

interested in traveling?"

I sighed. "It's probably because I haven't gone anywhere." I held up my hand. "And before you say I shouldn't exaggerate, it's true — I haven't gone *anywhere* at all. I've never been on a plane nor a train, and until today, not even a boat."

"So that means you're from Atlanta."

"I am. Born and received all of my brains here."

"Don't forget your beauty."

I ignored his comment and started again. "I got all of my brains from Stone Mountain, to be specific. And while I love home, I'd also love to leave it every once in a while."

"I'm surprised you've never gone anywhere. Surprised that you didn't just one day get on a plane."

Spoken like someone who'd received a windfall from his grandmother, spent a year bumming through Europe, and was now a millionaire who'd traveled a continent just to learn a new language. He didn't even have a poor person's name. Harrison Wellington didn't understand the everyday person's struggles. I shrugged, then tried to explain, "I had a turbulent twenties, but once I crossed into my thirties, I became responsible." I paused and wondered if I should share exactly how much Stephon had helped me to get on the right financial course. After all, Harrison and I were just buddies.

But I decided to keep Stephon's name out of this.

"So I spend my money cautiously, focusing on my needs rather than my wants. At least for now. But when I hear about people traveling, I guess it raises that desire in me, and I kinda live vicariously through them."

"Well, we're gonna have to change that."

"How? You know people giving away free trips?" I laughed.

He didn't laugh when he said, "I do."

And those two words stopped all my laughter. Had I heard him right or had all of this boat rocking jarred my hearing?

He continued, "Most of my travel now is basically paid for. It's technical, industry stuff, but I can show you how it's done."

"Are you serious?" I slipped to the edge of the bench. "Regular people can do that?"

"You, beautiful, are far from regular."

"You know what I mean. How can I travel for free?" I sounded like a kid asking what he was going to get for Christmas, but I didn't care.

"We'll talk about that," he said. "Right

now, there's something else I want to show you."

I tilted my head and Harrison reached down into the bag he'd carried on the boat and lifted out a small box, black velvet. "This is for you."

I paused, I stared . . . Déjà vu. No, that was only if you felt like something had happened to you before. Once. What was it called when I kept having the same experience over and over and over?

"For you," Harrison repeated as if he thought I hadn't heard him.

"Why are you giving me . . ." I paused.

"See, you can't even finish the sentence to ask why because you don't know what's inside." He nudged it closer to me.

My hands were shaking when I reached for the box, and in that instant, I knew that was a sign — though for what, I did not know. Still, I took the box and held it for a moment before I lifted the top.

I gasped.

"Do you like?" he asked.

How was a woman supposed to answer that question — *Do you like . . . diamonds?* Especially a woman who'd never had a diamond anything in her life.

The diamond studs glittered, and if I had to guess, this was at least a carat — a half for each ear. But it didn't matter. No one had ever given me anything like this before.

"This is not the reaction I expected."

Finally, I blinked my eyes away from the loveliness and looked up at him. "Harrison, I can't . . ."

"What?"

"I can't accept this."

And then . . . he laughed. I mean, he leaned his head back and laughed. The shock that had been inside of me turned into frustration, and I sat there and waited for him to finish so that he could let me in on the joke.

He finally did when he said, "Look, Zuri. I bought these for you as a way to apologize for Thursday. Even though I didn't lie to you, I didn't completely tell you the truth. I twisted it a bit."

I flinched, thinking how I'd used that twisted thinking to justify my own actions so often.

He continued, "So this is my way of saying I'm really sorry because I do like you and I want us to be friends." He held up his hands as if he were surrendering to the police. "Just friends."

"Do you give all of your friends gifts like this?"

He shrugged. "A few." And then he

pressed his lips together, holding back a laugh.

I smirked.

He said, "No, just special ones. Special friends."

What did he mean by that? A special friend? How did he define that, especially if it came with gifts like this?

Shaking my head, I told him, "Still, I can't accept this."

"Yes, you can. And you know what? You will. So I don't want to go through this little back-and-forth where you say no, I say yes, and we go over and over it until — you end up taking those earrings home anyway. Because we both know that's how this will end." He leaned forward. "I really want you to have these. Please, as a friend who is saying I'm sorry. And who wants to be friends with you for a very long time."

I wanted to be a little insulted by his words, but Harrison had just read me, and he'd read me right. I *was* going to take these diamond studs because I wanted them. Just like I'd wanted Julian's bracelet and Alexander's purse.

"Just say thank you," he instructed me.

And I did. But then I added, "No more gifts, Harrison."

A slow smile spread across his face. "Now

let me tell you what I love about what you just said." He said, "By saying no more gifts, that implies that you plan to hang out with me again. And by saying no more gifts, that implies that you know that if I wanted, I could give you plenty more of this." He paused. "And you're right. I hope we can hang out again, and if you would let me, there is plenty more where this came from."

His words took my breath away. No, not just my breath; what he'd said took my words away — there was nothing I could say.

He pushed himself up and strutted away from me, I guessed to head to the controls to guide the boat. We'd had lunch, I had new diamonds, I guessed it was time to go back.

My stomach fluttered a bit, and I placed my hand over it. Glancing down at the earrings again, I knew these were why I felt a bit woozy. But the truth of it was that it was more than the gift that made me feel this way. It was Harrison's presence, his words, his being that made me feel a bit off-kilter in a sweeping-me-off-my-feet kind of way.

I inhaled as much oxygen as I could and thanked God my man was coming home tomorrow.

30

There had never been a time in my life when I was happier to see Stephon Smith. If I could have lifted him from his feet, that's exactly what I would have done. Lifted him up and spun him around. But while I couldn't do that to Stephon, that's what he did to me.

And then, we kissed. In the middle of baggage claim for the busiest airport in the world, we kissed like we were home alone.

"I missed you so much," I said.

"I thought you were going to meet me curbside."

"See? This is how much I couldn't wait. I parked. I just had to see you."

He held me in his arms and led me to carousel eight. As we waited for Stephon's bag to come up, I leaned against him and sighed. With his arms around me, I felt like I had landed in heaven, and this put an exclamation point on the thoughts I'd been having about Harrison since he'd given me those diamond studs.

The lunch, the boat ride, and even the earrings couldn't measure up to Stephon just having his arms around me.

For more than fifteen minutes, he held me that way, every so often pressing his lips against my head. And each time, I sighed. Wanting more. And more. Hardly being able to wait. Until we really were home alone.

When we finally rolled his bag to my car and he dumped it into the trunk, he asked if I wanted him to drive.

"No, you've got to be tired from that long flight, and I want you to save what little energy you may have for me."

"Oh, you don't have to worry about that."

Inside the car, I asked him about his first plane ride, then we chatted about his mom, and the joy in his voice made me so glad he'd gone to Portland. "She's gonna be fine, and the doctor said seeing me and my brother served her better than any medicine."

"Well, you know what? We'll just have to make a point of going to see her. Maybe we can set that up for once a year. Just work it into our budget."

He gave me a glance that I couldn't read and that lasted too long, and for a moment,

I held my breath. But then he massaged my neck as he said, "I like the way you said *we,* the way you say *our.*"

"When it comes to you and me, that's all I see."

He gave me such a slow nod, and I knew Stephon well enough to know there were thoughts tumbling inside his mind. Was it about his mom? Or . . . was it about me?

I shook my head. Why was I being paranoid?

But then the talking stopped. Stephon turned toward the window and didn't say anything else. Now, there had been plenty of times in our relationship when we were quiet together. That was the beauty of who we were. Our desire to be with each other didn't have anything to do with being verbal or being physical. We transcended all of that, just wanting to inhale the same oxygen.

But this felt different — a heavy kind of silence. What did it mean? I peeked at Stephon through my peripheral vision, but his head was turned toward the window, and he just stared. Intensely. As if the study of all that we were passing were imperative to his life.

Paranoia.

Or was it guilt?

Either way, this was not something I was

used to feeling.

The quiet remained as we parked the car and entered our apartment, and for a moment that felt awkward; we just stood in the middle of our living room/art studio and stared at each other. What in the world had happened between the airport and home?

I asked, "Do you want something . . . to eat?" It was a line that was meant to offer him food . . . or the other kind of nourishment that he sought from me.

But he shook his head. "Nah." He turned down my offer with a quickness. "I'm gonna unpack."

Really? Now? He'd been away from me for all of these days, and this was what he wanted to do? "Okay?" It came out as a question because now I had so many.

As he rolled his suitcase toward the bedroom, I sat on the sofa, something that neither Stephon nor I often did because the plastic that covered the furniture was for preservation, not comfort.

What had happened? In an instant, Stephon had totally changed. Had he seen something? Thought something? Had I let something slip?

I rewound what we'd talked about and then . . .

"Zuri, can you come in here, please?"

341

I sprang up from the sofa, but my feet didn't move that fast. I heard it in his tone. Somehow, he knew, he knew, he knew. He knew about Julian and Alexander and Harrison. His greeting at the airport was a setup, made to make me feel like he didn't know.

But he knew.

The thing about our apartment was that it wasn't very big. So no matter how slow my steps, I got to the bedroom much sooner than I wanted. I stepped over the threshold and blinked. And blinked and did the same again. It was because I couldn't make sense of the scene in front of me.

Stephon on one knee.

Holding something in his hand.

A little box.

Black velvet.

Just like the box I'd held, what? Twenty-four hours ago?

And then, Stephon opened the box and faced it so that I could see its contents. He said, "Zuri Maxwell, I have loved you for a long time. Far longer than you ever knew. I admired you in high school, and then when I met you again on your thirtieth birthday, I knew that was a sign we were meant to be.

"I know neither one of us is where we want to be, but I know the most important place I want to be is in a world where you are my wife.

"So, I know we kinda did this already, but it wasn't formal, and we didn't have a ring." Now he stood. "Zuri Maxwell, would you change my life, make my life, and become Zuri Smith?"

His words were more wonderful than his paintings. I felt like I was hyperventilating, and when I pressed my hands to my face, that was when I felt my tears.

Stephon took my left hand from my face and slipped the ring onto my finger.

"It's so beautiful," I said.

"So are you." He kissed me softly, gently. It was the definition of our love: pure, real. When he leaned back, he said, "You haven't given me an answer."

I said, "Yes, I will marry you. I will marry you from here to beyond infinity."

My man had been exhausted, but still Stephon had given me what I'd wanted. Rolling out of the bed, I glanced over at him, then traipsed to the bathroom, my nakedness shivering against the cool air. I grabbed my bathrobe that hung on the hook, then as gently as I could, I closed the bathroom door.

Standing in front of the mirror, I held up

my finger and stared at the ring. Even with my naked eye, even with the little that I knew about the 4Cs of diamonds, I knew the earrings that Harrison had given me were more expensive than Stephon's ring.

There was just no comparison.

I loved this ring on my finger more than Harrison's earrings, or more than anything I'd ever received in my life, because I loved the man who'd given it to me.

Bringing the ring to my lips, I turned off the light, dropped my bathrobe, and crawled back into bed to be close to the man I loved.

31

I had such a good time with you on Saturday. And can't wait to see you again. I have a huge surprise.

Lord help me, was all I could think as I read that text. This was, what? The fifth or sixth time he'd sent this text today — as if he had some doubt that the last text he sent had made its way to me.

On my desk were two files from potential clients I was pitching this week, so what I needed to be doing at this moment was getting my head in the work game — and not thinking about Harrison Wellington.

But how could I focus when I had all of these warring thoughts inside my head?

I swiveled my chair around and faced my window. Stephon's homecoming last night was another one of our times that would be a memory for the ages — the night we officially became engaged. The night we'd share with our children and grandchildren for all of the decades in front of us.

Looking down at the ring now, there was no doubt in my mind, and certainly none in my body — I loved Stephon Smith and couldn't wait to become his wife.

So what was this draw that I felt to Harrison?

That was what I felt — a draw. Even as I had waited for Stephon's plane to land, I'd checked my phone to see if Harrison had texted me. Then last night, I'd done the same thing. When I'd received the first text from him this morning, I was almost relieved. As if I'd been afraid that he'd forgotten about me.

What was it about Harrison? His looks? No. Was it his business and how much he traveled? Maybe. Or was it his financial status (the man was a multimillionaire)?

Bingo.

I shook my head at that thought. Please, God, don't let me be that shallow.

But I didn't need God to break this down for me. I *was* that superficial, which was a sad self-awareness moment for me. The good thing, though, about being aware was I knew what this realization meant. I had to stay away from Harrison and his surprises. Why would I get caught up in a lifestyle when I had all of this love? I needed to break this down and break it off with Harrison.

Standing, I closed my door (it was never good to have anyone walking by seeing you on your phone), then returned Harrison's text:

> I had a great time, too. Thank u for the boat ride . . .

I paused, wondering if I should say anything about the earrings. After a moment, I did:

> And for the amazing gift. But I think it would be best if we ended our . . .

What was this?

> friendship here. It was wonderful meeting you for so many reasons. And I wish you well in everything you do.

And then I did a sign-off . . .

> All the best, Zuri

. . . because I wanted him to really understand that this was it.

Then I stared at the phone, waiting for the return text. So when it rang in my hand, my heart almost leaped from my chest. It was still pounding as I stared at the screen. *Mr. Wellington,* it said. That was the way I'd locked in his name just in case Stephon ever saw it, and I'd explain that Mr. Wellington was just a client.

My first thought was to not answer — let Harrison know for sure that I meant what I said. But then I wondered, for someone who'd been so nice to me, didn't he deserve more than a text?

By the time I decided to answer, it had stopped ringing. But then a second later, it started again, and I clicked ACCEPT right away.

"Harrison."

"Zuri, how are you?" he said, and the way his tone was so casual, I wondered if my text had made its way to him.

"I'm really good. But listen, I know you read my text, and I just wanted to say that it won't be possible for us to see each other again."

"Really? Why not?"

"Just not a good idea." I glanced down at my ring. "For where I am at this point in my life."

"So you can't have friends at this point in

your life?"

"I can, and . . ." Then I paused. Why should I have to explain this? I'd said it, I meant it, and that was enough. "Look, we both know . . . so, like I said, I wish you . . ."

"So you don't even want to know my surprise?" he interrupted.

If there was a moment in my life when I needed God to give me strength, this was it. Because did I want to know about the surprise? Yes! What had he bought for me now?

But it was the love I had for Stephon that made me say, "No. Whatever it is, I don't want to know."

I was so proud of myself until, "That's really too bad. When I got these tickets to see Michelle Obama tonight at the Georgia World Congress Center, I couldn't wait to invite you, and . . ."

I didn't hear another word he said. Actually, after "Michelle Obama tonight," my senses shifted. Yes, I'd known she was in the city and would be speaking about her new book. But by the time I'd checked the ticket prices, they'd started at five hundred dollars.

"I was sure," Harrison's voice broke through my musings, "that you would want to go to this."

Oh, God. I did, so much. It was Michelle Obama.

"The tickets are actually VIP. We'll be in the front few rows, watch her speak from there, and then we'll get a copy of her book and have a photo op after."

How was I supposed to say no?

"I met her during Barack's first term."

The way he said the name of the man I would always claim as my president was like he really knew the Obamas.

"I'd given a sizable donation to her Let's Move! campaign, and she asked to meet some of the donors. So when I found out she was coming to town, I called for tickets, and she told them to give me two VIPs." He paused. "So . . . would you like to go tonight?"

I didn't have the fortitude or character or whatever it was that I needed to say no. So all I said was, "That would be great. What time should I meet you and where?"

This time, it wasn't very difficult to twist the truth. When I had called Stephon and told him that I was going to be late coming home tonight, at first I'd heard a little bit of disappointment.

But once I said, "I'm going to see Michelle Obama," there had been nothing but joy from my man.

"Get out of here. Where? With whom? And can I go?"

It was only then that I had to twist the truth a little — I told him I was going with one of my clients.

"Do you think she can get another ticket?"

"I already asked," I told him, leaving that *she* out there. "You know there's no one I'd rather go to this event with than you." At least that was the truth.

"Well, do you need me to drive you?" I was glad he asked that question with a laugh. Then he added, "Babe, go, have a great time and tell Michelle I said what's up. And don't worry about me. I'll be here waiting for you."

He had told me he loved me, and I ended the call with how infinity couldn't even describe the depth of my love for him.

But what was great about telling the (almost) truth about going to this event featuring Michelle Obama was that now I could share this with my father.

As I turned my car onto my dad's street, I couldn't wait to see his face. My dad loved Jesus and he loved me, but President Obama had been right up there with us, and a time or two, I was sure that the president had nudged me out of the way.

I jumped out of my car and trotted up the walkway after I hit the car's remote. I was already running too far behind. After the call from Harrison this morning, it had been easy to focus on work — the idea of seeing, hearing, and meeting Michelle Obama made me want to get some things accomplished.

But I hadn't watched my time, and now I had less than an hour before I'd be meeting Harrison. He insisted we arrive together because between the security and the crowds, we would never find each other. So I agreed to have him meet me at my job — picking me up there was innocuous enough.

At my dad's door, I used my key. Since he had aides, he allowed me to come into his house without waiting for him. Not that it would have mattered; after finding him on the bathroom floor, there was no way I'd be standing outside waiting for him ever again.

"Hey, Daddy," I called out when I stepped inside.

Every time I saw my dad this way, it warmed my heart. He was leaned back in his recliner, his eyelids halfway closed. The days of my father working long, hard hours at the barbershop, standing all day, were still felt fresh in my mind.

Now he rested with his feet raised. And

though I didn't like the reason why he was like this, I liked that he was — he deserved this life after working so hard for so many years to take care of me.

Leaning over, I kissed his cheek. "You're tuckered out, huh? What did Brenda have you doing all day?"

"Nothing." Brenda came from the back already laughing. "He just finished having some ribs. So you know how that is."

She greeted me with a hug, then returned to the back, she said, to clean up. But I knew she was giving me and my dad some personal space.

He pushed his recliner to its upright position. "So . . . what's going on, my daughter?"

"Well . . ." I was excited, but wanted to draw out the drama just a little. "I wanted to come by and tell you something in person rather than calling."

His lips spread into such a wide grin that I laughed. "Got something to tell your dad, huh?"

I nodded, and for a moment, I felt like I was back in the third grade, giving my dad a report card that I knew would please him. I paused a little longer before I said, "I'm going to see Michelle Obama."

There was silence as my father blinked

and blinked, looking confused, as if that was the last thing he'd expected me to say. "What?"

"I know, it's hard to believe, right?" I said. "Mrs. Obama is speaking in Atlanta tonight, and I'm going to see her."

"Who got you a ticket?"

The way he asked that question didn't sound as if he was excited for me at all. "It's . . . I'm going with my job."

"Hmph." He pushed his chair back just a little bit. "Your job sure be doing a lot these days. A gathering on Saturday, Michelle today. So who you going with?"

I frowned now, totally befuddled by his reaction. "Why are you asking me all of these questions? I'm going with people. From my job. I can't believe this. I thought you would be excited."

"These people got any names?" He'd ignored what I'd said about Michelle.

"Daddy, why all the questions? I come over here to share this good news, and you're interrogating me. What's up with that?"

He nodded slowly as if he was waiting for what he wanted to say to come together. "Because you come over here all excited, and then I get excited, too. 'Cause I'm thinking you're about to tell me about that ring on your finger, and instead you're telling me you're going to see the First Lady and don't mention your engagement at all."

There was a whole lot wrapped up in that statement, and I waited for a moment to digest it. "But, Daddy, you already knew that. You've known forever that we would get married eventually."

He shook his head. "Nothing's official until it's official, and an engagement isn't official until he puts a ring on it . . . and until he calls and asks your father if he can have your hand in marriage."

My eyes widened. "Did Stephon do that?"

"Saturday," he said with a nod. "While he was still in Portland. He was at the jewelry store, and he said he knew this wasn't the correct protocol, that he knew he should be here asking me in person, but he was there and got a good price on a ring, and so he wanted to know if it was all right with me.

"I told him he was a fine young man and I'd be honored to have him as a son-in-law. Then both of us laughed about how you'd be over here first thing this morning telling me all about your engagement. When you didn't show up, I just figured it was work. And when you came here now, I was sure you had rushed over here, especially the way you barged into my door. So . . ." He held out his hand for me to put mine inside of his, and after a moment, I did. He stared at the ring, turning my finger a little to the left and then to the right before he nodded. "That's a mighty fine piece of jewelry right there," he said. "He gave it to you last night?"

"He did."

My father shook his head and dropped my hand. "So either you didn't want to share this big deal with me or it's not really that big of a deal to you."

"That's not it," I protested. "I just assumed since everyone knew and —"

"What's going on, baby girl?" my father interrupted me.

I sighed.

"You don't have to answer me, but this is what I know. I've lived a long time, and I've lived with you for your whole life. I know when a person has changed."

I held out my hands. "How have I changed?"

"The daughter I love, a year ago, would have driven over here first thing this morning to show me her engagement ring. If she had an early meeting, she would have gotten up an hour earlier and brought her tail over here before work. But the daughter I love now, seeing Michelle, who I adore, don't get me wrong . . . but seeing someone she doesn't even know is more important than telling me about the man she's going to spend the rest of her life with." He shook his head. "Nah, something ain't right."

I had come over here on such a high. And all I wanted to do now was get away.

"I'm sorry if I'm a disappointment to you, Daddy."

I paused, waiting for him to tell me what I'd just said wasn't true. But all he did was shake his head. So I did the only thing left for me to do — I stood, kissed his cheek, then walked out of the house.

When I got into the car, all I felt like doing was crying.

32

Seeing Michelle Obama changed everything.

From hearing her speak about her new
book and finding out so many things I
didn't know about her, to having the opportunity to take a picture with her (though
it was a photo with me, Michelle, and Harrison, so that picture would have to remain
in the back of my closet), and then stopping
at Pinnacle, just to grab a drink and an appetizer, I was back on top, feeling the way
I'd felt before I'd spoken to my father.

When we sat in the exact seating area
where Harrison and I had talked the first
time, I marveled that just ten days had
passed. Polaris, Lake Lanier, and today,
Mrs. Obama. Harrison Wellington was living some kind of life.

He asked, "What's wrong?"

"What do you mean?"

"You were staring . . . at me, not that I mind."

I shook my head. "Sorry, I didn't realize I was doing that."

"Oh, no; when a beautiful woman is looking at you the way you were looking at me, trust me, I don't mind."

I smiled . . . and then I looked around, suddenly feeling not only a little uncomfortable, but a bit exposed. It was interesting to me that all of the other times I'd been out, whether with Julian, Alexander, or, now, Harrison, I never considered running into anyone I knew. Not that I had a lot of friends — it had always been that way. But I still had people: Audra, folks from work, and even Ms. Viv — she could certainly afford some of the places I'd been. I could have run into anybody, and they could have thought anything.

But I was quick on my feet, so in the past, I would have been able to explain any of the situations . . . If they saw me at dinner, it could've been a new account; even on the boat, I could have been entertaining a client.

But here in the middle of this lobby bar under lights that weren't bright, but felt as if they were all shone on me — right now I felt exposed primarily because of the hour.

How would I explain sitting in this bar with this man at one hour before midnight? Guilty — that's what anyone would think of me right now. He said, "We've returned to the scene of the crime."

"What?"

"The crime. Where we met," he said. "And I believe we sat right in this section."

I wasn't going to tell him we had. I didn't want him to believe that I remembered meeting him all the way down to that detail.

"You know what?" I glanced at my watch. "It's getting late, and . . . I have to be at the office early in the morning. So if you don't mind . . ."

"Are you all right?"

"Yeah, I just want to be . . ." I stopped and glanced around as if I felt someone watching me. "I just want to get home."

"Okay," he said. "I'll call for my car."

We didn't say a word to each other as we stood, though Harrison waved off the waiter on his way over. We had been in the bar for such a short time, so his driver was back in less than five minutes.

Inside the car, the silence continued, and I kept asking myself, what was I doing? What was I thinking? What in the world did I want?

At the parking garage for my office building, the town car eased up the ramp, and the driver pulled right up to my car.

Turning to Harrison, I said, "Thank you so much for tonight. It was really special to me."

"I'm just glad you came." When I reached for the handle of the door, Harrison leaned over and put his hand over mine. When he pulled away, I noticed his gaze on my finger — my ring finger.

When I turned to him, he said, "Would you mind waiting a moment?"

I nodded, knowing what was coming next. This was something that had been on my mind all night: When would Harrison notice my ring? What would he say?

This was the moment, I was sure, when he would tell me he didn't want to be friends with a woman who was engaged. I got it. He was right; this needed to be the end.

He said, "I really enjoyed our time tonight." He glanced at my hand again and then after a few silent moments, he said, "Let's go to lunch this week."

My eyes fluttered a couple of times, because clearly I didn't understand his English. What happened to the words he was supposed to speak — *I can't go out, not even as friends, with a woman who's be-*

trothed to another man?

I said, "That's not what I expected you to say."

His eyebrows raised. "Why?"

I glanced down at my ring, and when I did that, I knew that his glance followed mine. "It's just that . . ."

Before I could finish, Harrison said, "Zuri, look at me. Please." When my eyes met his, he continued, "I'm not trying to make you sad; I like hanging out with you. I like exposing you to opportunities and giving you a chance to do things you may not ordinarily do. I'm not asking for anything else." He shook his head. "That's the problem. People don't understand friendships. They always believe that a man wants something more." He shrugged. "I'm a man of means; I can have the 'something more' that you're thinking about any time I want. But that 'something more' always comes with situations and consequences that in the end cost me more than I am willing to spend. Sometimes a man needs a little break, and right now, I'm not looking for a situation or a consequence. What I am looking for" — with his fingers, he lifted my chin — "is a friend who I can make smile." He paused. "Can I get one of those smiles right now?"

I nodded. I smiled.

"So, lunch this week?" Then he held up his hands. "Just lunch. With a friend. And to prove it, we'll go someplace regular."

A chuckle now accompanied my smile. "I have no idea what 'regular' means to you."

"Someplace where two friends would meet in the middle of the day. What about Starbucks? You can't get any more regular than that, right?"

I laughed.

"See, that's what I wanted to do. I want to see you smile. I want to make you laugh."

I nodded, and then I said the only thing that I could. "Thank you."

He smiled, then knocked on the closed privacy window for his driver to get out and open my door. As the driver came around, he said, "So, we're cool?"

"Like ice."

He held up his fist, I bumped mine against his, and before I got out of the car, I told him, "Let me know when you want to do lunch."

Inside my car, I backed out of the space because Harrison and his driver were waiting for me to leave. But as I drove, I thought about his words. There were no lies in what he'd said. If Harrison were a woman, no one would think anything of this new friendship. So why shouldn't I take advantage of all the things that Harrison could expose me to? Why shouldn't I sit back and enjoy his lifestyle . . . the best restaurants, rolling around the city in a town car, attending events with the country's elite?

I shook my head. There was nothing wrong with what I was doing at all. I just had to make sure that my friendship with Harrison never interfered with my relationship with Stephon — and since Harrison had seen my ring, we really were cool like ice.

I felt so much better settling into that thought. Now I wondered, what would this mean? What kinds of things would Harrison have planned? More nights like this? More gifts? And then I wondered why I had even asked myself that question, and when I did, why had my stomach fluttered?

33

Saturday morning. And it was wonderfully the same. But it felt a little different because this was the first Saturday when I stood at the edge of our living room, taking in the sight of Stephon, and he was officially my fiancé.

Beethoven's Symphony No. 5 piped through the speakers and it made me smile the way Stephon's brush moved to the music, as if he were painting that symphony, bringing the notes to the canvas.

Easing up behind Stephon, I wrapped my arms around him, kissed the top of his head, and stayed there until I felt like I had disturbed him long enough. I stepped away, but Stephon pulled me back before I could get very far.

So I stood there with my arms around him even as he created.

It was only the ringing of my cell phone that made me break away. I trotted into the bedroom to grab it from the nightstand. Peeking at the screen, I clicked ACCEPT, then said, "Hey, girl."

"What's up? You and Stephon out of bed yet?" Audra said with a chuckle.

"Ha, ha, ha. We've been up for hours. I'm already showered and dressed, and Stephon, well, you know how it is for him. He was in front of his canvas early this morning. Working hard to bring his best in July."

"Oh, that's right. His show. Then you guys may not be able to do this."

"What?" I asked as I returned to the living room.

"Well, the four of us haven't gone out in a while, and Joseph and I want to take you guys out to celebrate your engagement. So what about tonight?"

"Dinner? Tonight?"

Stephon frowned, and I mouthed, *Audra, Joseph.* Stephon gave me a thumbs-up.

Audra said, "Yeah, that's what we were thinking. Do you think Stephon will be able to step away from his painting for a few hours?"

"Yeah, that'll be cool. It's been too long since we did this. So what are you thinking?"

"Well, I loved when we had drinks at Pinnacle . . ."

I flinched.

"And Joseph and I have wanted to go there for a while. Let's do that — our treat."

I wasn't sure why I was hesitating. I mean, it was a public restaurant, so there was no problem with me returning to the place where I'd had dinner with Alexander. It wasn't like he was going to be there.

But what about Harrison?

"So let's say seven?" Audra asked. "Is that good?"

"Yeah, that'll be fine. Thank you, I'm looking forward to it."

"Yeah, girl. We're gonna party until . . . at least midnight or so."

We laughed together because it was true — we were far away from those college days when we'd stayed up all night and went to class the next morning. I told her Stephon and I would meet them there. When I hung up, I filled Stephon in on the plan.

"That's cool."

"So, what I'm going to do is leave right now so that you can have a great day of painting, and then we can have a great night of . . ." When Stephon looked up, I said, "A great night of whatever you want."

He grinned. "Get out of here, woman, so I can get to painting."

We kissed, and I rushed out of the apartment, feeling like I wanted to dance. Until I saw my next-door neighbors, the two sisters, who grinned at me as if we were friends.

"Hey!" the blue-and-pink-haired, blue-eyed one said. "Where's your boyfriend?"

I stopped for just a split second. These were the first words that woman had ever spoken to me. And she wanted to know about Stephon? Shaking my head, I slipped into my car. I had too much in front of me today to worry about these chicks.

First up was heading to the mall for my Saturday stroll and then to my dad's. It had taken almost the whole week, but we were back to where we were before I'd told him about seeing Mrs. Obama. But my mind stayed on my dad for only a moment before my thoughts returned to tonight and celebrating at Pinnacle. Harrison had already shown me that Pinnacle was one of his favorite places. I didn't want to walk in there blindly; I didn't want to be sitting at the table looking to my left and my right the whole time I was there. Not that I could tell Harrison to change his plans, but if I found out that he was going to be there, I could change ours.

I pressed the button on my steering wheel, turning on my Bluetooth, and called Harrison, something I had never done, though I texted him all the time. But a call felt more intimate, though that was Harrison's preferred way of reaching out to me. He was considerate, only calling during the day, when I was at work, as if he gave consideration to the man who'd put the ring on my finger.

The moment he answered, I couldn't help but smile because I felt his energy, and then, in his voice, I heard his excitement.

"I was just getting ready to call you," he said before I even said hello.

"Really?"

"Yeah, I had a good time at lunch the other day."

Even though he couldn't see me, I nodded. Because I'd had a great time as well. It was the first outing with Harrison when I felt . . . regular, just as he'd said. We'd gone to Fridays, and we'd gone in the middle of the day. The venue and time had changed all the dynamics, and we talked and laughed like we really were good friends.

He taught me a few words in Swahili: *hello — habari* most of the time, but sometimes *hujambo* or *jambo* or *shikamoo. Good-bye — kwaheri.* And then, *I love you — nakupenda* (which fascinated me because it was a single word). We debated the Temptations versus the Four Tops, "Let's Stay Together" or "Sexual Healing," and we finally agreed that Prince and Michael Jackson shared the crown of king.

At the end of the lunch, which had stretched so far beyond noon that folks began to walk in for an early dinner, Harrison and I had strolled back to my office building just two blocks away and he'd left me right there in the lobby (in front of Starbucks) with a hug and a promise that he'd be in touch. Then he'd walked away. Without an offer of anything.

It had been a happy afternoon for me, until I'd returned to my office and a not-so-happy boss, who told me that it seemed like I had been distracted recently.

But the same way that I'd reassured my boss then, I told Harrison now, "I really did have a good time at lunch."

"And I want to continue that today," he said.

"Oh, I can't," I said right away. "I have plans tonight."

"Well, that'll work 'cause I'm talking about *today*. Right now. What are you doing?"

Right now? I glanced at the clock. I just had a few hours to do my Saturday mall walk before I made it over to my dad's.

He said, "I have a surprise for you."

I laughed. "Really, Harrison? What now?"

"Well, I'll give you a hint. It's not a diamond, but it's still a pretty good surprise."

It was ridiculous, the way his words made me feel giddy.

He said, "So, can you meet me? Just for a couple of hours?"

"I don't know," I said, taking a quick glance down at the shorts and tank top I wore. "I'm not even dressed."

"It's not that kind of party. Whatever you have on will be better than fine."

I paused again. "How long will this take? I have to be back by five," I said, calculating the time I'd need to get home and dressed for our dinner tonight.

"Not very long. A few hours; we'll be done and you'll be back by four," he said. "And remember, it's a surprise."

Saying *surprise* three times was the charm. There was no more hesitation inside of me. Once again, I found myself saying, "Okay, meet me at the parking garage at my office," because there was nothing that could beat a good surprise.

34

Because of the life I'd been blessed to live over the last few months, I'd become used to eating at the fanciest places and attending elaborate celebrity events. It was amazing how quickly I'd become acclimated. It wasn't my norm, but no longer did these kinds of things feel out of the realm to me.

But as I watched the long stretch limousine roll into the pretty much deserted parking garage, I got a tingly kind of feeling. Like I *was* living that life.

Now, it wasn't that I'd never been in a limousine — Alexander had sent one for me when we went to Usher's event. But with Harrison . . . this was just how he rolled. He jumped in a town car or limo the way most people jumped in and out of Ubers.

When the limo came to a stop in front of me, I waved at the driver, signaling that I didn't mind opening the door and sliding inside myself, which is what I did.

"Hey, beautiful lady." Harrison grinned, looking as sharp as ever today in just jeans and a white T-shirt under a navy blazer.

"Hey. What's up with the limousine?"

"Well, we have a bit of a drive, and since you don't have much time, I thought we'd eat on the ride over; this way we wouldn't have to stop to grab something. So a little picnic lunch in the car, and it's much more comfortable in this space, wouldn't you agree?"

"I guess, except I don't know where we're going. Wanna share?"

"Now how can I do that and keep it a surprise?" He shook his head. "Just lean back and enjoy the ride."

As the limousine began to move, he unpacked our lunch and we chatted about everything, the way we always did. We had been riding for I'm not sure how much time, when I glanced out the window just in time to see we were still on I-20, but now right outside of Birmingham.

"Oh, my goodness." I glanced at my watch. "We're leaving Georgia? Where are we headed?"

"We're almost there," he told me. Then he patted my hand. "But no worries. You said you needed to be back by five, and I promised you by four, so I have this all planned out. Really, it won't take long. Relax."

For the rest of the time, I looked out the window, not able to imagine what kind of surprise Harrison could have for me in Birmingham. Finally, we exited, then edged onto a smaller highway before the limousine slowed down to weave its long body through the shorter residential streets. We turned into a subdivision called Mountain Brook Estates.

My first thought was these homes had once been on plantations. And when the limousine finally curved into a driveway, I thought this particular house had probably been on the biggest plantation of all. It was massive, with eight columns surrounding the porch that led to the front door of the redbrick home.

When we stopped, Harrison looked at me. "We're here."

We waited for the driver to open the door, then Harrison slipped out first, and I was right behind him. I didn't ask any questions because I knew he wouldn't give me any answers.

But right before he rang the doorbell, I got an awful thought — was he bringing me to meet his family? Before I could digest the horror that would be, the door opened and I forgot all about whether this woman was a relative or not, because I was fascinated by her right away. She was statuesque, her height an advantage for anything that she'd want to do — particularly play basketball or strut down a runway. Her skin was golden, like bronze, making her look like a statue, almost, especially wrapped in the orange dress she wore. And that dress — it was fire. Not a color I would have chosen, but one that fit this woman with perfection.

"Harrison!" she exclaimed.

I tilted my head a bit. She looked familiar, but that wasn't possible. There was no way my world and Harrison's would ever have collided if we hadn't met by chance.

As they hugged, I did a deeper assessment, trying to figure out why it did feel like I knew this woman.

Then she turned to me and held out her arms. "You must be Zuri."

When she stepped back, I said, "Yes, I'm Zuri," wanting to give her a hint that she had the advantage because I had no idea who she was.

She must've caught my clue because she laughed before Harrison said, "This is your surprise. This is Terez Pruitt, though most people don't know her last . . ."

"Oh my God!" I pressed my fingers to my lips. "You're Terez!"

Now they both laughed.

Harrison said, "And here I had this whole introduction to tell you how special Terez is, but it seems you know already."

"Who doesn't know?" I asked him.

Indeed, everyone knew Terez or rather everyone who was into fashion. She was one of the top designers in the country, by far one of the most successful designers of color, who had studied under Vera Wang and Donatella Versace before she set out on her own. Now she clothed at least a dozen of the stars at every Oscars, and she had a line in Target as well as her upscale line exclusively in Saks.

But the best part: she'd gone to Spelman!

"I can't believe I'm meeting you," I said, understanding now why she looked not only so familiar, but also so fabulous.

"And I can say the same thing. Harrison said you're a special friend, and since I'm a friend, that's something we already have in common. Come on in."

She turned around, and I wanted to curtsy to the fashion queen. The cutout in the back of her dress dipped dangerously low. She'd taken slay to a level where few people would ever be able to go.

When we stepped into a grand room, there was an assault on my senses — the soft pastels: a pink sofa, light blue chairs, a soft yellow shag rug that hung on the wall. Oh, and then there was the white piano, covered with dozens of silver picture frames.

I sat on the sofa next to Terez, and Harrison was across from us. "This was a great surprise," I said to Harrison. "Thank you for this."

"Oh" — he raised his eyebrows — "you think the introduction is the surprise?"

When they laughed, I looked between them, waiting for either to bring me inside their joke.

Harrison said, "Well, I guess meeting her was part of the surprise. You had to meet her if she's going to design something for you."

It took a couple of seconds for his words to reach the comprehension section of my brain, but still I said, "What do you mean?"

"I mean, anything you want, Terez is going to design it for you."

Now, even though I knew Terez sold an affordable line in Target, the truth was, a private design would cost more than her line in Saks.

I shook my head. "Harrison, you don't have to do this."

"I know that."

"But . . ." I didn't want to go into it with

Terez sitting right there, but *another* gift? I mean, yeah, I'd expected a surprise, but nothing that would cost this much.

I guessed Harrison knew me well enough, because he said, "You're not going to stop me from blessing Terez, are you?" he said. "Let me bless her by having her design something for you." He paused. "She needs the money."

They laughed again, but inside I sighed. It made no sense to argue. Like Harrison had told me before, I was going to accept this gift. No way would I ever turn down a Terez original.

I pressed my legs into the sofa so that I'd stop shaking. Now I was a little annoyed — Harrison should have told me, because how was I going to decide so fast what I wanted?

"So, while you ladies work this out" — Harrison stood — "I'm going to get out of here." Looking at Terez, he said, "So, an hour and a half?"

With her eyes on me, she said, "Give me two. I want to make sure I capture everything about Zuri."

He nodded, then hugged Terez, though he only squeezed my hand, and once we were alone, Terez said, "Now let's get to work."

"You know," I began, "this was so much of a surprise, I don't even have any idea of what I want."

"That's okay," she said. "People think designers just work with cloth, but what fashion designing is all about is working with people." Her hands glided through the air as she spoke. "I design people; the dress must have a body. You can't separate the two. So let's just talk a bit."

She held a sketch pad in her hand, though she twisted so that I couldn't see what she was drawing. At first, it was a bit distracting, as I felt like one of those models in the middle of a classroom.

But Terez was a natural because after not too many minutes, I was leaning back on the sofa, and we were chatting like girls. I wasn't sure how some of the things we talked about had anything to do with design: food, the kind of television shows I liked, and if I exercised. But there were other things we discussed, where I could see how those topics might impact my fashion tastes. She asked me what I did for a living, and then we talked about my favorite places to go (though most of that came from my imagination — the places I'd love to see), what would be my dream vacation, and my favorite colors, my favorite songs.

It was almost like an interview without any of the pressure, but the thing was, while

Terez got me to talk, she shared a lot about herself, answering some of the questions she asked me. By the time she said she needed a break, I felt like I really did know a little about her.

Just as she stood and stretched, my cell phone vibrated, and I checked the text:

You good? How's Dad?

"Excuse me," I said to Terez. She gestured as if my texting was no big deal, but I'd been in enough situations to know how rude it was to text without excusing myself. I texted back:

I'm good, and Dad is Dad.

After just a second, Stephon texted back:

LOL. Can't wait till tonight. Before . . . and after dinner.

That made me smile. I texted:

Me too. I'll be home by five. Love you.

I tucked my phone back into my purse, but when I received a notification of a text a few seconds later, I knew what Stephon's response had been. I sighed with love for my man.

Terez had a bit of a frown when she asked, "Everything all right?"

I waved my hand. "Yes, definitely. Just checking in with my fiancé, and he does that to me."

"Fiancé?" she said as if she were surprised.

So quickly, I told her, "Oh, Harrison and I are just friends," making sure I waved my left hand so she could see my ring, which I guessed she hadn't noticed.

She nodded. "Yes, that's what he told me. But when you walked in here, there was" — she paused and circled the pencil she held in the air — "just a chemistry between you two."

I chuckled. "No, truly, there is nothing between us. We're friends. I'm involved, and I'm sure he is, too."

"Okay."

Her tone sounded like she was holding back a chuckle, but she could laugh all she wanted. This was not a twisted truth.

"Well," she said, "you're going to have my information because we'll need to get this creation completed, but maybe after that, you'll hire me to design your wedding dress."

"Oh my God. That would be amazing."

Then I rolled that thought back. "But I don't think I'd ever be able to afford you."

She was still sketching as she shrugged. "You never know. I guess it depends on who you marry."

Before I could object, she turned the sketch pad around, and I gasped. The image in front of me — this alone would have been enough. This alone would have made this surprise complete. It wasn't just the dress, but the sketch was so beautiful. It was a silver gown, a throwback to old Hollywood. What the starlets wore in maybe the 1940s or so. Fitted from the shoulders all the way down to the waist, highlighting the hips and then flaring out at the bottom. Every inch of skin was covered, but I had never seen anything so sexy — especially not on me.

But this dress *was* on me. Because Terez had put my face (and what I hoped was my body) on this model. It was almost like a penciled portrait of me — two images, the front and the back.

"What do you think?" she asked.

"I've never seen anything so beautiful," I said. "Oh my God. I couldn't have even come up with something like this."

"That's why I'm the designer. I'm glad you like it."

"But . . ." I shook my head. "I wouldn't have anywhere to wear this."

"Oh, come on," she said. "You live in Atlanta. There's always something going on there."

Again, she must've thought I rolled in Harrison's circle. But where I really lived — this outfit wouldn't go down well at Big Daddy's Burgers or Centennial Park.

"Well, even if you can't think of anyplace right now, every woman should have a dress like this in her closet because an occasion will surely come around."

Terez was right — Stephon . . . and his art shows. I was really believing that one day he'd have a showing at the Museum of Contemporary Art of Georgia, or when I was really thinking big, I thought about the Metropolitan Museum of Art in New York or even the National Gallery of Art in DC.

"Okay." I nodded. "So what do we have to do from here?" I hoped I didn't sound as anxious as I was.

She glanced at her watch. "Well, Harrison will be back in a little while, but I still have time to get your measurements and other vital statistics. And then we'll have to think about fabrics, but we can do that by email and I can send you samples by snail mail. But it all starts with the measurements."

With a wave of her hand, she stood, then led me up the stairs and into a room with mirrors at different angles and mannequins all around. She grabbed a measuring tape that was draped over a mirror and began to measure me beyond my bust, waist, and hips. She wrapped that tape around parts of my body that I never knew mattered.

"There!" Terez said, and when she glanced at her watch, she added, "Perfect timing. It's exactly two, and knowing Harrison, he'll be ringing my doorbell in five, four, three, two . . ."

But then, Terez could have said *one* a thousand times, and when my phone showed me that it was two thirty, I called Harrison.

He answered right away. "Hey, are you and Terez finished?"

"We are; I thought you would be back by two."

"Yeah. We were on our way, and the car started overheating. So we're at one of these auto stores. Gonna put oil in and be there in about fifteen. No worries, okay? I'll have you back in Atlanta on time, even if I have to fly you there."

But fifteen minutes came and went, then turned into an hour. It wouldn't have been bad if I'd just been out with Harrison, as long as he was all right. But my man was waiting for me at home. I calculated in my mind. If Harrison walked through this door right now, I wouldn't get back to Atlanta until well after five, going on six. I would already be late.

It seemed like I wasn't going to make this dinner.

"Can I use your bathroom?"

"Oh, sure." Terez pointed the way, and after two turns around two corners, I was in a bathroom where all I wanted to do was stand and admire the black commode, black marble floor, and gold fixtures. But all I did was lower the lid on the commode, sit down, and try to think this through. Whatever I was going to do had to be by text — I wouldn't be able to twist the truth to Stephon if I heard his voice.

What should I do?

One thing was for sure; I'd need an ally. Audra was out, not only because of what happened before, but I couldn't use her as an alibi if she was showing up to the dinner. And then there was my dad; he definitely was out.

I sighed, but then, right away, I had a thought. It wasn't the best thing I'd ever done, and it might not even work, but it was all I had left.

Taking a breath, I opened my text app. My fingers shook as I texted:

Babe, an emergency came up. I have to do something with . . .

I paused and asked for forgiveness before I typed:

Ms. Viv.

I figured she'd be a great alibi. Not in the typical sense. She wouldn't be in on this, but I wouldn't have to worry about Stephon calling her since he didn't have her number and he really didn't know her. I texted:

She's in such a bad way. I'll explain later.

I nodded. That would give me time to figure out what I'd say later. I finished with:

I didn't call because she's in front of me. I'll explain. Sorry I'm going to miss dinner, but you go. Please! I'll feel better if you do. Love you beyond infinity.

My thumb hovered over the SEND button for a moment before I finally pressed it. Then I watched the screen, knowing that I'd be able to count the few seconds that it

386

would take until the return text came back.

And then . . .

My cell rang. I dropped my phone because I was so shocked. I grabbed it from the floor, and the beating heart pumped on the screen. I let it ring, and when it stopped, I turned off my phone. Closing my eyes, I sighed. All of this just because I'd wanted Harrison's surprise.

After a few moments, I stood, splashed water on my face, and released a couple of quick breaths. Really, what I had just done was worth it. I'd fix it with Stephon; he knew how much I loved him. What was in front of me now was a dress from Terez or dinner with my friends, a dinner that I could make up to them, even if I had to pay for Pinnacle myself. If I'd told them the truth, and then, if they'd all sat back and thought about it, Audra, Joseph . . . and even Stephon would agree that I had to make this trip.

At least, that was what I told myself.

35

"You're so quiet; again, I'm really sorry."

Turning my eyes from the darkness outside the window, I faced Harrison. I smiled. "You've apologized so many times already. It wasn't your fault."

His head bobbed from left to right, the gesture telling me he wasn't so sure. "I need to choose my limousines better, though."

His laugh was light, and I joined him.

"Seriously, don't worry about it," I said. "I ended up having a really good time."

He nodded, and I turned back to the window. It wasn't that I wanted to see the scenery. There was little in my view along I-20, especially at this hour; it was well after eleven. But there was a lot that I had to process.

What I'd told Harrison was true. I did have a good time. Once Harrison showed up, an hour after I texted Stephon, I didn't have a choice but to sit back and relax.

"The car won't be ready for another hour," he'd told me and Terez. "I'm so sorry, Zuri. I took a cab over here. Ben will bring back the car when they're done with it."

Before I could answer, Terez had said, "There is nothing you can do about this. So let's just relax and have a party. I'll cook, y'all chill, and we'll have a good time."

At first, all I had done was shrug and agree. What was another hour? But it had turned into many more as Terez had made the best shrimp and grits I'd ever tasted and the three of us had shared two bottles of wine. We'd chatted and laughed, like we were all friends, Terez and Harrison taking turns sharing their adventures around the world.

It wasn't until I looked out the window and noticed that not only had the sun set, but it was so dark outside, I realized the sun had hit the horizon hours before. That was when I told Harrison that I really had to get home.

We wouldn't get back to Atlanta until a bit after midnight, and I still had to drive to my place once he dropped me at my car.

"What are you thinking?"

Again, I turned to Harrison. "I'm thinking I had a really good time."

"So you're not thinking that you're sorry you missed your plans?"

"Oh, no," I said quickly, to make sure that he understood. "I was supposed to have dinner with . . . some dear friends. So I'm very sorry about that." And then I added, "Really sorry."

He nodded, and this time, he was the one who faced the window.

That was fine with me because I needed this time, I needed the silence, I needed to get myself together because in a little more than an hour, I was going to have to face my fiancé.

Before I even walked into the apartment, I knew this discussion was going to be more difficult than I'd imagined. It was because of the music that played: Barber's Adagio for Strings, one of the saddest classical songs I'd ever heard. No words, but it always sounded to me as if the violins were crying.

I'd told Stephon I didn't like this song — so he hardly ever played it.

Slowly, I closed the door behind me and stood there looking at Stephon, who sat in front of his easel, barechested, barefoot, the way I'd left him this morning.

He didn't turn toward me; he stayed

focused on his canvas.

"Hey, babe." And then, because I wanted to keep this conversation as casual as possible, I said, "You didn't go to dinner?"

He tapped his brush against the edge of the easel, then dipped it into the water before he turned to me.

"Where were you?"

I took a breath to keep my heart calm. "You didn't get my text?"

"That's not what I asked. Where were you?"

Stepping farther inside, I dumped my purse onto the counter, the divider between the living room and the kitchen. "I texted to tell you where I was and that I wasn't going to make dinner."

"Well, since you're not going to answer me," he stood, faced me, crossed his arms (though that did little to take my focus from his chest), and said, "I called your father."

And now my focus was all on his face.

Stephon said, "Your father hasn't seen you all day."

"So you didn't read my text?"

"I texted you about your dad, and you said he was fine."

"That's not what I said." I shook my head. "I said he was being dad."

"Do you even hear yourself right now? Do

391

you even hear how you're ducking and dodging and . . . lying?"

Now I crossed my arms, but it was more to stop them from shaking. "So you're calling me a liar?"

He laughed in my face. "Yes. Because you weren't with your father, so were you even with Ms. Viv?" Before I could twist another truth, he said, "Were you with another man? Are you seeing someone?"

I was so glad of the order of his questions because with righteous indignation, I said, "Are you serious? Are *you* hearing *yourself* right now? You think I'm seeing someone else?"

"Well, what else am I supposed to think, Zuri? You've been out all day, you lied about seeing your father, you missed a dinner to celebrate our engagement, now you come in *after* midnight and you won't answer my questions." He paused. "Where were you?"

I sighed. "I'm sorry. I did lie." Reaching into my purse, I pulled out the business card. "I was here." Handing him Terez's card, I said, "I was in Birmingham, meeting with one of my favorite designers. About my wedding dress."

Confusion covered Stephon like a blanket. It was in his eyes as he squinted at the card, it was on the folds in his forehead, it was in the way he tilted his head. "You went to see a designer?"

I nodded. "I ended up spending the whole day with her, though that wasn't my plan. I got there a little after noon and was just supposed to talk to her for about two hours. But then, when I got ready to leave, my car . . . I don't know what happened." I shook my head. "Some guys, some friends of hers took care of it. They had to run and get some oil and some other fluids." I shook my head and waved my hands like I had no idea what had been wrong with my vehicle. "It took a few hours, but then I got on the road."

"You drove home from Birmingham and your car wasn't working?" Now his voice was filled with concern.

"Yeah, but it was cool." I waved my hand. "I made it, I'm safe."

"Why didn't you call me? I don't get it."

"Because I knew you wouldn't approve of me going to see a designer, that you would say we can't afford it. But Stephon, her idea . . ." I pulled the sketch that I had rolled up inside my purse out for him.

His eyes widened as he took in the image. "Wow."

"I know, right?"

"It doesn't look like a wedding dress . . ."

"That's what makes it so special. I mean, I'm not sure about the color, though the silver is so regal, but that dress would be fire in white, and I would be the only person in the world who would have this."

Slowly, he nodded, then handed the sketch back to me. I thought with the card, with the sketch, with the story, all would be well. From the look on his face, though, all was not.

"So why did you lie?"

"Because you wouldn't have approved. You would have told me we couldn't afford it, and I wouldn't have gone to meet her. But even knowing that I can't afford this dress" — I held the sketch up — "it was so wonderful for me to sit and talk to Terez. I just thought that I could get to Birmingham for the consultation and be back in time for our dinner. I'm so sorry."

He nodded. "But you still lied. And that's the part, Zuri, that I'm struggling with. Because I don't want to do this. I don't want to marry a liar."

I flinched. "I told you why I lied."

"It doesn't matter. If I know you'll lie to me, then I will never be able to trust you. Because if you'll lie to me, you'll cheat on me. And that . . ."

"I'm sorry," I said, wanting to beg for his

forgiveness, "and I really mean it."

He nodded. "This is what you can know about me. No matter how hard the truth is, you'll always get that from me. And I need that same promise from you."

"You have it, Stephon."

As perfect as our relationship was, this wasn't the first time we'd had a tough talk — never about lying, but we'd had our debates about me wanting to spend money, or me wanting to go out — but no matter what the talk was about or how heated it got, it ended the same way. Stephon always wrapped his arms around me.

And this time . . .

He nodded, then turned back to his canvas, sat on the stool, and turned up the music so that now the violins screeched.

I stayed in place for a moment. Surely, he'd forgotten about me still standing here. But all he did was pick up his brush and focus again, like I hadn't come home this late with a great explanation.

Swinging my purse back onto my arm, I paused behind him. He didn't look up.

"I'm going to bed," I said.

He said nothing.

"I'm sorry."

At least this time, he nodded.

I said, "I love you."

And this time, he spoke, but when he said, "I love you, too," I wished he hadn't said anything at all. Because *I love you, too* wasn't anything close to beyond infinity.

36

It had been two weeks since I'd seen Harrison, and watching him strut toward me as he approached our table at the Winery gave me a good view of him in all of his sophistication. And I realized how much I'd missed him. Well, not *him* — though I thought Harrison was a cool guy. But I'd missed the dinners, the driver, and the events. I'd missed Harrison's lifestyle.

The thing was, though, Stephon was more important than all of that. So over these last few weeks, I'd dove into fix-it mode. I'd gone to work (I had some things I had to fix there, too), gone to see my father, and come home. I'd talked to Audra on the phone, especially to apologize for missing our dinner, and then I'd checked in with Ms. Viv more than a few times — to see if she had found a mentee for me yet (she had not), to see if she was okay (she was, according to Psalm 34:8, which she recited to me), and to let her know that I was doing well (and she asked me to repeat Romans 8:28 with her).

But besides that, my focus was on my man. And it had worked. I knew that for sure because Stephon had shown me in the way he made love to me last night.

Finally.

I could breathe.

So when Harrison had called me this morning, I agreed I could have lunch. Just lunch.

"Well," Harrison said as he sat down at the table. "Finally. Where have you been?"

"I told you, I've been busy."

"Must be some project, huh?"

"It is. My life depends on it," I said. "But it's good to see you. I've never been here," I said, looking around at the place, which had wine bottles everywhere, even as table centerpieces.

He said, "As you can imagine, this is one of my favorite spots."

"For sure. They serve wine, don't they?"

We laughed, and then, for the next hour, we didn't stop. We chatted, caught up, and I was thrilled when Harrison told me about a college he was partnering with for their student exchange program.

"Oh my God. Aren't you excited?"

"Beautiful lady, I'm excited every day when I can look up, 'cause that means I can get up."

Yeah, but wasn't it easier to look up when you had at least a million in the bank? He was one blessed man.

We chatted until the waitress brought the check, and then she said, "Would you like your package now?"

He nodded, and I wondered what that was about.

Until she returned less than a minute later. With a thin box that she handed to Harrison, and when she turned to leave us alone, he held it out to me.

"This is for you," he said, "just to say I'm sorry."

I kept my hands in my lap when I said, "For what?"

"For what happened when we went to Birmingham. I know you had plans, I know I messed them up, and I'm sorry."

"It wasn't your fault." Because he still held the box in the air, I finally took it from him and with a breath opened it and sighed. "Hermès."

He nodded. "Their scarves are so beautiful."

And expensive, I thought as I held the red, white, and gold silk scarf in my hand.

"Now, before you say anything about this costing too much" — he paused as I glanced at him — "Hermès is one of my clients."

"Really?"

He nodded. "They're in my discount book. So I get great deals on these things. Practically free."

This may have been practically free to him, but I knew how much these scarves cost. I inhaled, trying to remember what he'd told me about friendship and gifts and these being just little things.

"So," Harrison said, "I hope you'll accept this and not do that back-and-forth thing."

I wanted to object — truly, I did. But . . . I knew in the end . . . this scarf was going home with me.

"Thank you so much" was all I said before I folded the silk back into the box.

He smiled as if my quick agreement made him happy. "Now, I have something else to tell you." He signed the check, handed the billfold to the waitress, then turned to me. "I'm going to the Bahamas this weekend."

"Wow."

"It's what I call a turnaround trip. Just for about forty-eight hours, but I have to put together an event for someone, so I'm doing some scouting and preplanning."

"The Bahamas." I sighed. "I always imagined going there because it seems so close," I said. "It's right there. Not like Europe or even other parts of the Caribbean." I stopped, thinking this wasn't about me. "Well, have a good time."

"Come with me."

"What?" The volume of my voice was much louder than I meant it to be, but Harrison was lucky that I hadn't screamed.

"Come with me." He leaned back and held up his hands. "We'll have separate suites, so you'll know this is all legit. But I don't want to go alone, so come with me."

"No."

"Yes."

"I can't."

"Why not?"

"Because."

That exchange amused him, because the ends of his lips did that twitching thing again. "You know 'because' stops working as an excuse after you're seven years old, right?"

I laughed. "Because . . . I have to work."

"Is that it? I thought you were going to say because you don't have a passport."

"Oh, no." I chuckled. "I've had my passport for over ten years. This is my second one."

"I thought you said you never traveled

anywhere."

"But I also told you that all I've ever wanted to do was travel. What would I look like saying that and not being prepared to do that?"

"See?" He held up his hands as if I'd made his point. "You were prepared for a time such as this. Now you *have* to come with me."

"I told you, I have to work."

"You'll only miss Friday; we'll be back Sunday afternoon."

I sighed. If only I could.

He said, "Well, I know you have to get back to work, but I can give you a couple of days to think about it," as if I'd given him a maybe. "Till Wednesday. I'd have to get your ticket by then. First class, of course."

I had never been on an airplane, and this man was talking about first class? I'd seen enough pictures, enough movies to know what that meant.

As we walked outside of the restaurant, Harrison continued to share the details of the trip, the things we'd do — a tour of the island, a sunset cruise.

"And the shopping sprees," he said as he walked me to where my car waited with the valet. "I won't buy you a thing, but I promise you because of the people I know, you'll be able to buy whatever you want. You've never shopped until you've been to the Bahamas. Especially their gold." He winked as he closed my car door and sent me on my way.

Harrison's words consumed me. All the way back to the office, the entire rest of the day at work, and then on the entire ride home.

The Bahamas.

My first time on a plane.

First class.

And if I knew anything about Harrison, the accommodations would be first class, too.

I'd lived a wonderful life these past months — the events, the clothes, the jewelry. What I'd experienced to this point should have been enough.

But to get on a plane. To be in a hotel suite. That would be the ultimate.

I sighed as I pulled into my parking space in front of my apartment and sat there for a moment. Was there any kind of way to make this work? Shaking my head, I knew there wasn't. There was no way I could get on a plane with another man and keep the one that I loved.

I was a bit surprised when I walked into the apartment and there was no music playing. "Babe?" I called out.

Stephon came from the bedroom, dressed in slacks and a white shirt. "I was hoping you'd get home in time."

"What's going on?" I asked right after he kissed me.

"I'm heading over to the art gallery with the first five paintings. They want to start figuring out the display."

"Babe!" I hugged him. "This is really happening. I mean, I know it's in what? Ten days?"

"Nine."

I clapped my hands. "I'm so excited."

"I am, too." He didn't have to tell me that. I heard the glee in his voice. "So you're gonna go over there with me?"

"Are you kidding? Do you want me to drive you?"

He laughed, kissed me, and then we jumped into his truck after he once again made sure the paintings were secure in the back.

On the drive from College Park to Midtown, Stephon chatted about things he'd told me before but I was always so happy to hear again. All of his dreams for the shows he'd have, all of the paintings that were still seeds waiting to be born of his brush.

"And then one day, babe" — he reached

for my hand — "I'll have my own studio, and next door, you'll have your interior design firm. Two creative minds, doing the dang thang."

I laughed with him, I dreamed with him, I loved him.

In less than twenty minutes, we pulled into the back of Le Blanc Noir Gallery, just down the street from the Four Seasons Hotel. I loved this part of Atlanta, right in between downtown and Buckhead, and I imagined that one day — after we got the art gallery and interior design firm, of course — we'd live in an expansive penthouse apartment that would be showcase-worthy, and we'd entertain friends and clients and live our best lives.

I'd never asked Harrison where he lived, but I imagined it was a place such as the one that just passed through my mind.

Harrison.

The Bahamas.

Shaking my head, I pushed those thoughts aside as I took Stephon's hand and we stepped into the art gallery. Even walking through the back door, the space was impressive — the bright white walls that would be the backdrop for the paintings almost glowed, as did the white marble floor, which gleamed.

"Stephon," a thin man who reminded me of the president of France greeted him. "It is so good to see you." He spoke with a French accent, too, and I wondered if that was where the name of the gallery had come from.

Until another man followed the white one, this one black, with the same slight build, same close-cropped haircut, same light gray suit with a narrow tie.

Now I understood the name, the gallery, and this partnership.

Stephon introduced me to both — Gabin (the French president) and Enzo. When they turned to me, even their smiles matched, and both greeted me with a double air kiss.

"This is going to be a marvelous show," Gabin said. "Let's get the paintings." He rubbed his hands together as if he were about to touch gold.

As the men went to Stephon's truck, I moseyed through the space, which was filled with about a dozen red, white, and blue pedestals of varying heights. I loved the look, but I imagined the gallery that Stephon and I would have and the things I would do to bring our personalities to our space.

When they returned, I joined the circle as they slowly stripped the coverings from the paintings, and I beamed as the two lauded Stephon's work, giving higher praise to each next painting as it was uncovered.

"So, we have five here," Enzo said, taking inventory. "You'll bring the other seven . . . when?"

"Well, that's what I wanted to talk to you about," Stephon began. "I have ten in total, and . . ."

"No, no, no," Gabin and Enzo exclaimed together, sounding like they were singing a song. "We must have a dozen."

"I know that's what I said," Stephon began as he stuffed his hands into his slacks, "but this is what it looks like."

"You don't have other paintings?" Enzo asked.

Stephon shook his head. "Nothing for a show."

Gabin said, "Well, you have a week," sounding as if that were a year.

Stephon laughed. "I'm not sure it's in me to paint two in a week."

"Well, just give us another one," Enzo said as if this were a negotiation. "At least one more. This has been all planned out: the space, the artists. We must have at least one more from you. And think of the money. Not one of your paintings will sell for less than a thousand."

Gabin nodded. "That will be the lowest. Most will be closer to five thousand. The opening will be filled with investors who love to discover artists. They will pay much to get their hands on these." He shook his head. "That is why we must have at least eleven."

I stood beside my man and tried my best to keep my expression the same. In my head, though, the numbers were flying as I did the calculation. Stephon and I had never talked about how much he'd make with this showing; I'd just been so excited about this exposure. But even with a percentage going to the gallery, this would be quite a bit of money for us.

Stephon sighed but nodded. "I guess I really don't need to sleep for seven days. But my fiancée" — all three of them looked at me — "isn't going to be happy about this." Stephon smiled when he said that, but I saw his concern.

"You understand, don't you?" Enzo said.

"Of course," I said. "The most important thing is Stephon having this show and doing it well."

"Well, there you have it," Gabin said, and then he, Enzo, and I clapped as if that would be motivation for Stephon.

I clapped because I wanted to support my

man. But I also clapped because I had just figured out how I would be able to support my man and get my first trip on a plane, too.

Even though we were on the interstate, Stephon drove slowly, as if we were just taking an afternoon ride. As Beethoven's Piano Sonata No. 14 played, I bobbed my head, feeling the romance of this song. The speed of the car, the song that serenaded us . . . I knew this was a moment Stephon wanted to savor. His first major art show. As he relished this, so did I.

Stephon was the first to speak. "It's going to be an intense seven days."

"It's going to be fine. I don't know if you can rush creativity, but I know you, and I know your talent and gift." I squeezed his hand. "I am so proud of you. And I love you."

He gave me a quick glance and a grin. "Beyond infinity."

I wanted to cry now, every time I heard him say those two words. Because, not having heard them that one time from Stephon, I now knew how precious the words were to me.

He said, "Okay, I'm going to give it my best shot. I have an idea for one painting, and if I finish this in time, I'll come up with something else."

I let a few silent seconds pass. "This is so interesting."

"What?"

"This morning, my boss talked to a group of us about a convention this weekend." I paused. "In Miami. And I didn't think anything of it. I wasn't going to go, but now . . ."

"What kind of convention?"

"I didn't pay a lot of attention, but it's about how to be more effective in this digital age." I shifted in my seat a bit, surprised at how smoothly my lies flowed, and it didn't make me feel good. Because no matter how I dressed this up, this was no twisted truth.

"So you didn't want to go?"

"No, I did. But I was gonna talk to you about it . . . to see if maybe we could swing it and go together. I mean, my company would pay my part, and we would only have to pay for your plane ticket. You could share my room."

He gave me a quick glance. "That would've been something, huh?"

"I know." I sighed.

"But you should go, babe." He patted my hand.

"You think so?"

"Yeah, and I won't feel so guilty now about how I won't even be able to look at you over the next few days."

"I wouldn't mind that. It's not like you'd be ignoring me just to ignore me. This is about your work, and I know what this means to you. It means a lot to me, too."

"No, go," he said, nodding. "I'd feel great about you going, and then when you come back, babe, it's on. Wait . . . you'll be back in time, right? For my show?"

"Are you kidding me? First, I'll be back on Sunday. And if anything tried to slow me down, I'd walk back to get here by Wednesday."

He grinned. "I wished our first plane ride was going to be together, but I already blew that."

"Blew it? You do remember you went to see your mama, right?"

He chuckled. "Who's doing really well now."

"See? Like the doctor said, you were her best medicine."

He said, "I'm going to miss you, but this will be great." Right before he pulled into his parking space in front of our apartment, he said, "So, Miami, huh?"

"Yeah, I guess I need to call my boss and

let him know I'm going."

"As soon as we get inside."

He held my hand as we passed our neighbors, the sisters, and then, right before we stepped inside, he said, "So Portland for me, Miami for you. We'll just have to make sure that our first trip together is to the Bahamas or something."

I tripped over the threshold right when he said that, and he caught my hand. "Be careful, babe. I like my fiancées in one piece."

He laughed. I didn't. I just said a quick prayer that his words were not a sign.

37

If I thought the two-hour plane ride on that jet with leather seats as wide as an oversize chair, as much wine as I could drink, and that delicious pretzel burger for lunch were something, all of that paled to when we entered the presidential suite in the Cove at Atlantis Paradise Island.

"This is amazing," I whispered as a bellman led us into my room. I'd been saying that from the moment we landed at Nassau's airport, where an escort had met us just beyond the gate, grabbed our bags, then whisked us to a waiting car.

As I stepped farther into the suite, behind me I heard the bellman ask, "Both bags in here, sir?"

"No, just this one. I have the other suite on the floor," Harrison said, and I breathed. Not that I ever had any doubt about this man and what he'd promised. He'd kept his word to me with everything.

As he stayed behind to speak to the concierge who'd accompanied us so that we could check in inside our room rather than the front desk (I wasn't sure if that was because of this hotel, this suite, or Harrison), I roamed through the space, which was double — no, maybe triple the size of my apartment. In truth, my apartment could have fit inside this living room with the two white sofas, covered with dozens of pastel-colored pillows and an entertainment unit that framed a fifty-inch TV. Right off the living room was a full dining room (that sat ten) and a kitchen (which I had no plans to use). But even though I couldn't wait to see the bedroom, which I was sure was as fabulous as the rest of this suite, which felt more like a home than a hotel, I was drawn to the terrace that wrapped around the suite.

Stepping outside, I felt like I was floating high above Paradise Island. It was interesting — when Harrison said that we'd be on the beach, I was sure he meant we'd be *on* the beach. But we were twelve floors up, and this view was nothing like I'd ever seen. To the left was the Atlantis resort laid out, but the best part was the sparkling brine that was set out before me.

I inhaled the smell of the ocean's air and

almost wanted to cry; it was just like in my dreams.

"This is beautiful, isn't it?" Harrison came up behind me, and I jumped just a little.

I'd almost forgotten that I wasn't alone.

"I've never seen . . ." That was all I had to say.

"Come on," he said. "The ocean will be here for our entire stay; I want you to see the rest of the suite."

It took him a moment to draw me away, but then Harrison gave me a tour as if he was an expert or he'd been here before. He took me to not one, but both of the master bedrooms with vaulted ceilings and beds that were beyond any king-size I'd ever seen. Both had master baths that made me want to jump into the tub and stare out at the ocean through the massive window that was one wall of the bathroom.

Those were all what I called the normal rooms that you might expect in a suite. I didn't really know, but Audra had never talked about a suite that had these other rooms. Harrison led me through the study and a media room with another flat screen, this one about seventy-two inches as the centerpiece in front of the eight theater-style recliners.

When we walked back into the living

room, all I could do was shake my head and pray this wasn't a dream.

"This is unbelievable," I said.

"This is what seeing the world is all about."

I nodded, though I didn't agree. I had a feeling that this was what seeing the world with Harrison Wellington was like.

"So, I'm going to my suite; it's the other one on this floor. Why don't you unpack, chill, and give me about two hours to take care of some business, then we'll hook up. I'd like to walk through the resort before we have dinner."

"Okay," I said.

When he left me alone, I returned to the balcony, because this was where I would have stayed if I could. I would sleep out here, eat every meal out here, and then do what I was going to do now — just sit out here and take it all in.

My first time.

On a plane. In a hotel that wasn't in Atlanta. This was my initiation to traveling. I could certainly get used to this. Oh, yes, I could get used to this quick.

Turning back inside, I grabbed my cell. I couldn't wait to call Stephon. But I paused for a moment before I pressed his number. Oh, how I wanted to FaceTime and share all of this with him. But of course, I couldn't, and that made me sad. Still, I wanted to speak with him. He'd hear my excitement and assume it was because of my first plane ride. That would have to be good enough.

This didn't make any kind of sense. We hadn't left the hotel. All we'd done was saunter through the lobby, then onto the beach for an oceanside stroll, but when we returned, we came through a different entry, which, if I hadn't been with Harrison, would've had me turned all around in this resort.

But he'd led me through the Crystal Court Shops and now . . . there was a David Yurman bracelet on my wrist.

Standing on the balcony, I held out my arm and admired it — a Solari bead bracelet with diamonds. Of course I'd seen this bracelet, had appreciated the beauty in its simplicity, but it was always from afar. And now I owned one.

This time, though, I hadn't told Harrison that I couldn't take the gift. It was because when we walked in, the clerk had greeted him like he was her brother, and then after introducing me, she told me to pick out anything I wanted.

Harrison had beamed and given me the same explanation that he'd told me about the scarf: "She's in my discount book; I bring her a lot of business."

I'd been modest, chosen this fifteen-hundred-dollar bracelet, and now I sighed.

"You like it?"

Turning around, I faced this man who made me so happy. "I love it. Thank you."

He shrugged. "This time, it wasn't a gift from me."

"But it was a gift *because* of you. If I traveled around the world with you, would I get a gift in every city?"

Leaning toward me, so close I could smell the mint on his breath, he said, "Why don't you travel with me and see?"

My heart fluttered, and I held his gaze, but just for a moment before I turned my eyes to the sea.

He stood by my side, saying nothing, but I felt everything. It was the knock on the door that broke the trance, and I breathed as Harrison turned to answer it, knowing that it was the dinner he'd ordered for us.

Why don't you travel with me and see?

Did he really mean that?

No, he couldn't have.

And even if he did, it didn't matter. *That* was something I certainly couldn't do.

As two young men rolled two tables onto the balcony, I stepped back into the suite and watched Harrison direct the waiters.

Why don't you travel with me and see?

We'd only been in the Bahamas for seven or eight hours, yet I knew for sure traveling like this was what I wanted to do. But I could only have this life with Harrison, and he wasn't who I wanted; he wasn't who I loved.

Was there a way for me to have a life like this? Could I hang out with Harrison as a friend and love Stephon as my husband? If I had my way, *that* would be my life — with that, I would have it all.

No! Just thinking about it was ridiculous. How greedy could one person be?

But still, the possibilities lingered in my mind. The fantasy stayed when the waitstaff left us alone, as Harrison held out my chair for me to sit down, then as we ate what the staff had said was some of the Bahamas' best dishes: conch chowder, rock lobster salad, then fried grouper with peas and rice and johnnycakes.

Even as Harrison and I slid back into the comfort of our rhythm of chatting and laughing, and sipping sky juice, the question — *why don't you travel with me and see?* — didn't leave my mind.

38

I was surprised when my cell rang so early the next morning. Harrison and I had taken a midnight walk on the beach, and I wasn't sure which I liked better — the daytime, when I could see the ocean's blue, or the dramatic black of the night, where my sense of hearing became my sense of sight.

But I guessed when you were a millionaire, you rose early — at least that was a trait that I'd always heard about folks with that much money in the bank.

Reaching across what I'd come to call the Atlantean-size bed (since it felt like it was as wide as the ocean), I grabbed my phone and, without opening my eyes, touched the screen, hoping I'd hit the vicinity of ACCEPT. I said, "I cannot believe you're up so early."

"Why not?"

It was a torque reaction: I heard Stephon's voice, and my eyes popped open. "Stephon?" I pushed myself up, suddenly very much awake.

"Yeah, who did you think I was?"

"Oh . . . Carol, you know. She works with me. She's one of the people here."

"I thought you'd be up early. I figured with workshops only being held today, they would have you guys in sessions from six in the morning." He chuckled.

"They kept us in sessions till about ten last night." I pushed myself from the bed and moved to the window, taking in the morning view. "That's why I'm so tired."

"Ah, babe. I'm sorry."

"No, don't be. I knew what I was . . . getting into when I . . . came down to . . . Miami." I bit my lip. "Anyway, I want to hear all about you. What's going on? How's the painting?"

"Whew!" He blew out a breath that took about ten seconds to release. "I. Am. Working. But . . . it's coming together. I'm pleased. I think I'll actually have the two paintings to give me a total of the twelve Gabin and Enzo wanted."

"That's fabulous, babe. I'm so proud of you."

"Thanks."

"But what I want to know is are you eating properly?"

And just as I said that, I heard a knock on our door.

Stephon said, "Right on time. You'd be proud of me, babe. I ordered breakfast using one of those apps you're always talking about."

"Yay! I'm rubbing off on you." I laughed.

"Yeah, I was hungry, and I really don't have time to stop and fix something to eat. Hold on," Stephon said.

Through the phone, I heard the squeak of our front door opening, then, "Hey!"

A woman? I frowned. That had better be the delivery person. And then I backed up and shook my head. This was Stephon Smith, the man who'd promised that when he pledged his love, he gave me his complete fidelity.

"What's up?" Stephon questioned whoever was standing there.

"Is your girlfriend here?"

Now I stood up straight. It was a different voice, this time. The sisters. What the hell were they doing ringing my doorbell?

"Nah," Stephon said. "What's up?"

"We need to ask you something."

Now I paced in front of the bed, each step heavier as the seconds passed.

"Okay," Stephon said. "Hold up." Then to me, "Babe, let me call you back." He clicked off before I could tell him to let me listen.

"Ugh!" What were those women doing there? What did they need to ask Stephon? Why did they ask for me?

I awakened the screen to call him back, but then I paused. I needed to calm down. Maybe they needed to ask Stephon something about the apartment. Or maybe they needed help with their car. I stepped onto the balcony and inhaled the morning's breeze. This was my only full day in the Bahamas, so I didn't need to spend a moment on anything that was happening in Atlanta. This was my single day in paradise, and I needed to enjoy it.

I was living in the middle of a Bahamian whirlwind. It was a good thing Stephon had awakened me, because less than ten minutes later, Harrison called and told me to be ready in thirty.

And I was.

We began the day at the beachside restaurant, where the chef and much of the staff knew Harrison. Our table felt exclusive, even in the public place — we were farther out on the beach, compared to the other tables — and then I realized they had set this table just for Harrison.

As the waves came awfully close, we

shared a breakfast buffet of grits, souse, corned beef, tuna, stew fish, and, of course, more johnnycakes, which I loved. We chatted about the day ahead. Or rather, Harrison chatted, and I trembled with excitement every time he said, "I have a day of surprises for you."

That was the last thing he said to me before he left me at the door of the spa. "I have a couple of meetings, but when you're finished, I'll be right here waiting for you."

A spa attendant greeted me by name the moment I walked in, and right away, I had that zen feeling. I'd been to spas in Atlanta, but this was different. It was in the soft golden light that reflected off of the furniture and fixtures. And the lavender that permeated the air. And it was in the quiet.

That was the beginning of the three hours that started with an aroma stone massage. I was a noodle by the time that hour ended, and the next attendant dropped my body in an ocean wrap. Then, a facial, a manicure, and a pedicure, and when I got to the front door, Harrison was standing right there.

"How was it?"

"Do you even have to ask?" I wanted to give a nod and throw up the peace sign. That was how I felt; like I was high on serenity. This was probably the most relaxed state I'd ever been in. It was difficult to find my land legs as Harrison led me to a waiting car in front of the hotel.

"Now let's tour the island," Harrison said.

What I'd expected was to have the driver give us a tour of the Bahamian landmarks, but I should have remembered who was by my side. Harrison never did what was expected.

Still, when we pulled up to a heliport, I was in awe. The sound of the helicopter's whirring blades was deafening as a man greeted Harrison with a hug and me with a kiss on the hand. Then he led us inside the helicopter, and I snuggled into one of the four leather seats.

As Harrison and the man chatted, my heart fluttered a bit in anticipation as the helicopter rose high above the air. But any anxiety I felt faded away as we glided above the islands and I saw the Bahamas from a vantage point that I would never have imagined.

The first thing that took my breath away was the ocean — I would never have thought I'd be able to see marine life from this high up, but the crystal clarity of the ocean's blue made it possible to see the underwater life.

The man who'd greeted us was our guide, I discovered as he pointed out the island's landmarks and the homes that were owned by celebrities. I heard little of what he said because my mind couldn't encapsulate it all.

Twenty-two minutes later, our feet were back on land, and I felt like my life had been forever changed. Who had a chance to do this kind of thing?

Back at the hotel, we had lunch before Harrison left me in my suite with, "You have about four hours. I'll pick you up promptly at five."

I was pleased to have these hours to just linger in the peaceful beauty of this place. As I sat on the balcony, I thought about all that I'd done already on this trip — and we'd been here just twenty-four hours. From the David Yurman on my wrist to the helicopter ride to the suite where I now rested — I was immersed in the life of the rich and famous.

All because of Harrison. Being by his side gave me such a feeling of exhilaration. People greeted him like he had influence, like he had money. But what Harrison Wellington had was power. That was so attractive to me.

Sauntering back inside the suite, I filled the tub, then lowered myself in the tepid water, leaned back, and with the window framing the ocean before me, I just stared at the point where the sea kissed the sky.

I lingered in this place of peace until I realized the passing of time. Before I dressed, though, I wanted to speak with Stephon. Again, I hated that I couldn't tell him about this experience. Still, I wanted to share in this moment with him somehow.

But when I stood on the balcony, wrapped in just the huge towel and called him, Stephon's cell just rang.

I knew what that was about — he was into his groove, and I wasn't going to disturb him. So I texted:

Call me when you're free. Love you!

I waited for his — beyond infinity — but when nothing came through in a minute or so, I rushed to get dressed, knowing how my man got when he was in his zone.

By the time Harrison knocked on my door, I was ready, my thoughts far away from Atlanta and totally on this island. Back in Atlanta, having dinner at sunset was one of the things he'd told me we would do in the Bahamas, but without specifics. Like how, once again, he'd rented a private vehicle, this time a catamaran. So it was just the two of us (and the crew and staff) as we sailed from the Nassau Harbor. And even though I'd walked on the beach and spent the night in the resort, seeing the Atlantis from this view was breathtaking.

After being served rum punches, we went to the bow of the boat and watched the performance of the Lord. That was the only way to describe this — it had to come from God . . . the kaleidoscope of colors that began with a yellow blaze of flames bursting through the sky before the yellow bowed to its sister of gold, the beginning of the sun's good-bye. Then the gold faded to orange before the sky became ablaze in red, a bonfire of heat that cooled only after dipping below the horizon, the sun's farewell for this day. All I could do was put my glass down and applaud our God.

The sunset had been a symphony for our eyes, and now this buffet was its own wonder. I was becoming used to the island dishes of all kinds of soups, conch, every kind of fish along with grits, peas and rice, and pasta salad (Caribbean-style). They were all welcomed treats. By the time the rum cake and chocolate pineapple upside-down cake were set before us, all I could do was cry, *"No mas!"*

When the catamaran set its course to take us back to the place that I wished I could call home, Harrison and I returned to the bow to watch the Atlantis, with all of its grandeur, come into our view. We docked and gave our thanks to the crew, then, as he helped me off the boat, Harrison said, "I know we have to get up early, but shall we go for one last stroll on the beach?"

I nodded, then kicked off my sandals and sighed as my feet sank into the sand. Harrison joined me, and without saying a word, we walked along the shoreline. I inhaled, opened my eyes wide, and welcomed the sea's mist that dampened my face. I wanted every one of my senses engaged, so each of these moments would be etched forever into my memory.

"I hope you've had a good time," Harrison said.

"My goodness." I shook my head, trying to find the words that would capture what I felt about this trip. All I could say was, "This has been fabulous."

He chuckled. "I love the Bahamas, love coming here, but just know, this is a little corner of paradise." Waving his hand toward the ocean, he added, "There is so much more out there, beautiful lady. So much more for you to see."

This I knew, and my hope, my prayer, was that Stephon and I would have the chance to experience at least a little bit of it. But sometimes from the corner of my world, I couldn't fathom having the opportunity to see any other part.

"You'll have the chance," Harrison said as if he knew my thoughts. "If you want it, you'll have the chance." He took my hand and pulled me close, held me like we were about to dance.

And then we did. Right there on the sand, the ocean our music. Right there beneath the moonlight that shone onto the sea . . . we danced.

It was one of the most romantic moments I'd ever experienced, and that was why when we stopped, and he leaned back and looked at me, I moved to him. And my lips covered his. And I invited my tongue inside to meet his.

My heart leaped and skipped so many beats.

But then Harrison pulled back, and with a long look that I could not discern, he took my hand and led me into the hotel. Thoughts shot like stars inside my mind, but I couldn't catch a single one. There were so many things I wanted to say to him, so many things I needed to tell him. He needed to know that I wasn't sorry about the kiss; I'd been attracted to him for a long time —

I could admit that now.

But this would be it. Just this kiss. Because I loved Stephon.

I didn't say that, though. Neither one of us spoke a word, and even when we exited the elevator on our floor, we stayed silent. At my door, I trembled because I had to tell Harrison no.

He leaned forward, kissed my forehead, then turned away, leaving me watching and wondering. He tapped the key against his door, entered, then closed it, never looking back. *His* way of telling *me* no.

Still, I stayed and stared at his door. What had just happened? I replayed that question over again until I finally stepped inside my suite. And then I asked the bigger question — what did I want to happen now?

39

Rolling over, I glanced at the digital clock on the nightstand: two eleven. Was this how I wanted to spend these last six hours in paradise? Tossing?

The moment I asked myself that question, I pushed up and swung my legs over the edge of the bed. Wrapping myself inside the hotel's robe, I stepped onto the balcony and, for a while, just stood there, listening to the rush of the waves.

Even in the deep dark that came in the hours beyond midnight, I could still see the beauty of this place. Or maybe it was more that I could feel it. Oh, how I wished I could stay beyond the morning. If I could afford it, I would stay a week. Because I had some things to work out.

I was sure if I really wanted to do that, I could ask Harrison and he would arrange it for me without question.

Harrison.

But I couldn't do that because I had to be back — I wanted to be back for Stephon's showing.

Stephon.

Sitting down, I reclined onto the lounger, but even out here, my thoughts still warred. I didn't have clarity. But why did I need clarity? About what? I was clear: I loved Stephon. So why had I kissed Harrison?

"Because I care for him, too." I whispered my explanation into the Caribbean night.

There, I'd said it. I loved Stephon, but I was beginning to care for Harrison. No, that wasn't true; I'd been caring for him for a while.

So what did this mean? That I had feelings for two men? I moaned. This couldn't be. My heart couldn't beat for two, but I felt as if it was doing just that.

This was my fault. If I hadn't come here, if I hadn't craved just one more surprise, just one more gift, one more experience . . .

Tears misted my eyes; I couldn't believe what I'd done to my heart. I couldn't believe the confusion that I'd brought to my life. All I could do now was hope that this was all worth it.

I was dressed, but I was not ready. When I heard the knock on my door, I took a breath for courage before I turned the knob.

"Hey, beautiful lady." Harrison stood leaning against the doorjamb. Today, he didn't look like a model. No, this morning, he looked more like a movie star, making my heart sigh.

"Good morning."

"Are you ready to leave paradise?"

"No," I said, reaching for my roller bag and handing it to the bellman.

When he chuckled and said, "Good answer," my shoulders relaxed. That kiss last night didn't seem to have changed a thing. And then Harrison confirmed my thought with "Next time, we'll just have to stay longer."

Next. Time.

Now my stomach did a backflip.

Taking one final look around the place that I would always remember for so many reasons, I followed Harrison out of the room and into the elevator before we were led straight to our waiting car.

Still, as our car edged away from the front of the Atlantis, I wondered if Harrison and I needed to talk about that kiss. But his actions toward me hadn't changed at all.

Next time, we'll just have to stay longer.

That certainly didn't sound like someone who had been put off by what I'd done. I still had questions, though. Like how did he feel about the kiss? Did he have feelings for me? And when I asked myself that, I answered my own question — he had to feel more than a little something. Look at all the gifts.

Harrison patted my hand. "You good?"

I nodded. "I am." This was my chance to get my questions answered. "What about you?"

His smile seemed wider than I'd ever seen him smile before. "I'm better than good."

Better than good. Everything was better than all right. We were going back to America better than when we'd left.

Confirmation! All was fine — at least with Harrison.

But what about Stephon? What was I supposed to say to him?

That question stayed in my mind on the ride to the airport, as we checked in for our flight, and then as we boarded and sat in our first-class seats. As Harrison leaned back and closed his eyes, I kept my eyes on the window and the clouds below. It felt like we were gliding through heaven; really, that's how I'd felt these last two days. My question now — what would the next two days bring? What was I supposed to do with my relationship with Stephon?

I loved that man, but there was something with Harrison. It wasn't love, but it was curiosity. There was a part of me that wanted to see where our friendship would lead. But that brought me back to what did that mean? What was I supposed to do with Stephon?

By the time the airplane's wheels bumped down onto the tarmac in Atlanta, the answer came to me. I knew exactly what I needed to do with Stephon — nothing.

Really, there wasn't anything to do — at least not yet. I needed to let everything play all the way through. Not that I was foolish enough to believe I could have both men in my life. But though a decision needed to be made, why did I have to make it today?

When we exited, like in Nassau, someone met us, heralded us through customs, and in fewer minutes than it took most to deplane, we were outside at the curb, with our bags already packed away inside the trunks of matching town cars.

Harrison opened the back door of the first car. "This one is for you, beautiful lady."

I felt no tension when I faced him. Felt so natural when I palmed his cheek with my hand. "Thank you for such a wonderful time."

He covered my hand with his. "You're

welcome." And then, with his chin, he motioned for me to get into the car.

"I'll call you later," I said.

He nodded then closed the door, making me feel like this was going to be all right — at least on his side.

Now there was Stephon. And what was crazy about all of this was that I really couldn't wait to see my fiancé.

40

"Do you want me to take your bag to your door?"

"No, it's right there." I pointed to my apartment. "Thank you so much," I said to the driver, then turned and saw the sisters standing in front of their open front door.

For a moment, I wanted to stop — ask them why they'd knocked on my door yesterday. But I was sure Stephon couldn't wait to tell me, so I didn't want to spoil that surprise.

As I put my key in the door, I felt my heart flutter. It was like it knew that I was home and it knew the love that waited for me on the other side of this door. I paused . . . Did I really want to risk what I had with Stephon for what I *might* have with Harrison?

I stood for a moment reflecting on that question. As beautiful as the Bahamas were, as wonderful as it was to be with a man who could give me everything — was that love?

Stepping into the apartment, I smiled. Because right in front of me was the answer — the man I loved. Right then, I knew that Stephon was the only one I really wanted.

But then I paused. This picture was a little off.

The apartment was dark, or at least much darker than it usually was when Stephon was perched in front of his easel. Usually, all the blinds were lifted high so the sun could shine through. But this afternoon, there was more darkness in here than light.

Stephon was out of place, too. No bare chest, no bare feet. He wasn't in front of his easel, kneeling before his latest creation. Instead, he sat on the sofa, fully dressed as he'd been last week when we went to the gallery. The heavy plastic that covered our couch had been removed. Along with his easel and the cans of paint that were always strewn around our living room — gone. All gone.

All signs of him were gone.

But he was still here, sitting, motionless, waiting for me.

"Hey, babe?" My questions were inside my greeting. I moved toward him, but when he stayed silent and still, I froze. And my heart did, too.

"Stephon?"

I was closer now, so I could see his eyes, glassy when he looked straight into mine.

And then his first words. "What is this?" He reached for something on the side table. He reached for . . . the box that held my earrings. That had been tucked deep inside my closet.

My eyes narrowed. "Have you been going through my things?" I snatched the box from him.

He shook his head, and the chuckle he released had no humor in its sound. "We're not doing this. You're not going to answer my question with one of your own. You're not going to twist this and deflect this."

"I don't go through *your* things," I said.

"Fair enough." He held up his hands. "You don't want to answer that. Then maybe you'll tell me about this."

From the floor, he picked up a tabloid magazine that I hadn't noticed before. Stephon and I didn't read those kinds of things. We were so far beyond that. What in the world could this be and why . . .

My thoughts screeched to a halt when Stephon opened the magazine to the centerfold.

Usher's party.

Right below a picture of Usher and

Onyx . . . there was me and Alexander. And even though my hands were in full sight, Alexander had me wrapped in his arms.

"What you got to say about this?"

I snatched the paper from his hand. "Where did you get this?"

"Zuri!" He screamed my name so loud it sent me flying through the air. Literally. I took at least five giant steps back. "Don't ask me a question. Just answer mine."

I stayed silent. That was all I could do. Because my lips trembled.

"Oh my God," he said, as if before this moment he thought I might have a plausible explanation for what he'd found in my closet, what he saw in this picture, what he imagined in his mind. "Do you know how embarrassing it was for those girls next door to bring this to me? Do you know what that was like?"

The sisters. Next door. Yesterday. The knock on our door.

He stomped across the room and grabbed the jewelry box from where I'd laid it down. "Did he give you these earrings? What about that purse?" He pointed to my bag on my shoulder. "Did he give you that, too?"

I didn't know what to say, because when Stephon said "he," he meant one man. But because right now that was just a technicality, I nodded.

He groaned a sound that reminded me of the violins in Barber's Adagio for Strings. "Where were you this weekend? Did you go away with him?" He held up the tabloid.

Again, Stephon had the wrong "him," but there was no space to explain that now. So I nodded, but said, "It's not what you think, though. Nothing happened."

"Nothing happened?" he said with a laugh. "You go away with a man who's buying you diamonds and purses and nothing happened."

"I know the way it looks, but we were in separate rooms. I just wanted to go away because I'd never been anywhere."

He shook his head. "Do you love him?"

In the moment when he asked that question, my only hesitation was that I needed to find a way to explain that whatever I felt for Harrison, it was no comparison to what I felt for him. But the thing was, my brain didn't move faster than time. Because too much time passed . . . Really, it was just a second or two. But it was a second or two too much for Stephon.

His glassy eyes opened wide. "Oh my God."

"No. I don't," I said, rushing out the

words now. "I don't love him the way I love you."

He shook his head. "I'm out."

"No, Stephon, please," I said as he crossed the room. "We have to talk about this. I haven't cheated on you. Not once."

It wasn't until he reached the door and he grabbed the handle of his suitcase that I noticed the bag.

"I got half my stuff in here," he said, without looking at me. "I'll be back for the rest when you're not here."

I pressed my hands together to stop them from trembling. But when I held them against my lips, they shook anyway, because of the way my lips quaked. "Stephon, please. I love you. I love you so much."

My words did nothing, because he said nothing. He just opened the door and stepped out without taking a single look back at me.

I stood in the middle of the living room, which didn't even feel like my home without the easel, the paint, the music, the plastic on the couch.

Without Stephon.

I stood there feeling like a stranger in this place that had made me so happy.

Making my way to the sofa, I curled up in one corner, and with my eyes on the door and my heart in my throat, I cried and cried and cried.

41

I hadn't had too many hangovers in my life, but this sure felt like one this morning. Because there was this sound, this ringing, that just wouldn't stop. When my eyes were able to flutter open a little, I realized it was my cell phone. I rolled over to grab it from the nightstand, and I tumbled over, falling onto the floor.

My eyes popped open. What the hell?

It took me a moment to realize and remember — I hadn't gone into the bedroom. I couldn't fathom sleeping in there alone; that would've made me miss Stephon even more.

I didn't move from where I was, just patted my hand along the carpet until I found my cell that was no longer ringing. Staying on the floor, I leaned against the sofa and checked my missed-call log.

Ms. Viv.

Oh, God. The last thing I needed right

now was for her to tell me that after all this time, she'd finally found a mentee for me. But while I didn't want to talk to her about that, I was glad to see her call because I needed to talk to her. I needed to talk to someone, and what I knew for sure: my father and Audra were not options. When they heard this story . . . I might be excommunicated from their lives.

Checking my phone, I was shocked to see that it was ten thirteen. I missed our Monday meeting, but there was nothing I could do now. There was no way I could go into the office today at all.

But first there was another call to make. Stephon.

I stared at his number for a while, wondering if time apart had softened his heart. My hand trembled as I held my phone. Really, I didn't have enough courage to do this, but what I had was more than enough love. It was that love that propelled me. I pressed his number and closed my eyes, but it never rang — just went to voice mail. I hung up and tried again. Did it again and again, though I didn't know why.

Stephon didn't have his phone turned off. He couldn't afford to do that with his show in two days. What he'd done was block me.

That brought fresh tears to my eyes and

another thought to my mind.

Harrison.

I was a little surprised that his name hadn't shown up in my missed calls. Usually, after lunch or dinner or an event, he would call to say how he'd enjoyed our time. Certainly, he would call after the days we'd spent together.

I scanned through my calls, just to make sure I hadn't missed him or a message. But the only call I'd missed was Ms. Viv's a few minutes ago. He was probably as tired as I was, but now I needed to talk to him. Not that I was going to tell him what happened with Stephon — I just needed to hear a friendly voice. Someone who cared about me, understood me.

Pressing MR. WELLINGTON, I took a couple of deep breaths, wanting to sound as natural as possible when he answered.

"The number you have dialed is not a working number. Please check the number and dial again."

Shaking my head, I couldn't believe I was that tired. Whose number had I called? Returning to Harrison's name, I dialed again.

"The number you have dialed is not a working number. Please check the number and dial again."

My movements were slow as I set down my phone, but my heart? That muscle raced at supersonic speed. The number was not a working number — just like Julian's.

But I shook that comparison away. Julian had nothing to do with Harrison. I picked up my cell again. Something must have happened. Maybe Harrison left his phone in the Bahamas or on the plane. And he had to get a new one. And if he did that, would he still have my number?

He would be desperate to reach me, so I had to get in touch with him somehow. I took a couple of quick, shallow breaths and it came to me: I'd just call him at work.

But . . . I'd never called him there before. What was the name of his company?

I searched my memory. Travel . . . something. Travel . . . Edge.

Releasing a breath of relief, I opened my browser and typed in Travel Edge. When the name of the company came up, I wanted to leap. But what I did was press the phone icon.

"Travel Edge," the woman said with an accent that I couldn't place, "how may I direct your call?"

Another sigh of relief. "May I speak to Harrison Wellington, please?"

Without a moment's hesitation, she said,

"I'm sorry, there's no one here by that name."

And so I repeated Harrison's name, slowly this time, and told her, "He's the owner of the agency."

"Uh . . . ma'am, I don't know what to tell you, but there's no one here by that name and no one by that name has been here since I started seven years ago. Is there anyone else who can help you?"

My response to her: I clicked END on my cell.

I tried to think, but couldn't make any sense of this. What had just happened? And then I wondered, how many times had I asked myself that question in the last thirty-six hours? It was like I didn't have control of my life anymore.

Or maybe that was the problem — I had control, but I'd focused on the wrong thing.

My phone rang again, and I prayed before I looked at the screen that it would be . . . who? Did I want it to be Stephon or Harrison?

I closed my eyes, told God the desire of my heart, then hit the screen without opening my eyes.

"Zuri?"

"Hi, Ms. Viv."

It wasn't Stephon.

"Do you have a moment, dear? I would love to speak with you today, maybe even during your lunch hour?"

I held my head with one hand. "I'm not going to work," I groaned.

"Are you okay?"

"No, I need someone to talk to."

"Well, you get over here, and I'll have some tea and scones ready for you. And then we can have a nice long talk."

"Okay," I told her and hung up. But then I paused. For the first time since I'd met Ms. Viv, she hadn't quoted a Scripture.

I had no idea why that stood out to me now, but one thing I knew for sure — it was a sign. The only problem was . . . what did it mean?

42

It didn't take me more than twenty minutes. Because all I did was get up from the floor, stumble into the bathroom, splash some water on my face, rinse out my mouth, and grab my purse. The dress I'd traveled in, I'd slept in, and now I was going to visit Ms. Viv still wearing it — wrinkles and all.

That was why I showed up to her house less than twenty minutes after I hung up the phone from her. When Ms. Viv opened her door and then her arms, I stepped into her embrace and sobbed.

She held me, giving me comfort, the way I imagined my mom would have done. She let me cry until I stepped back. Then she said, "What's wrong?"

"Everything."

After closing her door, she led me to her designer sofa, where, even though I'd rushed over here, the tea service was prepared on the table before us.

She said, "Before you begin, let me pour you a cup. I want you to get settled, get centered."

Even though it was July-hot outside, the heat of the teacup on my hand was soothing. Then I sipped it, and the comfort I felt was almost as warm as Ms. Viv's hug. I wanted to stay in this place for a moment, even though I'd rushed over, ready to pour out my soul. But this tea, this quiet, gave me moments to calm my head and my heart.

As I sat, Ms. Viv closed her eyes and leaned back as if she were thinking, but I knew she was waiting.

Inside the quiet, I felt so content. Inside Ms. Viv's home, I felt so protected. But I knew I couldn't stay in this place, physically, mentally, emotionally, for too long. So, finally, I said, "Ms. Viv."

Her eyes opened slowly, like the rising of curtains. "You're ready to talk?"

I nodded, but then not a single word came out of me because I wasn't sure where to begin. "It's a long story. Do you have some time?"

"I have more time than you know, especially for you. And this is a story I want to hear."

So after taking a very deep breath, I exhaled the history of the last three and a half months. I started at the beginning, with meeting Julian.

"In fact, it was the Monday after we first had tea," I told Ms. Viv.

Ms. Viv nodded and took another sip as I continued.

I told her about the places I'd gone with Julian and the bracelet I'd received from him. Then I turned the story to Alexander.

"He gave me a job. It was only part-time, but I was able to do interior design for the Enclave — new lofts downtown. And if it hadn't been for you, if you hadn't introduced my dad to Brenda and Ebony, I never would've been able to do it."

I told her about the money I earned, Usher's party, and the purse he'd given to me.

And finally, I got to the story of Harrison.

"I met him at Pinnacle, the night I told you I was going there to meet my girlfriend."

The story with Harrison took the longest of all, of course. But Ms. Viv sat nodding, listening, and from her expression, I imagined she was empathizing with me.

"My experiences with him made meeting Julian and Alexander seem like nothing, from the diamond earrings to the Hermès scarf and then the events and the dinners in between. He even introduced me to a fashion icon who is going to design a dress for me — at least I think she is — and he took me to the Bahamas this weekend. We just got back yesterday."

I paused and waited for Ms. Viv to show some kind of surprise — a raised eyebrow, a twitch of her lip, something, because certainly she wouldn't have approved of my going away with a man like this. But there was nothing from her. She just nodded, her lips pressed together.

It was odd, but then I wondered if it had something to do with her age. My dad always said there was nothing new under the sun, so maybe she'd experienced this herself. Or knew someone who had.

When she didn't stop me, I continued, telling her how wonderful the trip had been, then about our time on the beach.

"I didn't mean to kiss him," I said. "It was just where we were, I think. And Harrison has been so good to me. I just got caught up."

I was about to get to the real part of the story for me: coming home, and my breakup with Stephon.

But for the first time, Ms. Viv spoke, "And that right there, Zuri, was the problem. You got caught up, you caught feelings, and you weren't supposed to."

"I know, because of Stephon, but . . ."

"No, not because of him, but because Harrison didn't want any feelings involved in this. He just wanted a lovely lady to spend time with, someone who wouldn't bring him a situation or a consequence."

Those words made me stiffen. Harrison had uttered those same words to me.

"But you brought a complication . . . which would turn into a situation. You caught feelings."

My heart was beating as if it just might be trying to kill me.

With a deep sigh, she shook her head, then stood and reached for the photo album with GFF embossed on the cover.

She opened it, flipped through a few pages, then set the book down on my lap.

I gasped at the page that Ms. Viv had turned to . . . It was a headshot of me, the photo that was on Silver Sky's website.

"What is this?" I whispered, though my eyes didn't lift from the page. Because beneath my picture were notes, I guessed. My age, height, weight (though whoever had gathered this information had that wrong — I was eight pounds heavier), and then there were bullet points:

- Takes care of her father in Stone

455

Mountain. Visits every day.
- Works in the Maxim building, downtown Atlanta.
- Visits Starbucks in that building. Coffee every morning.
- Lenox Square on Thursdays and Saturdays.
- Very professional, very well spoken.

There were more notes, more information about me: I loved to dine in top restaurants, was a designer connoisseur, wanted to be an interior designer, and had never been on a plane.

"Ms. Viv." Now I looked up. "What is this?" And when I asked that question, I asked with complete innocence. Because not a bit of this made any sense to me.

She sat back and crossed her legs. "You know what's so bad about this?"

I blinked. Her question made me think of Stephon's words — how it always got to him when I answered a question with one of my own. Ms. Viv had just done that to me — and now I understood Stephon.

She said, "You were one of my best girls."

Her words made me push the album away off my lap, as if it were a snake about to strike me with its venom. "What did you say?"

She gave me a half shrug, then, "I told you I was a businesswoman."

I pressed my hand against my chest, hoping that would be enough to keep it inside. "What are you saying?"

She picked up the album, closed it, dusted off the cover, before she returned it to its place on the table. "Along with my Girls First Foundation, I have a business called Girlfriend Fantasy. Actually, in a way, they kind of work together, but I started Girlfriend Fantasy long before this girlfriend experience became part of pop culture and ended up on television as a show." She shook her head.

"I . . . I don't . . ." I stuttered. "What are you talking about?"

"I have a business. I help men, sometimes women, create fantasy relationships."

"What?"

"Usually well-to-do men who have to be . . . careful about the company they keep."

Her lips were moving, and words were coming out, but they weren't making any kind of connection to the sensical part of my brain.

"And so these men," she continued, as if she was sure I was following along, "who are in town for a short period or who just want a girlfriend in Atlanta for a short time, they all come to me."

And then I had a flashback: Julian — Starbucks, Alexander — Lenox Square, Harrison — Pinnacle. All matched up with things I'd shared with Ms. Viv.

"You used me?" My eyes narrowed. "In that way?"

"No." She tilted her head. "I didn't use you at all. Why would you think that?"

I pointed to the book. "You had my picture, you had a dossier on me, you . . . you set me up."

"Now, that, I did do." She nodded. "I set you up because you were concerned that you weren't living the life that you believed you should be living. So I set you up to get everything your heart desired. I set you up to be wined and dined. I set you up so that you could get fabulous gifts. I even worked with Alexander to set you up for the job. When I found out about his business, I was the one who recommended you, and you loved it. I set you up with men who gave you what you told me you wanted."

"But . . . but I had a boyfriend — a fiancé."

She held up her finger. "You didn't tell me that. You told me your relationship was casual. If you had been truthful with me, I would have been truthful with you. I don't normally hire girls who are in serious relationships — at least not without their knowledge." She continued, "But I have several young ladies who don't know what's going on, and there are men who like it that way. There are men who enjoy that fantasy. They know and the women don't. So the men get to meet the perfect, already vetted woman, have the real experience of connecting with her, and then when they've had enough, they move on. Sometimes to someone new, sometimes not.

"There are others who want the women to know who they are and what they're getting. And then there are men who want . . ." She paused. "Never mind. I just give the men the women they want. And I was always very careful with you."

"You're nothing but a madam, you . . ."

She held up her finger again, this time wagging it in the air. "No, there is not one woman who has ever had sex *because* of me. I just make the introduction, and I tell the men that sex is off-limits. Now, if something happens that I don't know about . . ."

"You sent me out with these men."

"I did not. I set up the introduction. The connection was their fantasy and your choice."

I had to pause, to take in air, so that I could understand. "I was out with those men. That was dangerous. Anything could have happened to me."

"Really?" She tilted her head. "You walk down the street every day, and you don't know who you're walking next to. You get inside cabs, get inside Ubers — you don't know who you're riding with. And don't get me started about online connections. The world is a dangerous place. But my business is not. With GFF, every man you encountered had been vetted, and they pay me very good money to have my girls vetted, too. Really, if women were smart, they would all find this kind of company."

"I never gave you any kind of permission to use me, or vet me, or introduce me."

She shrugged. "What did I really do? It was all your decision to spend time with them, and you were paid well for it. Think about it," she said so casually. "You had the opportunity to go to the restaurants you wanted, to receive the gifts you wanted; you even flew on a plane, first class, for the first time in your life." Then the tone of her voice changed. "But you caught feelings, Zuri. You weren't supposed to do that. Harrison didn't want that. He'd just gotten out of a complicated situation and all he wanted was a beautiful, smart woman to keep him company. He may have gotten there and may have wanted to take your relationship to another level, but you pushed it. And now he wants a new experience."

All I could do was shake my head because I didn't have enough words to tell her how violated I felt. By her . . . by Julian, by Alexander . . . by Harrison.

I moaned at the thought of Harrison.

"Now" — she tapped the book — "clearly, you won't be in the group of a true girlfriend experience because now you know. But you are very good. Both Julian and Alexander recommended you highly."

"Oh my God." I wanted to cry.

"But that's okay. Now that you know, you can bring in even more money, depending on . . ."

My eyes widened.

She said, "Now, I'd be able to guide you, and when you're selected by a man, there will be much more money for you, and . . ."

Finally, I jumped up and away from her. "No!" I exclaimed. "I can't believe you." I paused and, in that moment, thought about all the conversations I'd had with this woman. "You go to church."

She squinted as if she was trying to see

me better. "I don't. At least not very often, but what does that have to do with it?"

"You believe in God," I said, feeling like she needed that reminder. "You quote Scriptures all the time."

Her answer to me: she laughed.

Now I was the one to squint at her. She thought this was funny? She thought my life was a joke? "I could go to the police and have you arrested."

"For what, Zuri?" she said, sounding as if talking to me was beginning to make her weary. "What did I do to you? Introduce you to men who gave you diamonds, gave you a job, gave you a vacation?" She shook her head. "I'm sorry to hear you say all of this. I really thought we were friends."

"That's what I thought, too. I thought you were going to set me up as a mentor. Is that even real?"

She shrugged and I stared down at her, still sitting on the sofa, with her legs crossed as if this had been a normal, casual chat. As I stood there, I calculated. What could I do about this? I hadn't had sex with any of them; they'd given me gifts that I'd accepted. I'd gone everywhere and done everything willingly.

Grabbing my bag (which had been a gift from Alexander), I sent a final glare in her direction before I marched toward her door.

"Let me walk you out," she said, standing behind me.

I spun around, facing her. "No, I don't need anything else from you."

She shook her head as if I'd confused her. "I don't understand why you're mad, Zuri. You're not the first one to find out, and while some are surprised, they continue because they love the lifestyle. That's what you told me you wanted. That's why it was so easy to pull you in. You wanted the lifestyle."

I wanted to slap her for those words. I wanted to slap myself because those words were true.

"And it's not like you were having sex with them. Not every relationship with a man is about sex. If you don't want to do that . . ."

"I already told you no."

"Are you sure you don't just want a little time to think this over? You've earned quite a bit in just three months."

Those words made me feel dirty. "I cannot believe you did this to me, and I don't want to ever see you again."

She clasped her hands together and sighed. "So be it."

As I grabbed the doorknob, she added, "One thing, though. Most of the men use throwaway phones. That's my policy." I stepped outside, but she continued, "So you can't get in touch with any of them. Of course, you know Alexander's company, but remember the nondisclosure you signed?"

She paused, but I didn't respond.

"There's a clause in there," she explained. "Let's just say you don't want to contact Mr. Gayle in any way."

I bit my lip to stop myself from crying out. I hadn't even taken time to really read the agreement, so I had no idea what Ms. Viv was talking about, but I knew that her words were true.

"And Harrison." She sighed. "He took you into his world more than he should have even though I cautioned him. But he called me the moment you landed yesterday and ended his fantasy. So do not try to contact him or any of his friends. He doesn't want to have anything else to do with you, and he will take appropriate steps, if necessary, to protect himself."

I slammed her door on those words, the same way her words slammed the door on my heart.

I didn't walk, I didn't trot, I ran to my car. I ran, then, with quaking fingers, I started the ignition. I screeched out of Ms. Viv's driveway, and then the tires screamed when I punched the accelerator. But then in a single moment of clarity, I realized I was speeding in a residential area.

The car swerved as I pulled it to the curb, then lunged forward when I slammed on the brakes. I had no idea why I panted, sounding like I'd just run a race.

I sat there until I panted no more. And when my panting was done, I rested my head on the steering wheel and cried. Because it had all been a fantasy for the men. And the only part that had been a reality had been Stephon.

But now the man I'd loved so much for so long was gone.

EPILOGUE

Almost Six Months Later

I clicked on the remote, slid inside my car, and dumped my bag onto the passenger seat. Then I just sat and stared at the envelope I held before I squeezed my eyes closed.

"Please, God. Please, God. Please, God."

I opened my eyes, blew out a long breath, and then ripped open the envelope. "Oh, no," I moaned as I stared at the numbers on the check — $427.23.

Before I'd gotten into my car, I was exhausted; now I was exhausted and sad. Once again, I closed my eyes, and now I searched for the bright side. This check was almost one hundred dollars more than my last check. I was working my way back at my job, keeping my head in the game. It wasn't difficult, though. There weren't too many other things that I had to focus on.

As I revved up the engine, all I wanted to

do was go home, climb into bed after this long week, and sleep until the New Year, which was only four days away. But I wouldn't be able to do that until well after midnight.

I maneuvered from the parking garage and then glanced at the clock as I hit Peachtree. It wasn't yet five thirty; I had thirty-three minutes to drive twelve miles. Friday rush hour in Atlanta — I'd never make it.

But since I was already tired, already sad, I wasn't going to add stress to that list. So I hooked up my phone to the car's speakers and then leaned back when Beethoven's Piano Sonata No. 14 pleased my ears.

This had become my favorite piece; it was so soothing, so calming. Made me feel like my pitiful check wasn't so pathetic. Made me feel the kind of hope that Stephon used to give to me whenever I faced disappointment.

The thought of Stephon made me sigh. Reaching for the volume button, I cranked up the sound. This was part of my challenge with truly moving on. I'd traded in much of my beloved R & B for the softer beauty of classical. In the beginning days of missing Stephon, I'd played the music to feel closer to him. The same way that I hugged his pillow at night or wrapped myself in his bathrobe that he'd left behind. But it hadn't taken me long to really begin to enjoy the music, since it reminded me of all the times when Stephon had tried to . . .

"Stop it, Zuri."

I tapped the volume button again and now blasted the music. Of course, classical wasn't meant to be heard this way, but I hoped that the sound would drown out my thoughts.

Then the sonata ended and Barber's Adagio for Strings came on. This was Stephon's playlist, and once again, I asked myself, how did I expect to go a day without thinking about Stephon if I kept doing this? And especially if I played this song?

But it was just that I had a new appreciation for the crying violins. I had a new appreciation for all things Stephon Smith. At least today was better than yesterday. Today, I didn't cry along with the instruments.

As song after song played, I drove through the rush-hour traffic, making my way to Ambience in thirty minutes. I was surprised — for once, I was going to be on time. That was my thought until I pulled into the parking lot, which was already packed with cars. It took four minutes of driving around to find a space — so now I was once again late.

I snatched my bag from the back seat,

then jumped out of the car. Before I even reached the huge double doors of Ambience, the Friday-evening din greeted me, the sound filled with the cheer of people still in holiday-celebration mode and now gearing up for the end of the year.

Stepping inside, I pushed through a group of waiting patrons, gave a fast wave to the hostess, but Rachel didn't even see me; she was surrounded by customers. This was going to be a long night.

After signing in on the digital time clock, I staggered into the employees' room.

"Dang." Diane, the only one inside the room, leaned back in her chair and looked me up and down. "You look horrible."

"Thanks," I said as I made my way to my locker.

"I mean, you're cute in that suit, though it might be a little uncomfortable to work in. But you look whipped."

I shook my head. "I'm exhausted. I've worked every night this week. And as for my suit, I had to come straight from work today 'cause Stanley . . ."

"Ain't no joke," she finished for me. "Has he docked you?"

I nodded. "And he knows that I'm coming from my job, but he doesn't care. So I'm gonna have to work it out somehow because I need every penny of every check."

"I hear you, and speaking of the boss and his paycheck-docking self" — she glanced up at the clock — "I better get back out there. I only have two more hours anyway."

"That's nothing. I'm here to closing."

"Girl" was all Diane said.

"I know," I said to her right before she scooted out of the room.

I didn't even bother to go into the bathroom to change my clothes. I was too tired and too late to care, so right there in the center of the break room, I shimmied out of my suit and then slipped into my black pants, white blouse, and black rubber-soled shoes, which at least gave me a little comfort from the stilettos I'd worn all day.

In two minutes flat, I was facing the mirror and had pulled my hair back into a tight ponytail per the employees' manual. I slammed my locker shut, turned toward the door, then paused. I sighed as I lowered my butt into one of the chairs around the table where we ate our meals.

I wished that I didn't need this money so much, or else, I'd go home and chillax, lie back in my bed and turn on Netflix . . .

That made me pop straight up, and as I made my way toward the door, I pushed aside my thoughts. It was tough not thinking about Stephon, but I was pleased that it was after six and I had not yet cried. This was progress. This was a sign . . . I was healing.

That made me smile. That was what I always said when Audra asked how I was doing.

"I'm healing . . . from my stupidity . . . from my greed."

As I stepped into the hall, the chatter and the clatter around me pulled me away from all memories. It was time to get to work. I checked in to get my table assignments, then grabbed my tablet before I headed to my first customers. It was only because I was still checking my tablet for the specials tonight that I didn't see him. Didn't see him until it was too late, too late for me to turn around and run away.

It was too late because when I looked up, he was staring at me and our eyes locked. I was frozen, except for my hands, which trembled so much I had to grip the tablet so that it wouldn't fall. This was a moment I'd dreamed of so many times. I dreamed of seeing Stephon while I was strolling through Centennial Park, grabbing a burger from Big Daddy's, or even while pumping gas at some random gas station.

But of all the places I imagined where I

would see Stephon for the first time, this restaurant was not one of them. No, not as I was dressed in my waitstaff uniform with my tablet in my hand, ready to serve. Not as Stephon was sitting at one of my tables . . . with another woman.

It wasn't until Stephon smiled that my feet were able to move. I pushed back my shoulders, lifted my chin, and made my way to the man who was still my love in my heart.

By the time I made my way to his table, Stephon was standing. "Zuri." He whispered my name the way he used to.

Wine and time had nothing on my ex. He was still Idris and Kofi and Morris and M'Baku and Michael B all wrapped up in those black jeans and black turtleneck that he wore.

He leaned into me; I did the same and cursed the tablet I still held. I wanted to put it down so that I could completely feel Stephon's embrace. But by the time I had that thought, he'd already pulled away.

"How are you?" he said.

"I'm good." I hoped that I didn't sound as out of breath as I was. "What about you?"

He nodded, sat down, and then stretched his hand forward. I reached for him, then snatched my hand back when I realized his gesture wasn't for me. "Zuri, let me introduce you to Stacy."

He paused, and I turned my glance to the woman who sat across from him. It was amazing — in those few moments, I'd forgotten about her existence. I mean, I saw her when I first walked over, but Stephon had taken all of my soul's attention.

Now I had to face her, and when I lowered my eyes, I had to face the fact that she was the one Stephon had been reaching for; she was the one whose hand he held. But unlike the way he'd released me so quickly, he held on to her as if he didn't have any plans to let her go.

Blood oozed from my heart. Or at least that was what I imagined happened inside as I felt my heart crack into two.

"Stacy, this is Zuri," he said.

"Hello, Zuri." She spoke with a bit of an accent — Caribbean, I thought. I didn't do my normal assessment. I couldn't. It was hard for me to see past her Halle Berry look-alike face.

Because I couldn't yet figure out how to speak, I just nodded my greeting.

Stacy said, "So you and Stephon are friends?" She looked between the two of us, and that was when I found my voice.

"We were —" I started, but Stephon didn't let me get to the part where I was going to tell her that he loved me first and that I still had the ring he'd given me tucked beneath my pillow to prove it.

"Friends," Stephon finished for me. "Yes, we were very good friends."

"Oh." Stacy nodded knowingly, though I could tell she didn't know anything about me before this moment.

I wanted to pull up a chair, sit down, and explain it all to her. But it was time to end my torture. I tapped to awaken the tablet's screen and said, "So, can I start you off with something to drink?"

"You work here?" Stephon asked.

It was only because I knew Stephon that I knew he wasn't throwing shade. But why else did he think I was standing here wearing these shoes and tapping on this tablet. I guess he was just surprised.

"Sweetie," Stacy said to him with a bit of an eye roll.

I guess that was her way of letting him know he'd asked a dumb question. And the *sweetie* was her way of letting me know not to get the hand-holding twisted — they were doing more than that.

Already, Stephon? Really?

I found the strength to say, "Yes, I work here. I'm still at the agency, but this helps pay the bills, you know." I needed to end this, so I asked, "Drinks?"

"Sweetie, let's do a bottle of wine," Stacy said, and then she turned her attention to me. "We're celebrating tonight. My baby . . ."

Oh, God.

". . . is an artist."

I know.

"And he had this great show at a gallery in Midtown."

I was there before you.

"And yesterday, he sold the last painting. Twelve in six months. Isn't that unbelievable?"

As much as I wanted to cut and run, I couldn't. Because Stephon had made it. He'd sold all twelve paintings.

"Oh, my goodness, you did?" I turned to him. "You sold them all?"

He grinned. "Yeah."

Though every bit of my heart was aching and bleeding, I smiled through tears that had blessedly not yet fallen. "Congratulations, ba— Stephon." I had to take a baby step back from the table so that I wouldn't pull him up and into my arms. "I'm really happy for you."

With a wave of her hand, Stacy put down the drinks menu. "So bring us your biggest, most expensive bottle of wine."

They laughed together, and I cried inside.

"No," Stephon said, holding up his hand. "Just bring us two glasses of champagne," he said as smoothly as he used to order a chocolate shake for us to share.

"Sure, and I'll be back to take the rest of your order."

Without even sharing the specials with them or asking if they had any questions, I rushed away. I put in their order at the bar, then made a mad dash to the restroom. A moment alone, on my knees, with my face over the toilet was all I needed. Then I'd be able to go back out there and face Stephon and Stacy.

My God — even their names went together. I couldn't take it.

But as I pushed the door open, Diane stepped out of a stall. She gave me a quick glance and said, "What's up with you?"

"Stephon," I breathed as I stumbled over to one of the sinks.

"Oh." She waved her hand, then turned on the water. "Well, I know it still hurts" — she spoke to me through the mirror — "but you'll get over him soon."

"Not soon enough — he's here."

Her eyes widened as she grabbed a paper towel. "What? Where?"

"Here. At Ambience. At the first table I

served tonight."

"Wow!" She leaned back against the sink. "What were the chances of this happening?"

"I know," I said.

"So, do you think you two will talk?"

"Not with his girlfriend here." I turned the hot faucet on — full blast.

"What?" She slapped her palm against the sink. "He's with a woman?" But she didn't give me a chance to answer before she continued with, "Maybe it's not his girlfriend. Maybe it's a coworker."

"He works from home. And with the way they were holding hands . . ."

"Oh, Zuri," she sighed. "I'm sorry."

"I can't believe it. It's not even a full six months yet. He was supposed to love me. We were engaged." I stated all the facts, all the reasons why Stephon should have been sitting home alone — exactly the way I'd been doing.

"Well, six months . . . that is half a year, and you know guys. Once they have a woman taking care of all of their needs, when that part gets broken, they need a replacement piece quick." When I moaned, Diane added, "I'm just sayin'."

"I thought he loved me more than that." I splashed water on my face, not caring at all about my makeup.

"How much he loved you has nothing to do with him moving on. His rearview mirror is cracked. He's looking through the windshield and maybe now you'll be able to, too."

This was one of the things I loved about Diane — she served the truth straight up. She'd been a great outlet for me when I met her here, six months ago. My dad and Audra had tried to be supportive through the pain of what I'd done, but too many times I'd caught both of them giving me the side-eye when they thought I wasn't looking. So Diane had been the one I turned to.

"Do you want me to take over their table?" she asked, once again her friendship on full display. "You don't need to go through this."

I patted my face dry and stared at my reflection. "No," I said. "I've got this."

And that's what I did. For the rest of the night, I served not only Stephon and Stacy, but my other four tables as well. I worked as if my heart had not stopped pumping. I worked as if I weren't running into the bathroom every ten minutes and whimpering like a baby.

The whole time, I tried not to notice the way Stephon and Stacy ate together (they shared an appetizer before their entrées), the way they laughed together (every time I approached their table, they had to apologize as they worked to gather themselves), and the way they seemed to love each other.

It was a relief to me when Stephon asked for the check. I gave him the over-one-hundred-dollar bill with a smile, and right away, he pulled out an American Express card. I raised an eyebrow but said nothing as I closed out his bill, then returned to their table.

Just as I handed the billfold to him, Stacy said, "Excuse me." She stood, squeezed his hand (and my heart at the same time), and said, "I'm going to the restroom; I'll meet you up front."

He nodded, and as she walked away, he said, "I'll take care of the bill now, Zuri." He signed the way he painted; every bit of him was in each swerve and dip of every letter.

When he added fifty dollars as a tip, I said, "You don't have to do that."

"I want to," he said. "It's not even enough for how you believed in me."

"You don't have to pay me for that."

"I never would be able to."

I nodded.

He said, "So, how are you really?"

I miss you with everything inside of me. "I'm hanging in there" was what came out.

"Doing good."

He nodded as if he approved of my response. Then his face lit up with a smile. "And how's Dad?"

It pleased me that he still addressed my father that way. "He's still Dad."

Another nod. "Brenda still there with him?"

I shook my head. "No. He has an aide, but she's part-time." I paused. "I moved back home to take care of him."

"Wow." He paused as if he needed a moment to let that sink in. "You're in Stone Mountain now."

"Yup. And it's different. But it was best. I had to let Brenda and Ebony go."

"Oh." He frowned. "I hope there was no problem."

"Not with them," I said. "I just wanted to use a different agency, but it's working out. While I'm at work, and the nights I work here, the aide is there, and then she leaves when I come home. It's more affordable this way." I didn't tell him how I'd been able to afford the aide. There was no need for him to know that I'd sold everything that I'd received as gifts during what I called my period of greed: the earrings, the clothes, even the purse and the bracelets.

"Well, that's good, I guess," he said. "How

does it feel to be back home?"

I miss you! "It's different. I'm not going to stay there forever, but for now . . ." I needed to change the subject. "I'm really happy for you, Stephon. I knew you would sell all of those paintings."

"Yeah, I can't believe it. I have five more there and two at another gallery."

"Really? That's a lot of paintings. You've been busy."

He nodded, and then his smile faded. "Yeah, well, for a while there, all I did was paint. That was all I could do."

In his words, in his tone, I heard the pain I'd caused him, and my bleeding heart really wanted to stop now.

He asked, "So you and ole dude, y'all still together?"

I tilted my head. "Who?" But before he could answer, I figured it out. Had he thought this the entire time we'd been apart? Had he thought I'd been with another man, when every night I'd been crying for him? "No, Stephon, we were never a couple. We really were just friends, and we're not even that anymore. Haven't been since the day you . . ." I left it there.

My answer seemed to surprise him. Made him nod once again.

"Stephon," I began, "I never had the

chance to say —"

"Stephon?" Stacy's voice floated over my shoulder. "Are you ready?"

His eyes stayed on me when he spoke to Stacy. "Yeah, yeah. I'm ready." Then, to me, he said, "It was really good seeing you, Zuri."

I blinked and pressed my lips together, hoping that would be enough to keep my emotions from exploding out of me. When he pulled me into another hug, a sob pushed its way from my heart.

"I really wish you well, Zuri," he whispered in my ear. "I want everything good for you." He pulled back, and his eyes were glazed like mine. "And I wish you love. One day, I hope you find it all."

I nodded, and then it felt like everything around me became silent as I stood and watched Stephon and Stacy. He slid his hand into hers, and even from where I was, I could see him squeeze her, wanting to hold her tighter, never wanting to let her go.

He held her the way he used to hold me.

The cost of my greed was such a high price to pay.

"I love you, Stephon," I whispered into the air. "I love you, and I always will. Beyond infinity."

I stood my ground, not flinching a muscle, watching Stephon and Stacy, until I could no longer see the man that I loved.

ABOUT THE AUTHOR

Victoria Christopher Murray is the author of more than twenty novels including: *Greed; Envy; Lust; The Ex Files; Lady Jasmine; The Deal, the Dance, and the Devil;* and *Stand Your Ground,* which was named a *Library Journal* Best Book of the Year. Winner of nine African American Literary Awards for Fiction and Author of the Year (Female), Murray is also a four-time NAACP Image Award Nominee for Outstanding Fiction. She splits her time between Los Angeles and Washington, DC. Visit her website at VictoriaChristopher Murray.com.